Secret Promise is a love story you don't want to miss.

Secret Promise—this historical romance takes place in a world of hate, deprivation, and peril. Its thrilling message of tender love conquering all will continue to play in your mind long after you've finished reading it.

Patsy Rae Dawson
Author of the *Marriage: A Taste of Heaven* series

Against a backdrop of prohibition, inadequate school systems, racial tension, and domestic abuse, a compelling romance emerges. Having walked along life's treacherous paths, Mary depicts realistic characters trying to resolve their conflicts.

Paul Elliott, M. D.
Marketer

Mary demonstrates her deep personal understanding of the dreams and dramas of the Southern way of life. She leads the reader into the deepest recesses of her characters' lives as they struggle to overcome the fears that stand between them and their heart's desires.

Paula Taylor
Author

Also by Mary Lou Cheatham

Solomon's Porch: The Story of Ben and Rose (pen name: Jane Riley)

Flavored with Love: Mary Lou's Family and Friends Can Cook (pen name: Jane Riley)

The Collard Patch (Co-author: Paul Elliott)

Do You Know How God Loves You? Successful Daily Living

A Prayer of Nehemiah, The Birth of Leadership

I'm Choking . . . But Life Moves On Along the Path of Grief: Insights about Grieving

Secret Promise

MARY LOU CHEATHAM

WESTBOW
PRESS®
A DIVISION OF THOMAS NELSON
& ZONDERVAN

All scripture quotations are taken from the King James Version of the Bible.

WestBow Press books may be ordered through booksellers or by contacting:

WestBow Press
A Division of Thomas Nelson
1663 Liberty Drive
Bloomington, IN 47403
www.westbowpress.com
1-(866) 928-1240

Because of the dynamic nature of the Internet, any web addresses or links contained in this book may have changed since publication and may no longer be valid. The views expressed in this work are solely those of the author and do not necessarily reflect the views of the publisher, and the publisher hereby disclaims any responsibility for them.

Any people depicted in stock imagery provided by Thinkstock are models, and such images are being used for illustrative purposes only.

Certain stock imagery © Thinkstock.

ISBN: 978-1-4497-3401-5 (sc)
ISBN: 978-1-4497-3402-2 (e)

Library of Congress Control Number: 2011962126

Print information available on the last page.

WestBow Press rev. date: 2/27/2017

For Christie

Covington Chronicles

Book One

*   *   *

The LORD liveth; and blessed be my rock; and let the God of my salvation be exalted.

Psalm 18:46

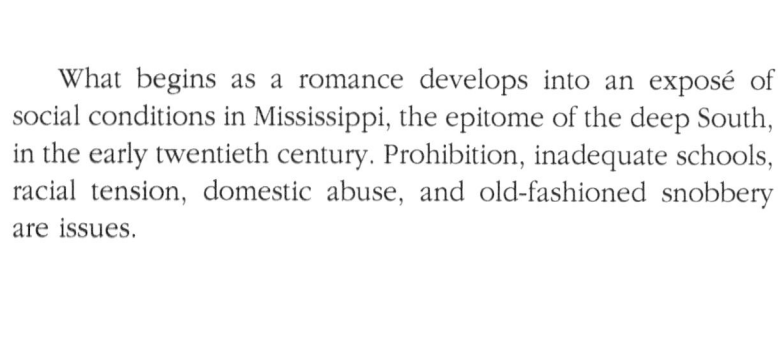

What begins as a romance develops into an exposé of social conditions in Mississippi, the epitome of the deep South, in the early twentieth century. Prohibition, inadequate schools, racial tension, domestic abuse, and old-fashioned snobbery are issues.

Chapter One

The Clemons Household

Spring 1907

The thought occurred to Caroline that no one would believe what went on inside the Clemons household. She slipped out of Millicent's bedroom. Glancing over her shoulder, she rushed through the dining room back to the warm kitchen, leaned by an open window, and drew the breeze into her lungs.

"Land's sakes . . . you done got too hot." Rachel brushed the thick soft back of her brown hand against Caroline's cheek. "Sit a minute. I'll fetch you some cool water."

Caroline swigged it down and set the empty glass on the worktable. "Thank you, Madear. Got to go."

"You can't let Miss Horsey catch you back here when you supposed to be at the front door."

In the parlor Caroline plumped the needlepoint-covered pillows on the sofa. A burst of wind blew a filmy curtain into her moist face. Reaching to straighten it, she looked through the window in time to see two Tennessee walking horses pull an elaborate surrey with fringe trim into the circle drive.

A dark-haired man perhaps in his early twenties stopped the team next to a hitching post. He jumped out to tie the horses and bounded up the steps to the high front porch.

*   *   *

Jacob MacGregor thought he was at the right place—the corner of East Main Street and Old Town Road. The steps led him onto a porch, which wrapped around the north and east sides of the pristine white house. When he raised his hand to knock, a young woman with sparkling blue eyes swung open the door with its etched glass panel to welcome him into the Clemons house. Smiling without speaking, she motioned him inside and then floated away through the dining room and toward the swinging kitchen door. Even though the door had a wide crack on the hinged side, he lost sight of her.

High hat in both hands, he stepped into the Victorian parlor of Mrs. Hortense Smith Clemons. She had sent him a formal invitation to come for tea. Delectable smells of baking food wafted from the kitchen to the front of the house.

"Oh, do come in. Place your hat on the table or hang it on the rack, whichever you prefer." Hortense, bustled in from a bedroom opening into the dining room on the left side. She tripped and almost fell.

Having plastered a solicitous smile across her face, Hortense stretched one hand toward him. She teetered in her high-heeled shoes to her wing-backed chair, where she sat too hard. "Caroline should have taken your hat."

"It's all right," he said.

"Girls, we have a guest." She turned her head and shouted, "Come here now." She looked back at Jake and forced a laugh. "How *are* you?" The left of her mouth turned up and the right side curved downward. "Do be seated on the sofa or the love seat." When she talked her voice went up and down two octaves.

"Caroline," she scolded. "Bring the tea." She clapped her hands. "Make haste." Almost losing her balance, she leaned toward Jake. As she recovered her composure, she daubed her flushed face with a dainty handkerchief.

Jake sat on the sofa. Mrs. Clemons was not at all as he had expected her to be.

She folded her hands in her lap. "Ah, here we are. This darling girl is Lydia." Hortense beamed with pride as she pointed toward the tall thin young woman. "This precious one is Millicent."

Jake arose and stood until the young women entered, curtsied, and seated themselves. "Pleased to make your acquaintance, ladies." He nodded his head in a polite gesture.

The server, whom he supposed was the person Mrs. Clemons called Caroline, entered with the tea.

He thought: *it isn't supposed to happen this way.*

In all of God's creation, he had never seen anyone so lovely. She was graceful but unassuming. He forced himself to focus on Mrs. Clemons and her daughters. What could be more uncouth than feasting his eyes on a servant in the home of the Senator's wife?

Caroline moved with fluid grace as she served. Her intriguing eyes remained focused on her task. Her facial expression was pleasant, but it seldom changed from a sad half smile. He leaned forward to take the teacup and saucer from her hands. The smell of her perfume—ah, what was it? A blend of roses, peaches, and sandalwood, all floating above the exotic black tea.

No one bothered to introduce her. "Come here, Caroline," Hortense tapped her spoon on her saucer. "Bring me my medication so I can add a spoonful to my tea."

At the mention of the medication, Jake thought he saw the slightest hint of a sparkle in Caroline's eyes accompanied by a covert grin.

"Here it is, ma'am." Caroline had anticipated the woman's needs. Mrs. Clemons doctored her tea.

"For my lumbago," she explained to Jacob. Caroline walked through the opened French doors with glass panels. She placed the bottle somewhere in the dining room.

"Now bring us some teacakes. Be quick about it," Hortense said.

Did he see her looking back? She gazed over her shoulder at Hortense Clemons. What was behind the expressive glance of her cornflower eyes?

Jake, despite his sensibility of etiquette, found himself admiring Caroline as she walked away. He noticed the way her skirt swished.

"I was saying, Mr. MacGregor, it is hard to get decent help nowadays."

"Oh, really?" he replied, as she jerked his attention back into the proper focus.

"Yes, I have Rachel, my cook. Jim is my flunky. He drives us. We have a serviceable buggy for every day and a surrey we use on special occasions. He takes care of the horses and yard. He goes to the Mercantile with our list and brings home our groceries. If the Senator would require Caroline to take boarding elsewhere, I'd have room to place someone more reliable."

Jake, not the least interested in her domestic affairs, gave the woman a blank look. She had rare grace and elegance for a serving girl. She hardly acknowledged his presence. Try as he might, he couldn't bring her into eye contact. Except for the look she gave Hortense, she looked away or down.

A braided cord held her hair away from her delicate face. Blonde waves flowed in rivulets down her back. At the neck of her navy dress, she wore a plain collar and a large locket hanging from a crimson satin ribbon. In her pierced ears she wore sparkling diamonds, out of character for a serving maid.

He noticed the sisters' elaborate hairstyles with pompadours crowning their heads and shiny curls streaming over their shoulders. He was amazed to see such professionally arranged hairstyles in Taylorsburg, Mississippi, in the middle of the week.

He gazed at Caroline . . . he was losing control. He admired the gentle pleasantness of her expression. Her apparent concern was to make everyone comfortable.

He blurted out the words on the tip of his tongue: "Beautiful hair."

"What?" Hortense demanded.

"Uh . . . ." He thought fast. "Excuse me, if I'm forward, but your daughters have their hair arranged beautifully."

"Oh, thanks. We do our best," Hortense said.

"You do it yourselves?"

"The sisters do." She spoke a half-truth.

Caroline appeared with a tray of crisp molasses teacakes, smelling of cinnamon and nutmeg. She placed them on the coffee table and retreated to the kitchen. Jake devoured more than half of them. As Millicent reached for her fourth, Lydia hissed, "Millicent, stop."

The three of them turned to smile at Jake. He wondered whether Caroline was watching from behind the kitchen door.

*   *   *

Caroline tried to watch the front room through the crack where the hinges supported the kitchen door. She felt a strong attraction toward the handsome young man.

Her father, Senator Chad Clemons, devoted his life to noble causes. Her precious friend Rachel was passing through life with all her dreams for her grandchildren deferred. Caroline's students lacked the textbooks, supplies, and creature comforts needed to develop their minds.

Helping others move a few steps along life's road to a better existence—a greater good—mattered more than whatever pleasures for which she could hope. Years ago she gave her word, she made a promise she had not failed to keep.

She would honor her commitment at any cost. No amount of understanding and forgiveness, however, could reverse the damage she received last winter; as a result, she would never marry.

*   *   *

When Jacob left a few minutes later, his mind was hazy. He would need to return to the Senator's home soon. He was sure Mrs. Clemons would invite him to see her two eligible daughters, since he was the newest bachelor in town. He could gain business in his mercantile from them, also from their friends. But what about Caroline? Having entered his mind uninvited, she lingered.

If she arranged her hair the way Lydia and Millicent had fixed theirs and if she didn't keep her eyes aimed at the floor, she would look like a Gibson Girl. She had the height—about five feet seven. The severely plain dress she wore drew attention away from her elegant proportions and tiny waist.

She obviously knew the finer points of etiquette, but why was she serving? Was she Hortense's personal maid?

She seemed ashamed. Had she done something in the past or was she afraid of someone? He couldn't help wondering what her story was. Where did she fit?

Hortense Clemens was the woman he came to see . . . the town's most prominent citizen. He didn't know how he could make the Mercantile succeed without her support. He wondered whether he could ever engage Caroline in conversation or if he would have the opportunity to become acquainted with her.

*   *   *

After the visitor left, Caroline started cleaning. Lydia went to her room on the west side of the parlor with Millicent following.

"Get me a dining chair," Hortense said.

"Yes, ma'am," Caroline said.

Straddling it backwards, Hortense pulled her skirt between her legs and mounted the chair. "You know what to do."

Caroline kneaded the loose grainy flesh on Hortense's neck. The color of the skin on the back of her neck resembled a pumpkin. The woman's face had a newly acquired sallow appearance. Something wasn't right.

"Sing to me," Hortense said.

But Caroline didn't feel like it. She cleared her throat in hesitation.

"I said, 'Sing.' Can't you see my nerves are frayed?" Hortense pointed toward her low back. "And keep massaging."

"Hush, little baby, don't say a word . . ." Caroline's voice, pure and sweet, floated across the parlor. She could feel Hortense relaxing.

Lydia's door flew open. "Give that back to me," she yelled. She and Millicent scuffed over a book.

Millicent scurried across the parlor to her room with Lydia chasing her. Blowing hard, Millicent ran as she held a tiny key. In the meantime, Caroline's percussion of the back of Hortense's chest provoked spasms of coughing.

"Give Lydia her diary," Hortense ordered in a wavy voice with gasps, but Millicent, ignoring her mother, ran through the dining room and into the sewing room. Lydia was not far behind. The sounds of furniture being knocked around made it evident that the fight continued.

"Take your hands out of my hair," Lydia's voice sounded from the sewing room.

"You pulled mine first." Millicent was breathless.

Lydia emerged with the diary and key, but Millicent followed. Dress ripped and hair disheveled, Millicent giggled. Lydia ran back to her room and slammed the door.

"Look at you," Hortense said. "You'll never catch a man the way you act. You're nothing but a fat little pig."

"Listen to this, y'all," Millicent ignored her mother's rebuke. She smoothed out a crumpled page from Lydia's diary. "Mrs.

Lydia Suzanne Smith MacGregor—that's what she wrote. She thinks she's going to marry him, but he's mine. Did you see the way he looked at me?"

Rachel peeked through the kitchen doorway. "Time for me to go, Miss Horsey."

"You come here," Hortense scolded between coughs.

With hesitation Rachel walked toward Hortense. "I done stayed later than usual 'cause you had that man over here."

"Yeah. Be here bright and early in the morning."

"Yes'm."

"Tomorrow I'll unlock the Senator's room so you can freshen it up."

Caroline didn't tell Hortense she had already cleaned it. She saw no reason to let her stepmother know she possessed her own key to the Senator's room.

"Is he coming home?" Rachel asked.

"That's an impertinent question, which is none of your business. You and Caroline have cleaned all the rooms on the east side and Lydia's room fairly well. You need to keep working down the west side. The library needs airing out."

"Yes, ma'am," Rachel said.

"What's in the sack?" Hortense asked.

"My own stuff. You can see I ain't toting nothing off." Rachel held up her flour sack, which contained only her personal items.

Caroline carried the dishes to the kitchen. Rachel followed and closed the door. "Go home. Get some rest." Caroline hugged Rachel.

"Okay, sweet baby. I'll see you in the morning."

"Bye."

"God watch over you . . . I can't stay no longer."

"Do you need a ride home?" Caroline asked.

"No, my preacher man, he's done out here waiting in the wagon," Rachel said.

"You've got Brother George trained."

"He knows how my legs has been bothering me, and he wants cornbread."

"I bet he's done made you some cornbread to have with buttermilk for supper," Caroline said.

"Maybe." Rachel's eyes flashed as a smile illuminated her face.

"Go with God." She hated to see Rachel leave. They needed to talk.

In the corner of the big kitchen was the laundry area. A pile of starched and ironed curtains lay spread across the ironing board.

"Oh, Lord," Rachel said.

"What's the matter?" Caroline asked.

"I didn't get back up the stairs to hang them curtains today. If Miss Horsey sees them here, she'll have my hide."

"Don't worry, Madear. As soon as she goes to sleep—and it won't take long the way she's been nipping from her medicine bottle today—I'll go hang them."

"You's tired already," Rachel said.

"No, I'm fine. I'll do it."

Caroline returned to the parlor with a polishing cloth to remove the crumbs and smudges from the oval coffee table. Seeing Hortense still sitting backwards in the dining chair, Caroline jumped back.

"Okay, Car-o-line." The name *Caroline* sounded ugly spoken by Hortense's mouth. "What did you do?"

Caroline backed out of reach of her menacing stepmother. "Nothing, ma'am."

"Don't give me that. I saw how Mr. MacGregor was ogling you."

"I didn't do anything, ma'am."

When Hortense stood and took one step forward, Caroline placed her left hand behind her.

"Don't start your pitiful act. It won't do you no good. Nobody here's going to pay you any attention."

Caroline guarded her left lower back with the top of her hand touching her dress and the palm turned outward. Backing away, she continued to straighten the chairs in the room.

As Hortense loomed closer, she could feel her skin tighten in pain. The portly matron raised her hand and made a fist. Caroline danced out of reach.

Hortense, losing her balance, fell onto the sofa. "You've got to stop wearing your hair down. Put it up in a bun or something not so showy." She pointed her finger to emphasize what she was saying.

"I'm sorry. I didn't want to take the time to fix it." Caroline offered a hand to help Hortense stand.

"Don't give me none of your backtalk. Just do as I say."

Caroline reached for the dust mop and started pushing it across the wooden floor. She watched Hortense wobble to her bedroom and slam the door.

I would have helped her walk to her room, but she would have slapped me.

A second later Hortense returned and went to the dining room cabinet to get the brown bottle of medication. "I'll expect a sandwich on a tray in my room at six."

As soon as Caroline finished cleaning the parlor, she took the pile of curtains up the staircase next to Millicent's room. She was glad the Senator had included three landings; otherwise, she could have tripped with the cumbersome load. Hortense had furnished the spacious upstairs room with couches, chairs, and tables, but the family seldom used it. She loved to entertain and the Senator built the room according to her specifications.

Caroline enjoyed the view from the west windows as she hung the curtains. She could see all the way down the low hill to MacGregor's Mercantile. Her thoughts drifted to Jacob's dark blue eyes with gray flecks in them. They had a piercing quality—clear but brooding. She thought it would be easy to tell when he had something on his mind but difficult to guess what it was. When he smiled, his eyes squinched along the outer edges. She could imagine he was aiming his sincere eyes at some customer that very moment.

Upon finishing the curtains, she walked over to the south side of the room. Double doors enclosed a suite consisting of an elegant bedroom and a private parlor. The Senator had built these rooms for her. She tried the doors just in case she might find them unlocked. As always, the secure locks kept her out.

Making as little noise as possible, she walked back across the vast party room and descended. Before she could step off the stairs, Lydia moved in front of her and extended her long arms from one banister to the other.

"We can work something out, Caroline." Lydia loomed in front of her. Caroline knew she was stronger than Lydia, but she was too much of a lady to push or shove.

"I won't tell Mama you've been messing around in the upstairs apartment where you are not supposed to go if . . ."

"Wait a minute. I was not in the upstairs apartment. Anyway, Papa built those rooms for me."

"Right." Lydia stood in front of Caroline to prevent passage. "You say he did. You know Mama keeps you down here for good reasons."

Caroline bit her tongue.

"We keep you close to the kitchen so you can help with the meals and earn your keep. We're saving those upstairs rooms for guests."

"You've finished?" Caroline asked.

"No," Lydia emitted a coarse laugh. "We can't trust you to manage a chamber pot on the second floor."

Caroline felt her face grow hot. "Please move over."

"I will when we finish our little talk." Lydia smiled in a condescending way. "Here's the deal. I'll keep quiet about you messing around upstairs if . . ."

"I was hanging curtains," Caroline said.

"Oh, doing Rachel's work. That fat so-and-so is too lazy to do it herself."

Caroline stood in silence waiting to take the last two steps of the stairs.

"If you'll keep away from Jacob, I won't tell Mama you've been snooping around upstairs," Lydia said.

Caroline glared at Lydia.

"And I won't tell her you've been covering for Rachel," Lydia added.

Millicent popped out of her room by the stairs. "What's going on here?"

"Oh, nothing of any concern to you," Lydia said.

"I heard every word," Millicent said. "It is my concern."

"You're nothing but a fat baby," Lydia said. "Shut up."

"Jacob is mine," Millicent said. "If you don't let me have him, I'll tell Mama you smoke cigars."

"Liar," Lydia said.

"No, it's the truth."

As Lydia turned to face Millicent, Caroline passed by them.

"I was on my way out," Lydia said.

"I'm going with you," Millicent responded.

"In a torn dress? With your hair messed up? I don't think so."

"Does Mama know you're going?"

"I don't have to ask her," Lydia said. "I'm old enough to do as I please. As drunk as she is, she won't remember what happens tonight anyway."

Leaving them arguing, Caroline went to her room. To reach it, she walked from the kitchen through the pantry. The exact size as the pantry, it was a chamber intended either for a second pantry or for a servant's quarters. The latter seemed to be the case; at least Caroline felt like a servant in her own home.

Life was easier when school was in session. She had her work. Most of the time she could stay out of her stepmother's reach. The best part of the summer vacation was spending time with Rachel. Caroline valued every minute. The old cook's health was failing.

Her little room had two beautiful windows, matching the others in the house. Crisp white lace curtains hung from the tops, and she had cloth shades she could raise or lower. Along the bottom halves were thick curtains, which made it possible to have privacy even though the shades were raised.

On her bed was a colorful quilt Rachel had helped her make. The room was a haven other family members seldom entered. She looked into the mirror above her bureau. She thought: *What will I do with my hair? I know. I'll braid it.*

She brushed her hair and parted it in the middle from her forehead to her neck. She made two large braids. Next she wrapped the braids around her head in a circle. The ropes of hair felt slightly heavy, but she would grow accustomed to them. Having a new hairstyle was fun.

She had a little time before serving the evening meal left on top of the wood stove. She'd check with Hortense again to make sure a sandwich was the final order. The collard greens, hot water cornbread, and fried chicken on the stove would be almost impossible to resist.

On the shelves in the corner of her room were schoolbooks she needed to review. She wanted to be familiar with all the material in the McGuffey readers.

Her Bible lay open on the top shelf to Ephesians 4:32: "And be ye kind one to another, tenderhearted, forgiving one another, even as God for Christ's sake hath forgiven you."

She sat in her straight chair by the window. "Lord, Mama Hortense doesn't intend to be hurtful. She seems to be having a bad day. Forgive . . ."

What a handsome man . . . what a kind expression on his face . . . no, I can't dare think about him. I could never marry any man.

His thick hair was close cropped and brushed back. She'd observe every little detail about it next time

"Lord, please don't let me have sinful thoughts. I'm just admiring your handiwork." She laughed at herself. "Surely you have made this man in your own image."

13

He had a broad forehead. His masculine nose was slightly prominent. It was narrow, but it flared at the nostrils. Something about his mouth gave him a pensive expression. His white teeth were perfect. When he smiled, he had dimples. She could see he would have a heavy beard if he let it grow, but he was clean-shaven. She loved the way he looked.

I wonder which of my stepsisters he'll court. Probably Lydia. She's older. They'll make an attractive couple. She needs someone tall.

"Father in heaven, if Rachel has to quit working, how I can keep my promise? What will happen? Please watch over Lydia. Don't let her get hurt. Keep her from dishonoring the family."

She must have dozed in her chair. She heard a bell clanging in the kitchen. Millicent called, "Caroline, it's supper time. I'm hungry."

Chapter Two

Dreams of Love

"Caroline, come here. Put my hair up," Millicent yelled from Lydia's room after breakfast the following morning.

"No, me first. I'm older," Lydia said.

"But I asked first," Millicent said.

Hortense shouted across the house from her bedroom, "She's busy working on my hair. You girls will have to wait." Caroline arranged a pompadour on the top of Hortense's head and a chignon in the back. On the right side she pulled down a dramatic wave.

Then she went to Lydia's room. "It's Lydia's turn. You were first last time." She reworked Lydia's Gibson Girl style. In Lydia's hair was the distinct smell of residual cigar smoke. "Start brushing your hair, Millic. It's a wreck."

"Make me look cute," Millicent said. We're going to the MacGregor Mercantile Store, and I want to look real good. I can't get over the way Jacob looked at me yesterday. I know he thinks I'm an eye-catcher. This dress I'm wearing today is the cat's pajamas."

Caroline repaired Millicent's hair. "You look great, Millie."

"Come on, girls," Hortense shouted from the kitchen. Just outside the open door, Jim—the yard keeper, generalized errand runner, stables keeper, and driver—stood ready to take Hortense and her daughters for an outing.

"I look beautiful." Lydia, entering the kitchen, flounced about in a new pink dress with a matching parasol.

"I'm prettier," Millicent said. "Jacob MacGregor can't keep his eyes off me."

Addressing neither Rachel nor Caroline, Hortense talked to the air in a high-pitched proud voice. "We're going downtown to MacGregor Mercantile, and we're having lunch at Anna Belle's." She swished her head from side to side and batted her eyes.

Caroline thought: *I'd love to go down to MacGregor Mercantile and run into Jacob. I can only imagine happening upon him. One day soon I'll think of a reason to go. It won't mean anything. I just like to look at him. It's silly of me but I like his eyebrows. Maybe I can put in a good word for Lydia. He'd be quite a catch for her.*

"We need to plan our social calendar," Hortense continued. "We'll host all sorts of soirees and matinees this summer."

Caroline kept her head down as she dried the breakfast dishes. The girls went out the door, and Hortense followed. Before walking out, she turned. "By the way, Caroline. Do something about your hair. Those braids are dreadful."

"Yes, ma'am."

As soon as Jim drove the buggy away, Rachel threw down her dishrag and poured two cups of fresh coffee. She placed one across from her on the high worktable and one in front of herself. Caroline drank hers black, but Rachel added generous servings of rich cream and sugar.

"The law ought not to allow crazy folk like them to run loose. I could've told you she wasn't going to be pleased with your hair. Child, if you get any more beautiful, I don't think them three mean ones can handle it."

"I still have hope for Millie, Madear."

"Let's see your hair," Rachel said.

"Mama Hortense doesn't like it hanging down. She said it was making that man Mr. MacGregor look at me too much. She told me to pin it up."

"She didn't mean for you to doll yourself up," Rachel said.

"They didn't notice my new lingerie dress."

*   *   *

Business was much better than Jake expected. It seemed all the young single women in and around Taylorsburg ran out of thread at the same time. Trying to help select items in the fabric department was not his forte. He sneaked out the back and left Mrs. Bently to deal with the customers. He wanted to drop a book off for Mrs. Clemons to read. Maybe she would enjoy an anthology of British poetry.

He took the pleasant walk up the little hill to the Clemonses' residence. Caroline appeared in the quiet parlor. He thought she was a vision with her hair braided and pinned in a crown. She wore a loose cream-colored linen dress, decorated with little tucks and elaborate lace made from cords, beads, and braids. He studied every detail of her as he stood in the doorway. She smelled like fresh honeysuckles.

Hat in hand, he waited on the threshold. After an awkward moment passed, he asked, "May I come in?"

"Please do." He stepped inside and she took his hat.

"I came by to see Mrs. Clemons."

"She took Lydia and Millicent on an outing," Caroline said. "Come meet Rachel."

"What an interesting dress. It's such a change from what the other ladies are wearing."

"Thank you."

"Where did you get it?"

"My aunt mailed it to me from New Orleans. It's imported from Paris. She bought one for herself and one for me exactly alike."

"Really?" He was incredulous.

"Fashions are changing. The tight bodices with the big skirts touching the floor are going out of style, even though women will probably keep wearing them around here for years."

"Interesting. I should look into stocking some of these in the Mercantile. I like that lace."

"*Passementerie.*"

"What?"

"The name of the lace."

He decided not to hand her the book of poems for Hortense. He'd save it for another time. Instead, while she was gazing out the window, he removed a cuff link and slipped it onto the coffee table.

"Come on back to the kitchen for a cup of coffee. Maybe we can talk Rachel out of some of her cinnamon rolls."

Her regal demeanor amazed him. As she walked the shimmering dress floated around her. "Rachel, this is Jake MacGregor."

"Pleased to meet you, Miss Rachel."

"Same here. Young man, pull up a stool. I'll pour you some coffee."

"Madear, could we have cinnamon rolls, please?"

"Sure, baby."

Soon three warm plates, each with a mountain-high roll appeared. Rachel placed two on the table and one on the farthest cabinet counter. She propped her massive arm on the counter to brace herself as she leaned over.

"Thank you, Miss Rachel," Jacob said.

"Oh, come on. Bring your plate and sit here at the table with us," Caroline insisted.

When Rachel took her food to the table, Jake felt one of his eyebrows raise. He cleared his throat. In his twenty-three years he had never experienced such social awkwardness.

"Go ahead. Sit down," Caroline whispered.

I can't believe she said that. Jake caught himself before he gasped. "Don't mind me," he said. He filled his mouth with the rich roll, but Caroline stared out the window instead of eating. Bored beyond measure with his presence, he supposed.

"Stop your fretting. They won't be home till after two o'clock," Rachel said.

"Are you sure?" Caroline asked.

"You heard what Miss Horsey said."

"Have you been working for this family a long time?" he inquired. He was directing the question to Caroline.

"Sure have," Rachel said.

"This is a nice community," he allowed.

"Uh huh," Rachel agreed.

"It's been hot weather already," he said.

"Young man, just sit and drink your coffee." Rachel bobbed her head at him.

Caroline seemed not to hear them. What was she feeling? Fear? He sensed her relationship with the others was bizarre. He wondered whether she was a fallen woman. Maybe Hortense had been kind enough to take her in. What was inside her locket?

"Your locket—it's a gorgeous antique." He wanted to ask her whose picture it held . . . a sweetheart, a child?

Did she sneak and change to her fancy dress after the others left? He wondered why this available woman remained distant. No eligible lady had ever ignored him before. Perhaps he had made a false assumption. Maybe she wasn't single, but she didn't wear a ring on her finger. It was apparent she found him uninteresting.

He finished his cinnamon roll with two cups of coffee. "I came back this morning because I misplaced a cuff link. I thought perhaps I left it here."

"I don't think so," Caroline said, "but we can look."

They went into the parlor. "Here it is." As she picked it up off the coffee table she grinned. He walked back to the kitchen and thanked Rachel. Caroline saw him to the door.

"Thanks for stopping by. I'm glad you found your cuff link."

*　　*　　*

Hortense and her girls returned in a flurry. Caroline observed all the commotion with an air of patience. All three talked at once but no one talked to anyone in particular. Periodically they would address their comments to Caroline.

Sometimes I feel like I'm their mother—all three of them.

"In June we're having a sort of pageant," Millicent said.

"It's called a revue," Lydia said.

"All the cultured young ladies of Taylorsburg are going to be presented," Hortense said.

"You're making our dresses," Millicent said.

At least they could ask. If I were their mother, I'd alter their behavior.

Lydia displayed a pile of peach colored satin. "This is mine."

Millicent held up a pale blue length of fabric.

Poor Millie. She needed to select a darker shade. A jewel-tone green would have been nice. She'll look even chubbier in pastel.

"Mrs. Bently cut the fabric for us," Millicent said. "We were so hoping to see Jacob MacGregor, but he was out."

"I wouldn't think he knows how to measure and cut cloth," Caroline commented.

"We just wanted to see him because he's cute. Haven't you noticed how darling he is?" Millicent asked.

"Caroline, you'll need to put everything else down and spend your time making the dresses." Hortense spoke in an authoritative tone.

During the summers Caroline had spent in New Orleans with her Aunt Mahalia and Uncle Sylvester, she had learned to sew like a professional. She had a talent for placing a piece of muslin over another dress and cutting out a pattern. Next she would baste it together to check for the fit. She would make the final adjustments on the satin garment.

While she thought about making the dresses, Hortense rambled on. "They'll walk across the stage at the school auditorium with Mrs. Harold playing music on the piano." After a second's pause, she threw up her hands. "I just had a genius thought. We'll ask Jake MacGregor to be the master of ceremonies. I'm sure he'll do it."

I'm going to have to stop this. I just don't know how. Sometimes I feel like I'm going to snap inside. These three have just stolen the next month from me. I could have taken a southbound train to New Orleans to visit Aunt Mahalia and Uncle Vester. Or I could have taken a northbound train to stay with Papa in Jackson for a vacation. I don't know how to stand my ground—no, I don't want to leave Rachel. Also I can't break my promise.

These dresses are going to be all wrong. The poor darlings don't know they'll be wearing out-of-date fashions.

It will take most of my time in between doing for them to make these complicated dresses. If I wanted to be in the revue, I wouldn't have time to make myself a dress.

Instead of taking a screaming dash away from them, she smiled. What if her aunt, her deceased mother's sister, visited soon? Not long ago Aunt Mahalia wrote her that it was time to visit Uncle Vester's sister, who lived near Taylorsburg. Sometimes they rented a room at the Covington Hotel. If they should visit within the next month, she wouldn't have time to talk to them.

After her mother died, her aunt and uncle lavished attention on her. They showered their sons with love, but she took the place of the daughter they never had.

The young men traveled as part of their employment. Mahalia was ready for them to settle down, marry, and give her some granddaughters. Caroline wished she could visit with her cousins, but they were birds no longer in the home nest.

"We both want our dresses decorated with lots and lots of beads and lace," Millicent instructed as she would order a steak with extra gravy.

"Girls, show Caroline those pictures of how you want your dresses to look."

Lydia produced two pictures torn from a magazine. "Give those back to me so I can show my friends."

"No, I need to keep them." Caroline, trying not to snap, bit her lip.

I'm going to take a month of my summer to make you an elaborate formal gown so you can charm a man I wish I could be interested in if circumstances were different, and you can't even let me keep the grubby little magazine picture of the way you want it to look.

Thank you, Lord, for giving me more practice in forgiving.

She sat with her face in her hands while they buzzed around her.

"Is something wrong, Caroline?" Hortense said with a threat in the undertone.

"No, I'm just thinking." *And praying not to explode.* Caroline maintained her composure. "First, I need to take some measurements. Lydia, if you'll remove your dress and put on the undergarments you plan to wear, I'll measure you."

"Me first," Millicent said. "Remember what you said this morning?"

"We were talking about hair." Caroline could not resist loving the child inside Millicent, even though it was a self-absorbed child.

"Oh, okay," Millicent said.

"Go ahead and get ready though. This won't take long. Both of you, meet me in the sewing room.

On the way to the sewing room, Hortense said, "Car-o-line, I thought I told you to do something with your hair."

"I'm sorry. I will as soon as I have time, ma'am," Caroline said.

"And what kind of outlandish dress are you wearing?"

"Aunt Mahalia sent me this lingerie dress. It's the new style."

"Mahalia has some wild ideas. It isn't decent."

How is it not decent? None of my body is exposed The dress is not too tight.

"It's suggestive," Hortense said as if she sensed Caroline's question.

Caroline let it go. She enjoyed sewing projects. Even though she held negative feelings about making the dresses, it would feel good to work with the exquisite cloth. The satiny-smooth feel, soft swishing noise, and nose-tickling smell caused her to be eager to start the project. She would do her best to make works of art as unto the Lord.

She was thankful for the long worktable in the narrow sewing room because it made it easier for her to do a professional job of cutting the material. She began working on the peach cloth. She laughed to herself.

Maybe the rapture will happen before I have to put the child in light blue. I'm disappointed in her lack of discrimination. I'll be happy for Lydia if Jake decides to court her. I don't desire any man to court me, because I'll never marry. I can't. Regardless, I'll wear a smile on my face.

She soothed the left side of her lower back with the top of her hand. Leaning over to cut the fabric stretched the tender scar.

Jake's complexion is dark with warm lights, kissed by the sun . . . why do glimpses of him race through my mind? When he finds a wife, I cannot think of him this way. Lord, help me stop now.

* * *

The remainder of the afternoon fled from Caroline. Sewing absorbed her.

Rachel stepped to the door of the sewing room and said, "You're going to put your eyes out straining over them tiny stitches. Excuse me for saying so, but it ain't worth it."

"When my eyes weaken, I'll get some glasses. By the way, Madear, how are your eyes doing?"

"They get by. I've got a pan of biscuits hot in the warm oven. I fried up some sausages, and the butterbeans are warm on the stove."

"It sounds fabulous," Caroline said.

"Let them get it theyselves. You don't have to jump everwhen they say *frog*."

"I try not to jump, dear Rachel."

"Sometimes trying ain't enough," Rachel said. "You got to just quit it."

"Like this sewing?"

"Like that sewing. Yes. You got to cut Miss Horsey loose. By the way *they* are all taking naps. Their morning tuckered them out. *They* ain't worried about nothing 'cause they know Caroline will see about everything for them."

Caroline put her pincushion down. "I take care of them."

"I know, but time comes when taking care of folks ain't necessarily doin' for them what they can do for theyselves."

Caroline walked over to Rachel. "You are such a wise woman. Good night, Madear." She placed her young slender hands around the sagging thick shoulders and planted a smacky kiss on Rachel's cheek.

Rachel patted her. "See you in the morning."

"Go with God," Caroline said. Rachel had told her the parting of loved ones, even overnight, demanded reverence.

*   *   *

Nobody stirred in the house. Caroline put the sewing aside and tip-toed to her room. She snuggled between her soft cotton sheets. "Dear God, help me live in peace with all those whose lives I touch."

The full moon sent mellow light through her window. Soon she dreamed she saw Jake riding by on one of his walking horses and then going away. In her dream she kept wanting him to look around so she could wave goodbye, but he wouldn't look.

After being jolted awake she returned to sleep with another dream of him. They were married. She stood at the front of the church. He came riding by on a white stallion and slowed, but without coming to a complete stop, he scooped her up and cradled her in his arms.

"I'll never marry. I can't. No man will accept me. I am grotesque." She awakened perspiring with tears streaming down her face.

It's just a dream.

She slept again, and another dream followed. "I can't remember your face. You must have looked like my aunt. People say I look like you, Mama."

She climbed out of bed. In the top drawer of her bureau, she had laid the delicate earrings that had been her mother's. She ran her hands over them. Next she picked up the locket. Standing in the moonlight streaming into the window, she could see enough of the daguerreotype of her mother mounted inside the silver locket to reorient her sleepy memory.

I hope I do look like her. She was a beauty.

Locket in hand, she returned to her bed, but sleep scurried off to others with fewer thoughts in their minds. Unable to get another nap, she went to her tiny writing table and lit a candle. On a sheet of linen writing paper she wrote to her Aunt Mahalia, whom she had called Tantaylee since she was a little girl. The pet word was a combination of the French word for aunt and the way Caroline first tried to say "Haley," a diminutive of "Mahalia."

Dear Tantaylee,

You and Uncle Vess are sorely missed by me every day of my life. I love the memories of all the wonderful times I had living in your home. I miss the boys too, but I know Will and Max are out conquering the world of commerce.

Words can never express enough of my gratitude for your leadership and support. I loved all you taught me and helped me learn. The special lessons, normal school, and finishing school helped prepare me for life. I hope to be able to practice piano again soon.

I'm so glad you wanted me to be an accomplished woman, and I hope never to disappoint you, Uncle Vess, or Papa. You've heard all this before. Now the news:

Mama Hortense and her cronies have organized a revue to present the refined young ladies of Taylorsburg into society. The entire town is in a stir. The goal is to entice the bachelors so they will start courtships.

Lydia and Millicent have selected such complicated dresses that I will be amazed if I finish them in time. I was hoping to visit you in New Orleans, but I'll be staying here and sewing for a month. I'm thankful to have my memories of all the fun we've had in the Crescent City.

You said earlier you might be coming up here to look in on Uncle Vess's sister. I'd love to have you stay with us, but conditions with Mama Hortense are worse than ever. I could not bear to hear her say harsh words to you again.

Give my love to Uncle.

With affection and admiration as always,

Your niece,

Caroline

P. S. Reading this over, I realize I forgot to tell you about a new well-heeled and handsome man in town, Jacob MacGregor. He's the nephew of the old Mr. MacGregor, who owned the Mercantile. The elderly MacGregor, you will recall, died in the tornado in Princeton. All the girls and their mothers think Jacob's the perfect catch. This revue is, in my opinion, a farcical parade designed to allow this bachelor to select a girlfriend.

Love, CC

She addressed an envelope to Mrs. Sylvester Schubert and applied a stamp. Writing the letter soothed her. Finally she slept.

At five o'clock in the morning—two hours before it was time for Rachel to arrive—Caroline awakened to the sound of the neighbor's crowing roosters. She made coffee. After drinking a cup and eating half a leftover biscuit, she went into the sewing room to get an early start.

She had been peddling steadily for more than an hour when her last sewing machine needle snapped. "Oh, no."

Caroline lifted her feet off the treadle and crawled on the floor until she found the point that broke off. She removed the piece of needle remaining in the machine. From the shelf she chose one of the little jars she used to store buttons and fasteners, dropped the parts into it, replaced the lid, and took it with her.

I'll have to go buy another needle.

She washed her face and put on a fresh dress, another comfortable cool one. It was white with eyelet lace trim and a scarlet sash. She put on her stockings and sturdy shoes.

Oh, my hair.

She had to stay on the project of making the two elaborate evening gowns, or she would not finish in time. As quickly as she could, she took down the braids and brushed her thick hair. She pulled a section from the front, tied it back with a ribbon, and plopped her quilted sunbonnet on her head.

The Mercantile had a tradition of opening at six for the farmers to get supplies early in the day. She assumed Mrs. Bently would have carried on the tradition.

Making a noiseless exit through the kitchen door, she found her little friend Bruiser waiting for her, Rachel, or Jim. She rubbed his face. Officially he belonged to the neighbors, but he spent most of his time at the back of the Clemons house. No matter how many times Hortense and Lydia chased him away, he always returned. "Good morning, Bruiser. We need to go buy sewing machine needles."

Looking up with his head cocked to one side, he seemed to comprehend.

"Let's go."

*   *   *

Jake stepped out of the Mercantile to breathe some fresh air. He looked at the deserted street. On his way back inside, he heard someone approaching. Caroline was moving at a face pace.

A tiny feist dog panted as it bounced along to keep up with her. He opened the door and invited her to enter. The dog stationed himself outside the door to wait.

"I'll be right back, Bruiser." She took time to reach down and scratch her friend's head. Turning toward Jake, she said, "Good morning."

"Caroline, what can I do for you?"

She held up the jar. "I need some needles for my sewing machine. I broke the last one."

He placed his thumb on his chin so he could think.

"Well?" Caroline asked.

From his shirt pocket he pulled out a pair of glasses. "Hmm. Let's see. Sewing machine needles. To be perfectly honest with you, I haven't a clue where Mrs. Bently keeps them. She isn't here yet."

"On the left wall behind the counter about midway. Third shelf. Look on the right side."

He followed her instructions and found a wooden box of needles. "You know more about my store than I do. Maybe you wouldn't mind working here on Saturdays."

"Thanks, but I'm busy. I have to make dresses for Lydia and Millicent."

"I meant later. Surely you'd like to do something more than work for Mrs. Clemons."

"I teach."

"Oh really?"

"Yes, I teach the lower elementary students at Taylorsburg School."

"Are you qualified?"

"I attended normal school in New Orleans."

He wasn't sure whether he believed her. From his vantage point she didn't add up, and he suspected her of fabrication.

"I have lived for long periods of time with my aunt and uncle in New Orleans. I'll take three needles. This is what Mrs. Bently charges." She handed him some change. "I don't need a sales slip. In a hurry."

"Oh, thanks."

"Have blessings today," she said.

He followed her and helped her with the door. Caroline and her little friend swished back along the street toward the east end of town. Her blonde hair cascaded in waves and curls from the back of her bonnet down her back. He felt his face flushing as he suppressed the warmth of attraction.

It's a hot day, nothing more.

After he propped open the door, he stared back up the low hill.

Where did she go? Oh, she's coming out of the post office.

She knelt to pet the little dog. To his amazement, she looked back at him and waved. He forced a deep fresh breath of air into his lungs. Was he smelling the blooms of flowers in the pots on the street, or was it the lingering essence of Caroline's rosewater and glycerin lotion along with her perfume? Every time she was around him, she had a different fragrance. As a student of chemistry, he was intrigued.

Skirt gathered in her hand, she ran with the feist scampering along. It was a fine morning. When Mrs. Bently arrived, a silly grin popped out on his face.

"What's got you so happy?"

"Everything's going well."

"Mac . . . that's a good name for you . . . I called your uncle Mr. Mac," Geneva Bently said. "You act like a man who's found himself a—oh never mind."

"I wonder where the men are shopping these days," Jake said.

"You ran them off."

"I didn't," he said.

"Just by showing up in high-waisted gray striped pants with pleats, a silk necktie, a stiff-collared white shirt and clean riding boots," she said.

"My uncle always dressed up. I was just . . ."

"They were used to him. Besides his clothes were threadbare." Mrs. Bently rolled her eyes. "Furthermore he had a pudgy corpulence no man found threatening."

Jake rubbed his belly as if checking to see if it was still flat.

"The women love the way you look, but the better you look the worse you make their men look."

"I need some male counsel to teach me how to farm. You know what I mean—men customers. Also I could use a few friends," he said. "I'm not a satin and lace person. The cash register has been busy, but I feel as awkward as a stray bull trying to help all those women with their sewing needs."

"What you need is a good woman to take you out of competition. Maybe you can select one."

Jake smiled as he shook his head.

"The men will come back here in time. Business will result from the efforts of the local settlers to get to know you."

"I need to develop relationships."

"What have you done to make friends?"

"Not much yet, but Mrs. Hortense Clemons is the person who can help me. I can form a bond with her because the Senator's wife is the social pillar of the community."

"Maybe so, but be careful with that one. She's dangerous."

"Oh?" Jake asked.

"I've said too much."

"What?"

"Later," Mrs. Bently said. "Your uncle left you a nice inheritance—a flourishing store and 320 acres of fine land . . . that's the equivalent of two homesteads. Many young men would be pleased."

"I'm confused."

She looked at him with sympathy.

"I wasn't ready to lose my daddy, mama, and uncle. I don't know where to turn."

"To God," she said.

"God did me a bad turn, and I don't know where to head next. I just need to sort it all out."

"Excuse me for being direct, but you need to change your attitude," she said.

"I don't know enough about farming," he said. "The farm is mostly timberland. At least I know how to take care of the horses. What am I supposed to do with the farmhouse?"

"Live in it or find somebody to rent it and help with the farm," she said.

"I can sort-of run the men's departments of the store with your help, but here I am peddling cloth and needles. I was sure I wanted to be a pharmacist, but now I have a whole new set of circumstances to work through. I need advice."

"Pardon me for saying so, Mac, but you need to stop grumbling."

"I thought I'd ride out to the farm this morning. Will you need help here or will you be able to keep it under control?"

"The way I look at it is like this. Every woman who was going to buy fabric bought it yesterday. Things will slow down today. Go ahead. I'll be all right. Folks will just have to stand in line. Where else are they going to shop anyway?"

"Right." He tried to chuckle as he left. "See you in a little while."

One of his two teams lived behind the store. He took time to curry them "Smoky and Firefly, are you two up to an outing?" He hitched them to the surrey.

I don't understand anything about farming except these horses. At least we get along well.

He considered himself a quiet man lacking the temperament for being a merchant. He wanted to spend his life doing something technical. Pharmacy, perhaps research in pharmacy, had been his dream; but the tornado that flattened his hometown of Princeton destroyed it.

He climbed into his surrey. His thoughts brought fresh anger. Riding along he shook his fist. He wanted to attend the Ole Miss Pharmacy School, scheduled to open in a year or two, but now he'd have to stay and take care of what he inherited from his uncle.

The farm was not far from the south edge of town. "Whoa." At the hitching post by the barn he tied Smoky and Firefly.

"Wait. Let me give Fancy and Montana a chance." He turned the horses out into the paddock. "Enjoy this late spring air." He slapped them with affection.

"I'm surprised a horse thief hasn't taken y'all off by now." He unhitched Smoky and Firefly from the surrey.

He changed to his farming clothes and laid his dress trousers across his uncle's bed. In his chambray shirt and overalls, he felt like a farmer. The stiff brogans he forced his feet into were not broken in. He completed his outfit with a new straw hat. Looking into an old broken wall mirror, he laughed out loud.

I'm trying to look like a farmer. These clothes are too new though. What would the women at the Clemons house think of me now?

He wished he could plant a crop, but it was too late. Furthermore, he couldn't farm in the country without living nearby to watch over it. Another problem—he hadn't the vaguest idea of what he should do to start row crop farming. He didn't know how to plow.

He wanted to work. He decided to commence tidying up the place, but first he checked the horses' water supply. He thought some physical exercise would help clear his mind. He walked outside just in time to see the horses walk through the gate and into the road.

"Come back here." He whistled. "Firefly, Smoky." He yelled, "Fancy, Montana."

They munched the tall green grass outside the fence. "Come on back," he yelled. He lowered his voice and approached them, but Fancy moved farther away. The others followed. He turned around and walked back inside.

"Oh, yes. I have carrots in the surrey." He rushed over and grabbed them. Instead of walking toward the horses along the outside of the fence, he stayed inside and approached them. All four horses remembered their way back inside the gate.

"You're a naughty bunch." They went running back to the barn, and he closed the gate. He fed them a scoop of mixed grain.

"I wish you could talk to me. I need help out this mess my life is in." He rubbed Montana's nose. "It would break my heart if somebody stole you beasts."

Jacob went from horse to horse with affectionate attention. He straightened their manes and gave Fancy and Montana a thorough brushing,

"I suppose I ought to start sleeping out here. But I need to guard the store. My assets are too scattered. It's hard to keep an eye on my stuff in two places. I see the problem, but I don't know the solution. Do you all have any suggestions?"

He replenished their hay, added fresh water, gave them a few ears of corn. "That's what I thought. You're not offering any advice. Until I find somebody to live out here as a caretaker, I'm moving all of you behind the Mercantile. I'll have to work harder and spend more feeding you. That paddock behind the store is too small. You'll be crowded.

"I know you ladies and Smoky won't like staying behind the store, but you wouldn't like someone stealing you either."

He checked their hooves. "I'll have to ask Mrs. Bently who a good farrier is. It's about time we got ourselves a puppy. You think you could help me train a dog?"

He sunk his head into Firefly's neck. "What to do? I just don't know. I have no one to talk it over with me—no parents, no uncle, no professors. My sister and brother-in-law have too much to think about to be concerned with me."

Firefly nudged him.

"No need to talk to you, God." He looked up into the sky. "Right now we're not getting along very well."

He looked at the trash on the ground. "This place is a mess." He picked up fallen limbs and stacked them in a pile. "One day I'd like to have a fine house with a good barn out here. I want a wife who won't mind living on this place. The right woman and I can conquer this land together. It will take time to develop it.

"Mrs. Bently does a fine job. If the business keeps up, I'll give her a raise. In the meantime, she deserves a bonus.

"Before it's time to plant crops again, I'll have to get someone to help manage this farm, a man I can trust. Or maybe I can find some people to work in the store. I have is a pile of opportunities, but so far they don't fit any better than my brogans. Should I clear more of this land? Should I raise cattle?"

He sat on the floor of the breezeway. "Now to complicate things I've found the one woman who looks like she'd be perfect for me. But first, I need to figure out who I am and how to manage my inheritance.

"She has something strange about her, even if she is splendid to look at and fascinating to talk to. All the single young women in this town are trying to get me to look their way, all except this Caroline. She is a mystery. This woman has no interest in me, but I haven't been able to think about anything else. When I try to sleep, I see her in my dreams, but I don't even know her last name."

Chapter Three

The Revue

"Madear, I have exciting news." Caroline was reading a letter. "Aunt Mahalia and Uncle Sylvester plan to come for a visit. They'll arrive June 22."

"The day of the girlie parade. You're going to be busy with them little fillies. Uh huh. Getting them combed and powdered. You'll have to scrunch the little dumpling into her getup so her dress will fit. She keeps coming back here and picking up extra food."

"You and I'll manage," Caroline said.

"You need to cut them apron strings," Rachel said.

"You know I can't."

"I tell you what I'll do," Rachel offered." Thursday and Friday beforehand I'll bake up plenty of cookies and bread. I'll make a cake."

"Maybe you could stir up some of your special egg salad and leave it in the icebox."

"I'll do it."

*   *   *

Tuesday Caroline asked Jim to hitch up the buggy. Hortense swished into the kitchen where Caroline shared coffee with Rachel as they discussed the supply list. "What are you up to? Why aren't you sewing?"

"The dresses are ready," Caroline said.

"How many times have I told you, Rachel, you are not to sit in this kitchen with the white folks?"

Caroline glared.

"Why haven't you tried them on for a final fitting?" Hortense asked.

"We did two nights ago," Caroline said. "You said everything looked perfect."

"Stop getting smart with me." Hortense leered at Caroline. Then she whirled toward Rachel, "Are they pressed?"

"Sure are," Rachel said.

Hortense crept out but turned in her tracks. "What is that awful smell? Is it coming from your body, Car-o-line?"

"I don't smell anything," Caroline replied with fake innocence, amused that Hortense noticed the new scent from Paris.

Hortense stormed out of the kitchen.

"Sugar, the Potter knows the clay," Rachel said. "He knows how much pressure it takes and what you can stand to make you a worthy vessel for him."

"I see no reason to tell Mama Hortense that Mahalia and Sylvester are coming to town. They'll stay at the Covington anyway."

"If she thinks she has to make plans for them, she'll just cause a bunch of confusion," Rachel said.

Bonnet and bag in hand, Caroline scooted out to the buggy, where Jim waited to take her to the Mercantile. Most weeks the Clemons family sent Jim with a list to buy the commodities required for the week. He would hand the list to Mrs. Bently or to Jake. One of them would fill the order. Once a month Jake sent the bill to the Senator, who paid it in full. This time she wanted to go with Jim so she could shop for some extra food.

Her New Orleans relatives, accustomed to the finest cuisine, would graciously accept whatever they were served in Taylorsburg, but Caroline wanted to give them the best of what she had to offer. She planned to provide extra snacks, although she would have to sneak them past Hortense. Maybe she could take food to the hotel during their visit. Papa would be glad for anything she did for Tantaylee.

"It's a special weekend coming up," she told Jim.

"Yes, ma'am. What with that revue and all," Jim said.

"I need to shop for a few extra items."

*   *   *

Jake had scarcely seen Caroline for three weeks. On Sundays at church she sat with the Clemons family, but she always seemed to drift away before and after church to talk to people he didn't know.

He filled his days with the details of trying to establish his new life in the fresh town. It seemed Caroline was avoiding him. He wondered whether he scared her away by asking her to work in the store.

Mrs. Clemons and her daughters had dropped by the Mercantile a few times. They introduced him to Loretta Larson, one of the high school teachers. He guessed she was in her thirties. Miss Larson prepared the script for the revue and insisted she meet him twice to rehearse it. When he saw how difficult it was to read her handwriting and how unusual some of the names were, he was grateful for her help.

He watched Caroline step down from the Clemonses' buggy that Mrs. Hortense's employee had parked and tied to the hitching post in front of the store. Since it was a steamy day, Jake had opened the windows and doors.

Bareheaded, she was a beautiful sight. Her hair was brushed neatly and tied in a ribbon. She seemed to be moving extra fast. "Good morning, Mrs. Bently," she said. "Here's Jim's usual list."

"Could I help you with anything?" Jake asked.

"Yes, I need to purchase some cheese." She walked toward his butcher counter.

"This is extra. Will it be all right with Mrs. Clemons?"

"Did the Senator not pay his bill last month?"

"Yes, he did. Right on time. Excuse me. My question was indelicate. Please accept my apology. Now what would you like?"

"Just put my extra items on the bill. Write 'Caroline' beside them on the list. Three pounds of the hoop cheese, sliced."

As he sliced and weighed the cheese, she looked inside the glass at the limited selections displayed.

"What else for you?" Jake asked.

"Let's see what you have." She peered through the glass. "Please allow me to taste the summer sausage."

He sliced a generous piece and handed it to her.

"Not bad. Give me two rolls. I'll need some crackers to go with it. Please select some crisp ones."

He went to work wrapping the sausage.

"How's your ham?"

"Extra good."

"Let me sample it."

He handed her a taste of one on display. "All right, I like that. I'll take one."

"One what?"

"Ham."

"Okay. You must be planning something special."

"Sort of. Give me three more dozen eggs than the list says."

"Check," he said.

"Do you have any chicory?"

"Mrs. Bently, do we?" Jake asked.

"Yes, it's behind the coffee beans." Mrs. Bently showed him.

"I'll need some dark roasted coffee beans and some chicory," Caroline said.

He rushed to keep up with her.

"What kind of cocoa do you have?"

"I don't understand the question," he said." Good cocoa."

She laughed. "It's all good. If you have Criollo, I'd prefer it. If you don't, I'll take Forastero."

He looked confused.

"We have some Criollo, but it's getting harder to find," Mrs. Bently said as she came by holding the list of the usual staples for the Clemonses' household.

"Give me the Criollo, please."

Mrs. Bently showed Jake where she had placed the rare cocoa out of view. "You'd better get plenty before we run out."

"Any fresh paprika?"

Mrs. Bently nodded as she scrambled to place some in a tiny jar.

"These must be some special guests the Clemonses are expecting."

Caroline ignored the comment.

He totaled the bill in a ticket book with carbon paper in it. With a glance he questioned Mrs. Bently about the purchases; she gave him a reassuring look. Mrs. Bently placed the groceries in one spot so Jim could place them in the buggy. Jake smiled ceremoniously as he handed Caroline a copy of the bill.

"Is it all right?" He waited.

Caroline glanced at it. "Yes, it's fine," she said. "It's about what I expected."

He helped finish loading the groceries and assisted her into the buggy.

"Thank you," she said.

As she left, he realized she had seemed to be in a hurry. Except for what was necessary, she had not engaged in conversation—no small talk.

What kind of housekeeper can prance into the Mercantile and buy whatever she wishes? It's odd that she can charge it to the owner of the house. How did she know about different kinds of cocoa? What is with her?

*　　*　　*

Wednesday morning Caroline told Lydia and Millicent, "Shampoo your hair in rainwater."

"When?" Lydia asked.

"Now."

"We need you to help us," Millicent said.

"I'm busy. You'll have to help each other."

"We'll fight," Millicent said.

Caroline ignored their protests. Because she had neglected her housecleaning chores, she needed to dust, sweep, scrub, and mop.

After the baths and the housecleaning, Caroline rolled their towel-dried hair and tied the sections with corn shucks. Then she shampooed her own, towel dried it, and rolled it.

Caroline went to the kitchen to enjoy a cool glass of tea with Rachel.

Hortense stormed in. "What about me?"

"Get your daughters to help you shampoo, and I'll roll your hair." In addition to two ornate dresses for ungrateful girls, the sewing project had produced a messy house and a testy attitude. Fatigue plagued Caroline.

Hortense's bottom lip pouted, but she flung the swinging door open. "I'll change into a dressing gown."

As soon as she left and the door closed, Rachel snickered. "Did you see how ole Miss Horsey stuck out her lip and puffed up?"

Millicent and Lydia helped Hortense shampoo her hair. They managed to get her sopping wet.

While the horseplay was going on, Caroline attended to the sour dough leavening.

"How was Mr. Jacob MacGregor yesterday?" Hortense asked.

"Oh, he was all right."

"Was there a problem?"

"He was nervous about how much I spent. I know Papa won't care. He'll expect us to help feed Tantaylee and Uncle Vess."

"I know, darling. I'm working on it."

"You're wonderful, Madear."

*   *   *

Millicent, rummaging through the pantry, found the extra groceries in the house. When she filled both hands with crackers and cheese, Rachel snapped, "Stop that. Put it back. You won't be able to wear your dress. Get out of here."

Friday night Caroline rerolled everyone's hair and laid out the clothes.

*   *   *

Saturday Caroline arranged the three hairdos. She helped Hortense dress. Then she helped Lydia into her peach colored dress.

"You look elegant, Lydia."

"I know." Lydia smiled as she kissed rose-colored crepe paper to color her lips.

She needed to complete one more chore: help Millicent dress. The girl's proportions defied the whalebones required for the costume. Caroline pulled with all her might to lace the back.

"Ouch. You're *hurting* me."

"I'm sorry. It's just a little hard to fasten everything the way we usually do." Caroline braced her leg on the footboard of Millicent's bed to gain leverage as she pulled the corset laces. "Suck in."

"Stop it." The girl spit as she slapped at Caroline, managing to dodge just in time.

"I'm through. That's it." Caroline raged out of the bedroom with Millicent tagging along behind her.

"I didn't mean it. Please help me finish dressing."

They reached the room and closed the door. Caroline said in a low no-nonsense tone, "Don't *ever* slap me or spit on me again."

With Caroline pushing and Millicent sucking in, they managed to fasten the underwear and pull the blue dress in place.

"Be careful, Millie."

"You didn't sew it right. I'm afraid part of me will pop out."

"The waist of your dress is under a big strain. I'm glad I triple stitched it. Let's just hope the satin doesn't tear."

With Jim and Caroline's assistance, Lydia and Hortense loaded into the surrey. Then came Millicent hobbling along.

"You're going to have to walk normally on the stage," Lydia said. "Stop acting weird just to get our sympathy."

"I'm doing my best," Millicent said. "It hurts. Caroline fastened my corset too tight."

Caroline was losing her patience. *Always my fault.*

Millicent stood, not knowing how to step up, since she couldn't bend enough to climb into the surrey. "I'll have to ride in the front. Mama, get in the back with Lydia."

"Jim, go around to your side. Take her hand and pull while I push," Caroline said. "Hold on, Millie." Caroline boosted the girl's rear.

"Pay attention to the top of your dress," Caroline said.

Off they went to the revue. How they would get Millicent out of the surrey when they parked on the school grounds was not a concern of Caroline's.

Her aunt and uncle didn't arrive. Feeling the quiet of the empty house, she collapsed in a chair. She wept. The tears caught her by surprise. "I suppose I'm just too tired. Forgive me, Lord. I wish I could have made a dress for myself." Even though she realized Hortense would have been horrified, she scooted over to the parlor sofa and lounged . . . dozed.

A loud knock and the clanging of the doorbell startled her. "Tantaylee and Uncle Vess." She shot up from the couch and threw the doors open.

After hugs, kisses, and joyful tears, Caroline asked, "Are you ready for lunch?"

"Yes, we're starved."

"I have some sandwich makings."

She took her aunt by the hand, and her uncle followed close behind. They went back to the kitchen worktable where she placed home baked bread, sliced cheese, summer sausage, and relishes. From Rachel's hiding place she brought out molasses teacakes and chocolate cake. She poured coffee. Her guests seemed comfortable on the kitchen stools.

After they ate a few bites Mahalia asked, "What time does the revue start?"

"Two o'clock."

"Eat fast," Mahalia said. "Girl, it's already 12:30."

Surprised, Caroline pushed her plate with its uneaten sandwich aside. "Do you want to go to the revue?"

"Yes, of course."

"How?"

"We drove up in our new automobile"

Her uncle asked, "You didn't hear the motor when we drove up?"

"No, I was oblivious to everything."

"It's my new Thomas-Flyer. I'll just need a minute to get it cranked. Let me know, girls, just before you're ready."

"Traveling in the new auto took longer than we expected because some of the roads were terrible," Mahalia said.

"We stopped ten or twelve times to open and close gates across the road. The map took us through cattle pastures," he said.

"Vester, could you be a sweetie and put the food up? But first, bring in the stuff from the auto. Come on, Caroline. We don't have a minute to lose."

He went out to the car and fetched a red dress on a hanger, a hat bag, and a small suitcase.

"What's going on?" Caroline asked.

"You're going to be in the revue," Aunt Mahalia said.

"How can I?"

Vester spoke up. "Your aunt thought of everything. Do this for her."

"It's too late," Caroline said.

"No, we can do it," Mahalia said. "Let's hurry."

"Do I have a choice?" A smile lighted Caroline's face.

"Not about this." Mahalia shook her head.

"Let's dress in the sewing room. We have more space in there," Caroline suggested.

Mahalia pulled a slender red dress from a bag.

"I won't look good in a red dress."

"Says who?"

"Mama Hortense."

"Stop hearing her in your head. You'll be gorgeous in a red dress. Now hurry. We don't have much time."

"What's this?" Caroline asked, holding up an undergarment like nothing she had ever seen.

"Oh, you wear it on the top section of your body. It's the latest style. Nobody fashionable wears those whalebone contraptions anymore. The Paris designers have cut corsets in two."

Caroline looked baffled.

"This lets you breathe and move," Mahalia said.

Caroline had quit wearing corsets since her worst injury . . . .

"Try it. We don't have time to dress you in whalebone anyway. This will look good under your dress."

Caroline chuckled.

"It's a blessing to hear you laugh," Mahalia said.

As part of her routine Caroline removed the saturated soft cotton dressing covering the wounds on her back and tied another one in place.

"Horrible—blood and pus." Mahalia's face blanched and then flushed. "I think I'm going to be sick. No, I'm going to kill somebody What on earth?"

"Oh, some scars. We're in a hurry, Aunt Haley, please. Can we talk about it another time?"

"Someone has beaten you within an inch of your life, right? Somebody pulverized your back. Who did this to you?" Mahalia's anger built to rage.

"Where's my slip? You said we needed to hurry, didn't you?" Caroline said as she placed her hand where she always did on her left lower back. The tender exposed flesh, not completely intact after wounds inflicted months ago, oozed. Caroline's face became contorted as the wounded flesh went into spasms.

Mahalia gasped. "I'm serious. I'll kill whoever . . ."

"My slip?" Caroline asked.

Mahalia assisted her.

"How do I get into this dress? Where's the front?"

"Okay. You've been hurt enough. I want to make things better for you. The dress goes on like this. Buttons in the front."

"I don't understand this dress, but it's beautiful," Caroline said.

"This is an original design by Paul Poiret of Paris." Mahalia told her. "Instead of the wide flowing skirts touching the floor with a train that drags behind, it's a slim gown with soft gathers of fluid fabric coming from a high waist."

"Wow—you shouldn't have." Caroline said. "I see now. The neck scoops all the way around."

"Right. It is supposed to hang from your shoulders."

A bodice of glamorous pearl-like sheer gray fabric overlaid the red layer. An ornate scalloped jeweled band of copper-colored fabric with sparkling red stones and shimmering gold beads scattered throughout embellished the bust line and mid upper arms. The semi-fitted sleeves came to her elbows. The dress had an empire waistline. In the front it had a buttoned placket to the waist.

"Here are your accessories." Mahalia adorned Caroline with a chain necklace for her locket, two wide copper bracelets, and some short gloves the same red color as the dress.

Mahalia took the locket to Vester so he could attach it.

"We'll do something snappy with your hair."

"We don't have time for a pompadour," Caroline said.

"No, but that's all right. Your curly hair is just perfect. Don't brush or comb it. Just pin it up in a chignon in the back with the curls blousing out as they please."

Caroline arranged her hair as her aunt suggested. "I have to trust you, Tantaylee. This is so different from anything I've ever worn."

"You've seen pictures like this in the magazines, haven't you?"

"I have."

Mahalia folded a red scarf into a narrow band, which she wrapped around Caroline's head and tied in the back at the nape of her neck.

Caroline rubbed tiny drops of oil on her eyelashes. Mahalia brushed a light coating of rouge on her niece's high cheekbones and a slightly thicker coating on Caroline's lips. From her bag, she obtained a makeup pencil, which she used to darken the eyebrows. Finally she dusted Caroline with a light coat of rice powder.

"Voilà."

Looking into the mirror, Caroline said, "I wouldn't have recognized myself in a photograph. I like the new narrow silhouette better than the old style of dresses."

"I thought the announcer would be introducing each young lady; so I wrote a little speech about you," Vester said. "We'll hand it to him. Looks like you're ready." He went outside, and the women followed. It was apparent that both Caroline's aunt and uncle had conspired to make this event happen.

"The new man in town, Jacob MacGregor, is announcing," Caroline explained.

"Did I detect a note of interest in your voice?" Vester asked.

47

"No, I'm not at all interested."

"As you walk out on the stage, hold your head up," Vester said. "Smile. You'll be the most beautiful girl in the revue and the most stylish. You don't have to look haughty, but you should look confident."

"I'll try," Caroline said.

"You'll do it," he said.

"What about my shoes?" Caroline asked.

"Those are fine," Mahalia said. "I'll keep your purse for you."

Caroline took care not to soil her fine dress as she climbed into the auto. They motored the four blocks north to the schoolhouse.

"You've got your gloves on," Mahalia said. "Good."

Her uncle drove around to the north side of the building. The children stopped playing on the grounds and ran to catch a glimpse at the new Thomas-Flyer. "Look. It's Miss Clemons in an automobile." Lively waving back and forth added to the dizzy excitement Caroline was experiencing.

"Take slow deep breaths," Mahalia told her.

The auto lurched and coughed as Vester steered it next to the building facing a hitching post. When he killed the motor, she started to hop out.

"Stay put. Let Vester have a chance to help us out of the Flyer."

*　　*　　*

In the hall the eleven participants stood in their array of gowns, almost all pastel. Because most of them wore hoops under their dresses, they couldn't stand close enough to whisper the latest malevolent gossip. Caroline was glad she hadn't allowed her stepsisters to wear hoops, which were passé. Matrons fanned the girls to prevent perspiration stains.

Millicent stood on the top of the three steps leading to the right edge of the stage. On the way to the back of the line

Caroline saw her. The Gibson Girl hairstyle, the bodice with the poufed sleeves trimmed in white lace, the cinched waist, the wide skirt supported by a layer underneath, and the big sash trailing into a train—all of it looked miserable and slightly quaint.

If they had been a little nicer to me, I might have tried to tell them how out of style their dresses are. I can't help laughing inside myself at the fools.

Hortense was presiding over her daughters. She looked flushed in her black silk-lined lace dress and her ostrich feathered hat—it was the ugliest hat Caroline had ever seen.

Lydia stood confident in her billowy peach frock on the bottom step. Caroline managed to sneak by undetected. So did Mahalia.

Girls in the line said, "Who is that?"

Sylvester said, "I'll give the paper to the master of ceremonies. You said his name is Jacob MacGregor?"

"Right," both women responded.

Caroline caught sight of Hortense escaping from the crowded little alcove by the stage and turned to the wall to avoid the woman's lethal view.

*　　*　　*

"Sylvester Schubert here. Jacob MacGregor, I presume."

"Yes, Jacob MacGregor." Hands were extended to be shaken.

In a matter-of-fact tone, Vester said, "One more young lady will be in the revue." He handed over the folded paper. "Here's her introduction for you to read."

"Oh, all right. Thanks."

At that moment Miss Loretta Larson from the top step on the left side of the stage smiled with firm politeness. "Let's go," she whispered. The piano fanfare grew louder.

"Here I come," Jake said.

Mrs. Harold, the piano player, looked toward Jake and Miss Larson as if to cue them. When Mayor Samson stepped from the edge of the stage to the lectern, the piano went silent.

"Welcome to all of you. You show your civic pride by coming out this afternoon to support our lovely young ladies. Let's give our master of ceremonies, Mr. Jacob Nathaniel MacGregor, a round of applause." The audience clapped and cheered

Mrs. Harold resumed playing as softly as she could. Jake laid his papers on the lectern. He dug in his pocket for his readers. With the revue in action, he read about Miss Millicent Leigh Smith. As the young woman swished onto the stage and twirled awkwardly when she reached the center, Jake read Millie's brief biography. Polite applause came from the audience.

Next was Miss Lydia Suzanne Smith, who moved with regal elegance as he presented her and Mrs. Harold played softly. The applause sounded much louder.

On and on the show went. Jake was glad he remembered how to pronounce all the names as the ladies paraded across the stage. When they finished, they exited on the south side. In the rehearsals they had planned to line up in the south hall as they waited to return to the stage a final time as a group.

At last it was Caroline's turn. Mrs. Harold had stopped playing, but she heard Jake say, "And our last participant is . . . ." Astonished, he looked up. The music resumed. He fumbled to unfold the paper. "Caroline." A long pause followed as he studied the script he hadn't taken time to read. His eyebrows went up, and he adjusted his eyeglasses. "Clemons?" He looked confused and hesitant. When Miss Larson nudged him, he glanced around. She gave him a reassuring nod. Caroline sauntered onto the stage. She smiled and walked near the front edge, over to the lectern, and back to the center.

The audience clapped with wild enthusiasm, the children called out, a hush fell over the audience. He read in a slow voice. It was apparent he was learning information he had not previously known. Although it was unrehearsed, the script could not be incorrect.

"She is the daughter of Senator T. Chadwick Clemons?" He finished his statements as though they were questions. From his pocket he pulled out a handkerchief to daub the moisture from his forehead; then he tugged at his bow tie.

Hortense rose from her seat on the front row and headed with her ostrich feathers ruffled toward the south hall. "Well, I never—they can't do this. They're breaking the rules." She muttered loud enough for the audience halfway back to hear her.

The mayor stepped forward and escorted her out of sight. "Come on, Hortense. Hush now."

"Let go of my elbow." She jerked her arm in protest. "We've got to stop her from making fools of her family."

Jake continued to read. To the music of Mrs. Harold's soft piano playing, Caroline, ignoring the fracas, strolled and twirled in grace and loveliness on the stage.

"She is presented today by her aunt and uncle, Mahalia and Sylvester Schubert, from the Gentilly section of New Orleans. She is the well-loved teacher of the lower elementary grades here at Taylorsburg School. She is an accomplished musician, having studied piano and organ. Her hobbies include dress design, riding, and baking. A talented seamstress and hair arranger, she prepared her stepsisters, Lydia and Millicent Smith for the revue.

"She is a graduate of a finishing school, riding academy, and normal school all in New Orleans.

"Her fashionable gown is a Paul Poiret original imported from Paris."

The audience thundered with a standing ovation. When she left the stage and the applause died down, the participants returned in a line, beginning with the last and finishing with the first. Millicent was crying. Mrs. Harold played as loud as she could to cover Hortense's voice.

Jacob walked toward the south backstage steps. Hortense, with Mayor Samson grabbing at her, stood in view of the audience in the front north corner. She elbowed him and jolted loose. At the top of her lungs she yelled, "Jacob MacGregor, you broke the rules. You ruined it."

The piano music thundered.

"Do you have a copy of the rules, Mrs. Clemons?" the mayor asked.

"Well, uh, no. They're not written down."

"That ends it. Unless the rules are written, there are none."

Hortense swooned. She fell just in time for Jacob to catch her. The curtain closed in rough jerks.

*   *   *

Back at the Clemons house, Vester told Mahalia, "Let's just wait out here and enjoy the sunshine."

Caroline tiptoed inside through the kitchen door, took her things back to her room from the sewing room, quickly changed into her white dress with the crimson sash, hung the Poiret original in her closet, locked it, and rushed back through the kitchen. On her way out she grabbed the chocolate cake.

They went to the hotel, where her uncle had arranged for a suite of rooms.

"You do know I'll have to pay for this," Caroline said. "Hortense will punish me."

Mahalia and Vester laughed out loud. "Stay out of her way," Vester said.

"I try to."

"Although I don't believe in backing down, I don't want to throw my precious niece into the line of fire," Mahalia said. "We have a room for you here. You can stay with us."

"She won't let me."

"Just do it," Vester said. "We'll take you to get your things. Tell her."

"She's probably in her room for the night. She'll say I caused her to have the vapors, but I suspect she's been swigging the spirits."

"This will be easy," Mahalia said. "Leave her a note."

"I need to take care of Lydia and Millicent."

"Lydia is a grown woman, and Millicent soon will be. They can solve their own problems."

"Write the note now since you think you won't see her." She took Caroline to the extra bedroom in the suite. "You have locks and dead bolts on the door to the outside hall and to the parlor here. It's just like being at home with us."

"Okay," Caroline said. "I'll do it."

"We need to unpack and settle into our room, and we want to rest a few minutes," Vester told her. "Afterwards we'll go get your things."

Caroline realized she could use a nap. She wrote the note and decided to rest too. She was more exhausted than she realized.

A little later her aunt called her. "It's four o'clock."

"Thanks. If I don't get up, I won't sleep tonight," Caroline said. As soon as she put herself together, she went into the parlor. "Let's go over to the house. I have my note ready, and I need to get some clothes."

"Good girl," Mahalia said.

"Let's go," Vester said.

All the rooms of the Clemons home were empty except one. Hortense's snoring rattled loud enough to resonate throughout the house, even though her door was closed. Caroline found a note clipped to her door: Mama, we've gone to visit the Byrons, Lydia and Mil.

Caroline attached hers to the same clip.

I have to hurry—get out of here.

"I'll come help you," Mahalia said. "I'm not afraid of that inebriated ninny."

They took the new Poiret gown and enough clothes to last a week to the auto. Heart throbbing in her chest, Caroline went back one more time. She filled a croker sack with cheese, summer sausage, ham, and crackers. On top she tossed in a loaf of Rachel's bread. She brought the egg salad, which she'd store in the dining room ice box.

I'm not stealing from my own house, even though it feels like I am. Papa would want me to serve snacks to my guests. I've got to get out of here before Mama Hortense wakes up and hears me.

She panted as she rushed. Seated in the auto, she heaved a deep sigh.

They motored through the few streets of Taylorsburg for the sheer joy of it. "I love it," Caroline said. "This new wonderful way to travel." When they stopped and Vester killed the motor in front of the hotel, she said, "I feel bad about leaving Mama Hortense there. The girls have gone, and she's all alone."

"I understand, but consider the alternative, he said. "You could stay there with her tonight and try to be available as her nurse-caretaker. It would, however, be as dangerous as trying to nurse a rattlesnake or a wounded she tiger. You wouldn't be able to help her. Let her sleep it off," Vester said.

"You're right," Caroline said. "All the stuff in the house is just stuff. I just pray the angels will protect her."

Mahalia said, "Pray the Lord's will be done."

With each passing moment, Caroline worried less and felt more of a growing sense of freedom.

*   *   *

Although Jake's original plan was to live in the farmhouse, he preferred to sleep on the cot in the back of his store. His meals, foods he selected from the Mercantile, required little preparation. Frequently, he ate out.

He had few choices of public places to eat. On Saturday evening nothing was open except the dining room in the Covington Hotel. When he walked inside, he heard a lonely harmonica playing a mournful rendition of "I'll Take You Home Again, Kathleen."

Having seated himself at his usual table, he looked over the little menu, which had no untried selections. It was his habit to eat the meal of the day. On Saturday the cook prepared something special. That night it was chicken pie with English peas and carrots cooked inside a double crust. Dessert was banana pudding. "I'll take it," he told the server. Not seeing anyone to talk with, he pulled out his glasses and started reading to keep from thinking about the way it felt to eat another meal alone. He liked the classics.

Absorbed in *War and Peace,* he didn't look up until his sweet tea was served. As he squeezed lemon juice into his glass, he saw three people at the next table—Sylvester Schubert; whom he met at the revue; a lady, who must have been Mrs. Schubert: and the loveliest young woman he had ever seen, Caroline Clemons.

"Come join us," Sylvester said. Soon all four were eating the special and enjoying a lively visit.

"Would you bring me some cayenne pepper?" Sylvester asked the server.

Chapter Four

The Sweet Life

Sunday, church . . . Jake stood around afterwards and chatted with his new friends. He accepted Mahalia's invitation to a picnic on the Gitano Creek bank by the waterfall. Back at the hotel, they collected the food Caroline had brought. On the way, they picked up Jake after he put up his horses and surrey.

Over lunch Mahalia said, "We need to go visit Vester's sister. Caroline; you are welcome to go with us or perhaps you would like to go back to the hotel to rest."

Jake seized the opportunity. Here was Caroline with time on her hands. Her aunt seemed to have a way of arranging things. "I'd be honored to have you go for a ride with me this afternoon, Caroline."

She blushed. After the meal, her aunt and uncle took them to the back of the mercantile, where Jake hitched the horses to the surrey so they could ride to his farm.

"You like horses?"

"Yes."

"You ride?"

"Yes."

"I believe I read that you went to riding school. What style did you learn?"

"English."

"Let me show you my other horses."

When they arrived at the farm, he led Smoky and Firefly to have a drink. He released the brake on the windmill so the pump would fill the holding tank, which was half-full. The wind turned the fan and the pump moved up and down. Fresh water bubbled out.

He let his other mares, Fancy and Montana, run into the paddock also. He pulled out some hay and placed some corn in the long trough.

She seemed to have a special affinity for the horses, but she showed little interest in him. He wondered why she answered most of his questions with monosyllables. Every time he thought he understood a little about her, she confused him all over again. She seemed to be preoccupied. Instead of responding to him, she kept placing her left hand on her back.

He wondered: *What is this all about?*

"We shouldn't have come out here. Are you uncomfortable with me and no chaperon?"

"Not especially," she said.

"Do your aunt and uncle like to ride?"

"Yes, they love it."

"I thought I might ask them to come for a ride tomorrow," he said. "Caroline, do you think it's safe to leave these horses out here?"

"If you don't ever stay here, it's just a matter of time until a horse thief comes through and takes them. Most of the people around here won't bother them though because you would be able to identify your horses."

"I need a dog to help protect the place."

"Yes."

"Any ideas about what kind of dog I need?"

"Whatever is available," she said as she patted the top of her hand against her lower left back.

The day before, every other single young woman in town had vied for his attention. Here he stood on Sunday afternoon with the one woman whom he found appealing, but she seemed uninterested in him.

What am I supposed to think? What is this nervous gesture she has?

*   *   *

Monday morning Caroline awakened refreshed. Before she heard any noise in the suite, she sat at the desk and read her Bible.

She had a new sense of freedom. In no time at all she had stopped worrying about Hortense, although she continued to have genuine concern . . . and she needed to stay on guard to keep her promise.

Lord, please heal this woman my father married, bless her, let her see thy love for her.

Using the hotel stationery, she wrote a note.

> My wish is that all is well with you. The people of the town of Taylorsburg and the state of Mississippi are grateful for all you do. I am especially gratified to have you as my father.
>
> How have you been? Are you taking good care of yourself? Do you eat the right foods and rest enough?
>
> I have done all in my power to take care of Mama Hortense, Lydia, and Millicent. Just when I thought I could no longer bear their mistreatment of me, Uncle Vester and Aunt Haley came for a visit. They motored up here from New Orleans. Their plans are to stay one week. The respite is surpassed in pleasure only by the fellowship.

Hortense has been on a rampage. She made a public spectacle of herself Saturday last. Her conduct is defaming the family reputation.

Please forgive me for worrying you, but I think you need to know that for the moment our ménage of four has dissolved. The girls left a note that they were visiting their friends. I think they'll do just fine.

Visiting Tantaylee and Uncle Vester here a few days at the Covington. We have some exciting adventures planned. When we see one another again, you will receive a more thorough report after you bring me up to date on your splendid life.

What's happening at home is strange. Hortense has taken to her room most of the time. She is out of sight, but I know she is all right because it is possible to hear her snoring. Rachel will return to work this morning, and I'll get reports periodically.

Rushing off to look in on Rachel and drop this off at the post, I remain

Your adoring daughter who loves you,
Carrie

In fast motion she bathed and dressed. She brushed her hair and tied it back with a ribbon. On her head she plopped her bonnet. As she left, she placed a note to Mahalia on the couch.

Without making so much noise as a cracking sound of the floor, she left. Toward the post office and the Clemons house, she sprang with light steps. Bruiser was waiting on the back steps.

"Good morning, fine doggy." She took time to pet the little feist.

"Come in this kitchen, Missy. I was wondering how you was."

"Having a great time with Tantaylee and Uncle Vess at the hotel."

"What about Lydia and Millicent?" Rachel asked.

"They're spending a few days with the Byrons. I saw them at church yesterday. They're doing fine. Has Mama Hortense left her room this morning?"

"No, but Miss Horsey's come through here some time or other."

"I didn't come to see her," Caroline said. "Have you felt well?"

"As well as usual," Rachel said. Somebody's got to eat these biscuits." She walked to the back door. "Jim's got the surrey hitched up already. Tell him to give you a ride back to the hotel. Meanwhile I'll pack y'all up some breakfast."

"You are sweet."

"I got biscuits and sausages in here and some of the best honey in the house. Let me pour some of this chicory coffee in a jug too."

"Wonderful."

"Child, take care. Don't you worry about us. She ain't going to mess with me. The Lord's angels are all around. As far as Miss Horsey is concerned, what's going to happen is going to happen."

"Madear, you are such an inspiration." She threw her arms around Rachel.

"Run along, little darling. Go enjoy this day of your life. None of us can predict what tomorrow holds."

When she returned to the hotel suite, she made noise. Her aunt and uncle had evidently needed a solid night's rest. They greeted her with sleepy voices.

"Here's breakfast," Caroline announced.

*　　*　　*

Jake needed to move his horses to the safer spot behind the store. Until he could make other arrangements, he would feed them and run them in the fenced paddock out back. He needed help moving them to town.

He sensed the men were not impressed with his role in Saturday's gala. He had their spare money, as well as the attention of their womenfolk.

How can I move those horses?

Four fine Tennessee Walkers with saddles and bridles. He wasn't sure how his uncle had managed them.

I suppose I could lead them in a train.

He decided to go down to the Covington for a morning cup of coffee and a sweet roll. As he sat there with an old newspaper, Sylvester, Mahalia, and Caroline came down the stairs.

After chatting a bit, Jake asked, "Would you help me move my horses from my farm to the back of the store?"

"We'll be right back," Mahalia said. "We need to dress a little simpler."

Jake and Caroline led the way in the surrey. Sylvester and Mahalia following as the shiny new automobile bumped along the dusty road to the farm.

At the farm he gave them a tour of the little old house his uncle had owned. "It's cute and quaint," Mahalia said. A breezeway about sixteen feet wide and open from the front to the back sat between rooms on either side opening into it.

"It's structurally sound, Sylvester added. It could be fixed up and used. It has possibilities."

Caroline looked around with what Jacob considered polite interest. From underneath her bonnet brim, she stole glances at him, but when his eyes met hers, she looked down or away.

They saddled and rode the horses into town. Jake tried to engage Caroline in conversation, but she seemed not to hear him.

"You're going too slow, Caroline. You said you went to riding school, but you act like you're scared. Pardon my saying so, but have you ever been on a horse before?"

She didn't answer; instead she made a horrible face. When her feet hit the ground after the ride, she started doing that little nervous thing. She placed her hand on her left lower back and patted herself. Her frown deepened. Tears streamed down her cheeks.

She must be miserable when she is around me.

He walked to her and patted her shoulder. "You all right?"

"I'm fine." Caroline was trembling.

Her nervous mannerism is starting to annoy me.

As soon as Jake stabled, watered, and fed the horses, he took his new friends through the store by entering the back entrance. "Come meet us at the Covington for lunch if you wish," Sylvester told him.

The day's lunch special was tasty—fried chicken and hot water cornbread with creamed corn, green beans, and sliced tomatoes. Dessert was blackberry cobbler. Over lunch the men chatted. Caroline continued with her nervous mannerism. Mahalia kept hugging her. None of the women's behavior made sense. Saturday on the stage she had been the most poised young woman he had ever seen, but today . . . strange.

"What kind of work are you in?" Jacob asked Sylvester.

"I buy cotton," Sylvester said.

"You what?"

"I deal in commodities futures, mostly cotton and sugar cane."

"Sounds stressful."

"Yes. The good part of it is that I'm not tied to my job. We have time to enjoy life. Tell me how you ended up here with a store and an unworked farm."

"I was going to Ole Miss."

"Ah, Ole Miss. Did you like it?" Sylvester asked.

"Loved it. Played on the football team. In fact I just graduated," Jake said.

"So you came to Taylorsburg and took over a general store."

"A big tornado came through my hometown, Princeton, and destroyed everything. My parents were killed. And so was my uncle."

"Oh, yes," Sylvester said. "So sorry. We read about the storm in the paper. It killed 400 people and turned the town into a pile of matchsticks."

Mahalia placed her hand on Jake's arm.

"My uncle was visiting them. My sister and her husband lost their house. She kept the farm and store down there, and I took what my uncle had." Jake was embarrassed when his tears flowed.

Over dessert Sylvester asked Jake, "What do you want to do with your life?"

"Ole Miss is getting ready to open a pharmacy school in a year or two. I was planning to go, but now I can't."

Near the end of the meal, Sylvester said, "Mahalia and I are planning a field trip to Laurel tomorrow. Do y'all want to go?"

"Count me in," Caroline said.

It was an invitation Jacob couldn't refuse. Mrs. Bently wouldn't have any trouble tending the store because business was likely to slow down after a land office week.

"We need a nap," Sylvester said. "Jake, why don't you and Caroline ride back out to the farm to get your surrey before someone comes along and takes it?"

"You don't have to go if you don't want to," Jake told Caroline.

"I'll be glad to. You need help."

*　　*　　*

Jake helped Caroline onto the horse. Again she crept along with a miserable expression on her face.

"You really don't like to ride, do you?"

"Love it," she said.

"I'm sorry I don't have a side saddle."

"This is better."

*   *   *

Later that afternoon when Jake dropped Caroline off at the hotel. Sylvester sat on the hotel porch in a swing with Mahalia. Jake saw an opportunity to discuss his business with a wise man. "Would you like to go with me to take care of the horses?" he asked Sylvester.

"One of the features of the Mercantile since my uncle opened the store three years ago has been the spit and whistle club," Jake said. "The men have spent hours of spare time at the store. Mrs. Bently told me about it."

"Yes, men need a place to go and exchange ideas," Sylvester said. "Great philosophy develops that way."

"On cool days she said they sit around the pot-bellied stove, drink coffee, and play dominoes or checkers," Jake said.

"Sounds like some serious entertainment."

"On the warm days they sit in front of the store on the covered porch."

"I haven't seen them," Sylvester said.

"That's because they've moved," Jake said.

"Oh?"

"They packed up their operation and moved down in front of the newspaper office."

"That's going to hurt your business."

"I asked Mrs. Bently what she thought was wrong. She said, 'Too much crinoline and lace.'"

"It sounds like you've been making a hit with the young women and their mothers," Sylvester said. "The men must not like it. They're losing their money to you. This is not good."

"She told me not to worry," Jake said. "Men will need hardware such as plow parts eventually, but I decided to try to fix things. I put up a sign."

"I saw it. *Free Coffee to Men*. How much coffee have you given away?"

"Not one cup."

*   *   *

Caroline loved her vacation from mistreatment. With the wind blowing on their faces . . . four miles down the road they removed their head coverings . . . and with their hair blowing freely in the breeze, the four of them motored in the Thomas-Flyer to Laurel. It seemed as though the Schuberts were the young people and Caroline and Jake were middle aged. Mahalia appeared to be in an especially carefree mood. When they had to sit in Soso and wait for the train to cross in front of them, she jumped out and ran around the car.

When she returned to her front seat, she announced it was time to enjoy some music; so she started singing. The others joined in. Caroline found her aunt amusing. She decided she didn't care what Jake, who was sitting beside her in the back seat, thought. He found it necessary to be nice to her because he liked her aunt and uncle; so she decided to lighten up. Who cared?

Soon she was laughing at some cows on the side of the road. Jake reached over and took her hand. He interlaced his fingers with hers. She tried not to look his way, but eventually she did. He eyed her and gave her a big smile.

Vester parked the vehicle on the street in front of the Pinehurst Hotel. Caroline and Jake waited in the courtyard while the Schuberts went to the tearoom and made a reservation for lunch.

"I like your aunt and uncle, Caroline. They're funny."

"Thanks," she said.

"Is she your mother's older or younger sister?"

"Much younger."

Caroline had decided to be as pleasant as possible, but she didn't want to encourage him. If he knew more about her, he wouldn't waste his time talking to her anyway. She was such a flawed person that no man would desire to take her as a wife, and Jake was looking for a woman.

"I've enjoyed this week," he said.

65

"Good."

"How about you?"

"Yes," she said.

"When I first met you, I thought you were Hortense's servant," he said.

"No one said that. You just assumed it."

"What's it like being her stepdaughter?"

She didn't care to give him any family information. "It's okay."

"She wants you to live somewhere else so your father can hire someone to do the things you do?"

"Right." His persistence caused her discomfort.

"But no one would?"

"No one would what?" Caroline asked.

"Be her live-in servant."

"That's right." She leaned forward and reached toward her back.

"She said you should live in someone else's home because you're a teacher, and teachers from out of town are provided living quarters with local families who have children in school," he said. "In payment they are supposed to help with the family chores."

"She told you all that?"

"Yes, she did," he said. "What I don't understand is why she doesn't treat you like family."

"She doesn't consider me her family. She thinks the house is hers. Could we talk about something else, Jake?"

"I'm sorry," he said.

"It's all right. Have you ever been to Fine's? That's where Aunt Haley wants to go."

"No, but I'm sure I'll enjoy it," he said.

"We have two hours to shop, and then we'll come back here for lunch," Mahalia said as her aunt and uncle returned.

It was not that she found Jake uninteresting. As a matter of fact, she considered him a joy to look at—even more attractive than she had found him that first day he had tea in the Clemons parlor. She knew, however, any man who thought he could make a commitment to her would encounter disappointment. Trudging along with the happy group, she tried not to think about her problem. She wanted to have a good time, and she enjoyed the time spent with Jake. She did her best not to attract his attention.

When they reached Fine's, Mahalia led them to the millinery department. She selected several of the newly popular hats with narrow brims. She tried them and had the group vote until they selected one for her. It was tan with a red band.

Next she went to work on Caroline. "I've been planning to buy you a hat so you won't have to wear your bonnet with your dress up clothes." She found a big floppy one of natural straw. It had a tan bow stringing down the back and huge multicolored silk flowers around the crown.

Also she selected a lightweight white one with a package of four scarves that were different colors. "See," she said. "You can change the scarves to match different dresses. Try them on, and we'll vote."

"I don't need a hat. I don't want to buy one today." Caroline didn't have enough money in her bag.

"This will be a special remembrance from us. Now try on the white one. Who likes the white one?"

Both Jake and Sylvester did.

"Now try on the other one. Who likes it?"

Both did.

"Which do you like best?" Mahalia asked.

"I like them both," Jake said.

"We'll take these two and this one in hatboxes, please," Mahalia told the clerk.

"You don't have to do this." Caroline protested.

"Just thank us."

"Thank you."

The rest of the time they looked around at displays in the store. Jake discussed with them various ways he could arrange merchandise in his Mercantile in a better fashion.

Jake took one of the hatboxes, and Caroline took the other. He offered his arm, and she slipped hers into his. As they walked back to the hotel, Jake told her, "You should model hats. You were incredibly beautiful in both of those."

"Thanks." She wished he had not said she was beautiful. He was making her life difficult. Poor man.

The tearoom was more than a place to drink tea and eat English biscuits. The meals were elaborate. They ate rib-eye steaks and fruit salad with iced mint tea and tender rolls. Dessert was jellyroll cake. Sylvester paid the bill.

"This means I'm treating you for lunch tomorrow back at the Covington," Jake said.

She dreaded to see the visit end, but she couldn't postpone Friday morning, when her aunt and uncle loaded her clothes into their automobile. They stopped by the Mercantile to say goodbye. Then they took Caroline to her back door. Hortense and the girls were not in sight, and they went inside to chat with Rachel.

A few minutes later they returned to stand in the backyard. Sylvester told Caroline, "I like that young man. He's a fine fellow."

"Ditto," Mahalia said.

Caroline devoted her efforts to shutting out any thoughts of Jake that invaded her mind. Thinking of him brought nothing but misery. If his motive was to build a business or to get to know the Senator, she didn't want to be used. If he was traveling on a track to fall in love with her, she would build a barricade. She regretted that she would disappoint her dear aunt and uncle.

"Thank you for everything. This week has been wonderful. Be careful, and go with God." As they drove away, her right hand waved to them, and her left hand patted her back.

Chapter Five

Tender Mercy

The note was scrawled on the back of the one Caroline had attached to the clamp on Hortense's bedroom door a week ago.

You just wait, Caroline. You know you've been out of line. You'll pay for your atrocious behavior. HC

"Miss Horsey left you a hateful note on her door," Rachel said.

"Yes, I saw it."

"She don't know I can read. She never bothers to turn things where I can't see them. Watch out for her. She's going to do something to you."

"When does she not?" Caroline asked Rachel.

She and the girls had gone somewhere. When they returned after lunchtime, life seemed to have settled to normal.

"Are you coming to the taffy pulling tonight?" Millicent asked without saying hello first, after a week of separation. "I'm starved, Rachel. Give me some cookies and milk."

"Yes, you're coming. We need you to help in the kitchen." Hortense's words cut into her.

"Where is it and what time?" Caroline asked.

"At the Kyles' at seven," Hortense said. "Be ready to leave by six."

Loaded with purchases, Lydia walked out of the kitchen with Millicent, also loaded, following her.

Orders were issued . . . a cage door slam shut around her. The latch snapped.

"Do something with your hair," Hortense said.

When the crowd cleared, Caroline said, "Rachel, could you fix my hair?"

"I'd love to, sweet pea. Let's go to the side porch where it's cool. Bring a straight chair and your hair things."

Rachel pushed herself back and forth in the swing.

Caroline brushed her long curly hair until it was smooth. *Squeak, squawk.* She made a mental note to oil the swing chains soon, but for the moment it was the time to fix her hair. She plopped into the chair. She could hear Hortense snoring through the open window.

"I'm ready, Madear."

Rachel smoothed pomade into the golden blonde mane and French braided it. She left a long braid hanging down.

"Take the pigtail and make it into a little bun at the top of my neck."

Using her hand mirror, Caroline viewed the back of her head in the mirror attached to the exterior wall by the front door. "I love it."

Rachel laughed. In a hushed voice so the resting ones wouldn't hear her, she said, "Just like molasses taffy. Them young men's going to be looking at your hair while they pull taffy with them others. You are about the prettiest thing that ever bore the Clemons name. One of these days soon some man's going to realize you're a treasure and see you pure and unblemished like Christ sees his church." She smacked her lips in admiration.

"I'm afraid not, Madear. You know the problem." Her hand slipped to its accustomed spot.

"When are you going to understand?" Rachel asked. "The church ain't perfect, but the bridegroom sees no flaws."

George drove the horse wagon into the backyard. "I got to go now."

"It's impossible to get any rest around here," Hortense shouted from her bedroom. "Rachel, you know you aren't supposed to sit on the swing. Bring me my cold spoons. Caroline is driving me to have bags under my eyes."

Caroline handed her the spoons from the icebox. "Rachel's left, but here are your spoons."

"Go slice me a cucumber. Set it in a bowl on my nightstand. By the time you slice it, the spoons won't be cold anymore."

* * *

Back in her little cubicle, Caroline drafted a note of appreciation to her aunt and uncle. She opened *Pride and Prejudice*, but her heavy eyes failed to focus. Lying prone to avoid disturbing Rachel's coiffure work, she dozed.

When the sound of the bell Hortense rang awakened her, she changed her dress and put on her apron. She looked into the mirror to make sure her face and hair were all right before she answered the signal to help her stepsisters and stepmother dress.

After a week with her carefree aunt, she realized she needed to stop jumping every time they rang her bell, but she didn't know how.

Jim worked at odd times. His original arrangement with the Senator was to have Friday night off, but if Hortense had other plans, he worked. He would take them in the surrey although there was nothing too difficult about hitching it to old Burl, their gentle gelding, and Ruby, the old mare.

Mama Hortense has all of us dancing on strings. One of these days she'll drop us all. I feel sorry for Jake because she is trying to fasten a hangman's noose around his neck.

*   *   *

Waiting for the taffy pull to start at the Kyles' house, the young men stood in clumps in the front yard or on the porch. Jake tried to join the small talk, but no one seemed to hear him.

Wilbur Mauldin stood with one leg bent and a cowboy boot against a porch post. He gazed into the distance.

Jake walked onto the porch. "Nice night, isn't it, Will?"

Jake stood and watched. With slow deliberation Wilbur peeled a Bugler cigarette paper from his pack and thumped his Prince Albert can in order to lay an even column of tobacco on it. Still silent, he inspected his handiwork. He licked the edge of the paper so it would stick as he rolled it.

Without looking at Jake, he stuck the unlit cigarette in the side of his mouth. "City boy, I don't need no free coffee or nothing else you've got."

Jake now had proof his coffee offer had offended the men of the community. Wilbur struck a match, cupped a hand to shield the flame from the wind, and lit the cigarette. He tossed the match onto the plank floor and ground it out with his boot.

The Clemons' horse-drawn surrey arrived. Jake stepped forward to help the ladies. First Hortense from the front and then Lydia, Caroline, and Millicent. He turned to Caroline and spoke in a soft tone, "Your hair is pretty like that."

"Thanks." she dropped her eyes.

Lydia hooked her arm in his and led him inside. He followed Caroline with his eyes as she disappeared into the kitchen.

Lydia sat in a dining chair and motioned for Jake to sit in front of her. "Roll up your sleeves," she said. She half-closed her eyelids in a seductive fashion.

Someone Jake didn't know handed them some butter. "Here, I'll help you." She rubbed the butter onto his hands and forearms. He was astonished. Why did she rub the butter on his arms?

"Now, help me." She fluttered her eyes.

Caroline walked over to them with a platter of hot taffy. "Be careful," Caroline said. Don't touch it yet. It's too hot."

"I've never done this before." Jake felt his face burning.

"You'll do fine. Lydia will help you. When you finish, bring it into the kitchen to have it cut. You'll know when it's ready, won't you, Lydia?"

"Sure."

"Braid it if you like," Caroline said.

He gazed at her. "I love braids."

He wondered whether Caroline had encouraged Lydia to seize him. For a week he had given Caroline almost constant attention.

When the candy cooled, they pulled it into a rope and folded it. They pulled it again. They twisted it and pulled it several times until the firm rope had a glossy sheen. Every time he looked up, Lydia was gazing at him. When it hardened, they twisted it into a braid and took it to Caroline. She showed him how to cut it with a butcher knife. He cut the rest of it into square pieces. All three of them popped pieces of the chewy candy into their mouths.

Caroline was too busy cooking to pull taffy with him. He realized Lydia was hooking her talons into him. To escape her grip he moved to a chair where another pretty girl sat alone. He had seen her in the store, but he couldn't remember where she fit in the social order of the town.

"Do sit down," she said. That second, Caroline arrived with another hot blob, which she stationed in front of him.

"You still cooking?" Jake asked.

"Yes," Caroline said.

He couldn't read Caroline. The unknown girl applied butter to her own hands, and Jake rubbed butter on his hands. The process of working the candy was beginning to make sense.

"I think I've seen you in the Mercantile," he said.

"I'm Geraldine Wiggins. I was in the revue." She paused and gave him a sideways glance. "The rose colored dress."

He remembered she had looked nice with her dark hair. The dress had accentuated her pink cheeks. He closed his eyes to clear his mind. When he opened them, he sensed a presence looming over him.

"Get up."

Jake recognized Wilbur's voice.

"Pardon me?"

"You're in my seat, city boy."

"Hi, Will." Geraldine sugarcoated her words.

Wilbur stood close enough to the back of Jake's chair to cause a collision when Jake pushed it back to stand. He created drama by hopping back just in time as though the chair's movement startled him. Jake ducked to avoid Wilbur's arm slung toward him on the way to grab the back of the chair.

In the kitchen, Jake wiped the butter from his hands, rinsed them, and dried them. "Goodnight, Caroline," he called over his shoulder as he made his way through the door.

*   *   *

Saturday business was slow . . . .

Sunday in church he found a vacant pew, where he sat in reverence. For the first time since his family's tragedy, he was starting to accept whatever it was God had planned for him. Absorbed in worship, he paid no attention to the people next to him until the close of the service. Geraldine Wiggins had sat by him with Wilbur Mauldin on the other side of her.

In his preoccupied state he walked outside. He found his horses tied in a difficult knot to a hitching post. He would have never tied them that way. After a frustrating struggle of trying to loosen it, he put on his spectacles.

From nowhere he was expecting, he received a sharp blow that crushed his glasses. Blood flowed from his nose onto his crisp Edwardian club collar shirt.

"What's the matter, city boy?" Wilbur snarled. "Can't you untie a simple knot?" Four brawny men flanked the attacker.

Jake wasn't too dazed to think fast. He faced a dilemma with unpleasant potential outcomes. He could strike back. The rough backup guys continued to stare with menacing expressions. Or he could take the blow without responding. If he took the second choice, his preference, the male boycott would accelerate as a result. The consequences could be severe enough to cause him to close the Mercantile. Some of the neighbors would pillage his farm.

If he struck back, he would have to punch hard. Although he was taller and more powerfully built than Wilbur, he was unaccustomed to coarse conduct unsuitable for a gentleman. He discounted the potential danger from the backups, standing in a row. Theirs was the herd mentality of cowards.

Lights resembling steel filings flew out like shooting stars through the darkness. Flashes of pain shot through the numbness. He saw the sad eyes of Caroline. Were they in his mind or were they outside of him? He was no longer sure. With the force of his trained athletic ability, Jake prepared to strike. From low beside his thigh came an iron fist gathering momentum and strength as it rose to its target. He felt the chin of Wilbur Mauldin only a second before he processed the sound of the strike. Knocked out, Wilbur fell to the ground.

Dizzy, he leaned against Smoky. "Let's get you into the back seat of our buggy." It was the sweet voice of Caroline, the woman who had shown him her ability to take charge when duty demanded it.

"You are so beautiful in your apron. I want to pull taffy with you."

"Lydia, come here."

Who said that? Was he talking, or was that Caroline?

"Sit here by Jake, and hold pressure against his nose. Lean him back. Use my cape to wipe the blood."

"Caroline, you are the most amazing girl I've ever seen." He gazed straight at Lydia and called her Caroline.

When he awakened, he was lying in a sick room at Dr. Woodley's home. Mrs. Woodley hovered over him.

"How did I get here?"

"Caroline and Lydia brought you Sunday."

He looked puzzled.

"It's Tuesday morning," Mrs. Woodley said.

"I walked out of church, and I was untying my horses. Wilbur hit me, and I hit him back."

"That's what we heard," she said.

"Is Wilbur all right?"

"Ask him." She folded back a screen to reveal the patient in a nearby bed.

"Wilbur." Jake was astonished.

"You sure can fight," Wilbur said.

"Are you okay?" Jake asked.

"I'm going to be fine and so are you in a few days," Wilbur said.

After a peaceful moment, Wilbur said, "I'm sorry I made a fool of myself. I thought you were trying to steal my girl Geraldine. I've been lying here listening to you talk out of your head. You're in love but it ain't with my Geraldine."

"In love?" Jake said. "No, not me."

"Keep thinking that way. You're a bigger fool than I thought."

"I don't know what you're talking about," Jake said.

"Any way I want to be your friend," Wilbur said. "I can't afford to have any enemies who can pack a wallop like you can."

"All right, Will."

Jake leaned back and fell asleep. At lunchtime he awakened to the smell of chicken broth. Caroline was at his bedside. "Where's Wilbur?" Jake asked.

"The doctor discharged him. He said you'll need to stay here another night."

"Where are the horses?"

"In the stables behind your store."

"Thank you for helping me," Jake said.

"Glad to," she said.

"If you hadn't helped me," he began a little sincere speech.

"Someone else would have." There was a briskness in her tone. "Lydia helped too. Drink this broth." She kept the focus on the business at hand.

He slurped down the liquid.

"I'll see you again before dark," she said.

*   *   *

The late afternoon sun shining in his eyes awakened Jake from a nap. Caroline reappeared with soup. "Your horses are fine. I fed them and made sure they had plenty of water."

"I want to go home," he said.

"Home?"

"The room in the back of the store—my home for now."

"Not until the doctor says you are able to go," she said. "I'll see you later. I need to get back to the house before dark."

"Bye," he said. "Thanks."

The following morning, Jim came to get Jake. They rode in the Clemonses' surrey. Back in the store Mrs. Bently fussed over him, but he felt fine. He sat at his desk and worked. Without his glasses, though, he couldn't accomplish much.

*   *   *

The next morning Caroline went to the Mercantile to talk to Mrs. Bently about ordering writing tablets for school. When she walked back to Jake's desk to check on him, he asked, "Would you ride with me on the train to Laurel to get some more eyeglasses?"

Caroline took a deep breath. She didn't want to give Jake any encouragement. He seemed to want to care about her—to think they were developing some sort of relationship. He didn't know the actual Caroline. When he knew more about her, he'd be repulsed. She wasn't sure whether he needed his eyeglasses, but maybe she should go to help him. She didn't feel she could say no.

If she postponed the date of her availability however, he might ask someone else. She could think of three attractive young women who would appreciate an invitation to spend a day with Jacob MacGregor. She considered suggesting someone.

"I'm sorry," she said. "I'm busy right now. Is Friday too late?" Hortense was planning to take Lydia and Millicent to New Orleans Thursday. They would have interviews at a finishing school and go shopping. She saw no point in telling Jake. Anyway he usually knew what that part of her family had planned before she did.

"Friday will be fine. I'll come by your place at eight. If it's all right, we can walk down to the depot."

"That's good."

She thought for a moment. Rachel would have the usual breakfast of biscuits, eggs, grits, and sausage waiting on the stove for anyone who came along, as well as a pot of hot fresh coffee.

"If you come to my house at seven thirty, Rachel will be glad to feed you a robust breakfast."

"I'll be there. Who could turn down an offer like that?"

*   *   *

Friday morning he showed up as planned. Rachel served the usual breakfast. Finishing his second biscuit, Jake said, "I don't know of a finer cook anywhere."

"It's clouding up," Rachel said.

"I brought my big umbrella in case it rains," he said.

Caroline took the hooded cape she wore when she was out in the rain. Off to the depot they went.

"Come here, Bruiser. Eat some breakfast," Rachel fed table scraps to distract the little dog.

In the crowded train car, Jake sat near Caroline. Although conversation was difficult over the noise of the train and the other passengers, he smiled at her every time their eyes met.

I shouldn't have come. The only reason I decided to was that Jake needs help managing without his eyeglasses.

The optometrist told him he would need to return on Monday to obtain his glasses from the optician. Jake looked at Caroline. She suspected he would ask her to return with him.

Back on the street, they walked until they arrived at a boarding house with a sign that said, "Lunch, Guests Welcome."

Diners sat in chairs around a large oval table with a lazy Susan in the middle. They found two places to sit and piled their plates with vegetables and meatloaf. The place was full of noisy workers and shoppers in addition to the boarding house guests.

Caroline was glad to spend some time with Jake and enjoy his company, but she feared the warmth she felt inside her heart every time he noticed her. That day on the streets of Laurel no other young ladies and no family members shared him. Consequently he showered her with attention.

Jake and me. I don't trust us. Not that we would behave as less than a lady and a gentleman. Our conduct is not the problem. What concerns me is the way he seems to be starting to feel about me. I won't let myself feel anything for him. I can't.

When they went back outside, the raindrops had started to fall. He opened his umbrella and guided her to stay close underneath with him. "We have three hours until time to go back to the train station. Do you need to shop for anything?"

"Not really."

"Let's walk," he said.

She had tried for weeks to avoid personal conversations with him when they were alone, but she had no choice.

"Jake, tell me about what happened to your family."

"My mother and father were killed in the storm. So was Uncle Marvin. My sister's ankle was broken. My brother-in-law and their son managed to go through it without a scratch."

"Where were you?"

"I was at Ole Miss. It hit April 24, and I had only two more weeks of classes and three weeks before graduation."

"What did you do about that?"

"My professors wanted to help me. They insisted I come back and take my examinations late and graduate."

"And you did?"

"Yes."

"Wonderful. I heard you telling my uncle you studied . . ."

"Football. Seriously I studied chemistry and physics. I enjoy studying science. I planned to go back to Ole Miss. I really wanted to go to the new pharmacy school that will be opening soon, but I need to stay in Taylorsburg and run Uncle Marvin's business and farm place."

"Do you want to go to pharmacy school still?"

"Not any more. I need to get my mind on the store and the farm. Maybe a time will come when I'll study some more."

"Taylorsburg needs a pharmacist."

By the moment I'm changing toward him. I feel for him. Now I feel sadness for his pain. I want to help him feel better. Lord, guard my heart. Please show me how I can help Jake. Maybe he simply needs somebody to cling to because of what he has faced. He may think he is falling in love with me, but I have many doubts that his feelings are real. He needs a friend.

"What exactly happened?" She'd overheard bits and pieces when he told her uncle. He had told her some of it, but she wanted to let him talk about it.

"A tornado swept through southwest Mississippi and on over into Alabama. In Princeton it left at least 400 people dead and 100 more injured. Some towns turned into piles of sticks."

She reached for his arm. "Yes, we read about it in the newspaper."

"Uncle Marvin had gone down there to visit for a few days. My aunt, his wife, had died a few months earlier, and he was lonesome."

"Jake, I'm so sorry."

"It was late Friday afternoon. My brother-in-law and sister were having a birthday celebration for my mother. Train cars blew off the tracks, houses were leveled, and buildings destroyed. Their house fell in on them."

"How about your parents' home?"

"It wasn't touched."

"So how did you and your sister work things out? I mean how did you decide what to do?"

"I told her to take my parents' house and store since she lived in Princeton. She gave me Uncle Marvin's store and farm." He wept. The tears, unbidden and uncontrolled, flowed faster than he could wipe them away with his handkerchief.

"My heart hurts for you. I suppose most people don't know what you've gone through."

"How do you tell them? How can you tell something like this without breaking down?"

Nestled underneath Jake's wide umbrella, they walked through the rain.

With his hand touching the back of her waist, they walked in silence down one street and up another along the boardwalks and brick streets of Laurel.

"If it hadn't been so terrible, the fight you had with Wilbur Mauldin would have been funny."

"I didn't realize I had offended most of the men around Taylorsburg."

"I know. Since you're not farming, they think you're a weakling."

"Am I supposed to go around telling the men I am a football player so they won't think I'm a milk toast?"

She smiled.

"By the way, I want to farm, but I don't know how. Now that Wilbur has decided to be my friend, things should be a little easier."

"Right. I don't think you'll have to show all the men how tough you are with your fists. Wilbur will tell them."

"Tell Lydia her special order has come in, please, if I don't see her when we get back to your house," he said.

"She's in New Orleans. Mama Hortense took her and Millicent down to apply for finishing school. They'll shop and take in the town for a few days too."

"In that case, we can't let you spend tomorrow evening at home alone. Could I have the pleasure of your company at the Covington Hotel dining room?"

She fell silent. How could she turn him down politely?

"Oh, all right, but I won't be home alone. Hortense doesn't like to leave me here like that. She says I don't watch the house closely. Loretta Larson stays with me. Miss Larson and I come and go as we please. We don't keep up with each other. She has her life, and I have mine."

"Is six o'clock all right?"

"Fine," she said. *What have I done?*

*   *   *

She decided to cook a big meal and invite people for Sunday lunch. It was her father's house. He would be glad. Her stepmother couldn't stop her. The farmers sold from their wagons on the main street every Saturday. She bought peaches, lima beans, and corn on the cob. Late that afternoon she pinched off some of Rachel's dough and made it into rolls to rise over night. She shelled the limas and shucked the corn, placed the vegetables inside the icebox, made a large peach cobbler, and prepared a chicken stew.

"Loretta, I'm cooking lunch tomorrow. You are invited to come and eat."

"I have other plans. Thank you though." Miss Larson always ate with her friends from the Methodist church.

When Jake came to accompany her on a walk to the Covington Hotel, she was ready. Dishes were stacked with silverware nearby. She had laid out some glasses and napkins.

*   *   *

Saturday evening over a meal of baked chicken and potatoes with gravy, they sat in a cozy booth in the back of the Covington dining room. She kept busy with her meal. "This is delicious chicken," she said.

"Yes, let's share a slice of chocolate cake."

After they finished he suggested they go for a stroll. It was a balmy evening. Although most of the farmers had gone home, the town seemed full of folks. The town people were having fun on the main street. In the bandstand at the west end a band consisting of an accordion, a fiddle, and a washboard played snappy tunes.

Despite the festivities, Jake was preoccupied, and Caroline was busy with her thoughts. They trudged along. "Let's go check on the horses," she said. The four tall, long-necked Tennessee Walkers were content. As usual, she petted each of them. They snorted in eagerness for her attention.

"You have a special bond with animals," he said.

"It's because I've often trusted them more than I could trust people."

"I think they see your beautiful spirit."

"I thank God for his beautiful creation," she said.

"I told you so much yesterday. Could I tell you something else?"

"Please do."

"You know I have been angry at God. In one afternoon I lost my mother, my father, my dear uncle, and my hope for a career. My sister lost her health. Did I tell you her leg is not healing well?"

"No."

"She wrote me and said her husband has been disloyal."

"No."

"He's staying around for what she inherited," Jake said. "Why would God do this to me?"

"Have you asked him?" Caroline asked.

"No, I haven't," he said. "I can't talk to him like that."

"He hears you now," she said.

"Last Sunday, I was finally starting to connect again with God. When I was a child, I felt very close to him. All through my college days, I behaved myself while my friends were out having wild times. I trusted God, but he turned his back on me."

"Last Sunday . . . you were saying?" She brought him back to the present.

"Yes, the preacher said some things that touched me."

"It was a good sermon," she said.

"Then lo and behold, I got hit in the face," he said. "What I minded more than anything else about that was the timing of it. At the moment when I wanted to make up with God, he sent somebody to drive me back away."

"Is that the way you saw it?" Caroline asked.

"God doesn't love me, Caroline. I believe in his saving grace, but for some reason he has it in for me. As I told you, he's turned his back on me."

She wanted to say something he would understand, but the words didn't come. Whatever she said would be misunderstood.

Finally before saying good night, she said, "Read Job."

"That's it? That's all you are going to say?"

"Then read Jeremiah and the letters in the New Testament. You are being tested, Jake. I don't totally understand it. All I know is that I'm being tested too. When my life gets difficult, God draws me closer to him. Give him a chance to heal your wounds. If you try to move closer to him, he will draw close to you."

"If most people told me that, I wouldn't believe it, but I've seen enough to realize you know what you're talking about," he said.

He told her goodnight at the door, as they shared a light sideways hug. "I'll give you a ride to church, if you'd like."

"That will be nice. Come early."

Watching him go, she held the back of her left hand over her back in her accustomed gesture.

How can I help him when I can't understand my own problems?

*   *   *

Early Sunday morning she made a big pitcher of sweet tea. She placed pans of water on top of the stove to cook the beans and corn. She placed pickles and fig preserves nearby, and she selected some tomatoes to slice.

When Jake arrived, she arose from the porch swing and skipped over to the surrey. On the way, she said, "I have a surprise. I'm cooking lunch for anyone who wants to join us."

"How can I help?"

"You can help me invite people, and then you can bring me back home as soon as possible," she said. "While I'm cooking, you can keep everybody entertained with lively conversation."

"That sounds like a good plan," he said. "Let's try to invite some of the young men and women."

Four couples of single young people came to eat.

*   *   *

Monday morning he stopped by the Clemons house early enough for breakfast and to talk to Rachel. Soon Jacob and Caroline strolled away to the station to go to Laurel for the glasses.

He told her, "Job had a hard time, but what was so special about the story?"

"Yes, he had a hard time, she said. "In a windstorm he lost seven sons and three daughters. Not long after that he lost 7,000 sheep, 3,000 camels, 100 oxen, and 500 donkeys. In addition, he lost his health."

"So?"

"The Lord is full of tender mercy. He brought Job through it."

"So what?"

"You're making this complicated. Let me ask you one question. Suppose you have everything you need and everything your heart desires, your health is good, and your family is well. Now suppose you have lost your family, your wealth, and your health. In which circumstance will you ask the Lord for help?"

"Point well taken. Now, let's talk about what we're going to do today. We have another whole day to explore Laurel."

*   *   *

Tuesday morning over coffee, she admitted to Rachel, "Jake MacGregor is trying to slip into my heart, but he doesn't belong there for more than one reason. My mind tells me to leave him alone."

"Your mind is telling you right."

"But my heart's walls are breaking down."

"I ain't raised you for a man that don't have his heart right with the Lord."

"How do you know his heart isn't where it should be, Madear?"

"Call it Christian woman's intuition. You need a man who's steady like a rock, not wishy-washy. As long as he don't reflect God's love, I'm going to think wishy-washy about him. My girl can do better."

Caroline sipped her coffee. "Maybe he'll change."

"No, sweet pea. Maybe the Lord will change him."

"My mind tells me I don't want *any* man."

"If the Lord sends him to you, you'll want him."

Chapter Six

Goody Two-Shoes

No doubt lingered in Jake's mind: Hortense Smith Clemons was a mean woman. However, he thought she was essential to his success. Even though he had observed the way she mistreated Caroline, he wondered whether Caroline irritated her stepmother.

Despite Caroline's sweetness, he was tired of her perfection. She was a little Miss Goody Two-Shoes from his point of view. She seemed sympathetic about his loss of a close relationship with God, but she lacked any real understanding of what true suffering was. He knew she had lost her mother, but she had told him she was too young when her mother died to remember the loss.

Furthermore, if he crossed Hortense, she could destroy his position in the community. It was too easy for girls and their mothers to hop onto the train and go buy their fabric in Laurel. He had merchandise to sell. Business was business.

Anyway she was keeping him at arm's length for reasons he could not fathom. She had potential, but her meekness irritated him. He was not accustomed to passive women.

It was time to stop showering her with attention. He thought she might consider him cruel or nurse hurt feelings, but that was life. If he didn't stop seeing her so much, the people of Taylorsburg, especially Caroline, would start expecting him to make a commitment to court her. What if her father came to town and asked him if he had plans? He could imagine the man speaking in a gruff voice. "Son, what are your intentions toward my daughter?"

He felt boxed in. Town gossips were circulating rumors that they were a couple. After their latest conversation about God, he thought about what she said. He expected her to give him more sympathy when he said he was mad at God. All she seemed to want to do was talk about faith. She was so unapproachable that he was sure she worked at keeping her distance.

His stomach hurt. He didn't want to be seen with her in public because he'd give the Taylorsburg news sources more material for their rumor mills. He made up his mind. Weighing the consequences, he knew he was making the right decision.

I need some space.

Wednesday she showed up at the store with her stepsisters. "We've been accepted into finishing school, and we need new uniforms." Lydia talked to him and rolled her flirtatious eyes while Mrs. Bently helped Caroline with the fabric needs. Millicent paid attention to the purchases. He spent his time conversing with Lydia about her trip to New Orleans.

*   *   *

Friday morning, Caroline appeared in the door of the Mercantile. He had hoped she'd stay away. "Mrs. Bently, I need a few more items." She presented a list.

He walked over to her as she waited. "I won't be giving you a ride to church this Sunday."

She surprised him. "I was not expecting you would. You haven't offered. I have other plans anyway."

* * *

In the middle of the afternoon, Caroline answered the door when Jake came calling. "Come in."

"I'm here to take Lydia and Millicent with their mother to see my farm. I didn't think you'd care to go, because I know you're busy. Besides you've already seen it."

"That's fine." She didn't mean to sound snippy.

After they left, she went back to the kitchen. Rachel poured her a glass of iced tea. "Leave that man alone."

"Okay. Madear, I'm so upset."

"Of course you are, but don't say I didn't tell you so," Rachel said. "I ain't never thought he was good enough for you."

Caroline sniffled.

"If you have to go in the store, go ahead, but try to avoid him. Don't pay him no mind whatsoever. Now that he's hurt you, don't go begging for him to lick your wounds no more'n you'd go up to a mad dog and say, 'You done bit me. It hurt. Can you fix it?'"

"Madear, you know how to explain things where I can understand them."

"That's what I'm here for," Rachel said. "If you hang around and let him see you being pitiful, you'll be acting like you've lost your mind."

"You're right. I see the point."

"Back off. Back way off from that fool."

"Okay."

* * *

Sunday morning Caroline visited the Methodist church with Miss Larson.

Monday Rachel said, "You know, honey, I've been thinking and praying about this all weekend. The Lord showed me something. I was remembering how kind Jacob was when he came here and ate breakfast with us. He really ain't no fool.

Lots of stuff has hurt him and hurt him bad. His sore's going to fester one of these days, and there'll be a good man underneath all that ugliness."

"You think so?"

"Has Rachel McBride ever steered you wrong?"

"No, ma'am."

"Give me a hug," Rachel said.

Caroline buried her face against Rachel's shoulder. "I've been fighting hard not to care about him, and now when I'm losing the battle, I'm losing the man." She shook as the tears poured out like rain in a blowing storm. "I thought I didn't want him until I pushed him away."

"Go ahead, honey. Just cry it out. That's what shoulders are for"

"I love you, Madear."

"Let it all out. There's more room out here than there is inside there."

*   *   *

Friday he came to tea, and Caroline met him at the door. "Mama Hortense will be here in a moment," she said.

"I wish you wouldn't call her that. It sounds so provincial, so Victorian. Several things you say are not good for a schoolteacher to make a habit of saying. You don't want your students to pick up your bad habits."

Ignoring him, she went to serve the tea.

He visited Hortense and her daughters, and Caroline returned to the kitchen. "Let's walk in the back yard," she told Rachel. "We've got to talk."

Bruiser, waiting on the back steps, trailed behind them as they walked through the yard.

"Hey, sweet boy," Caroline said. She reached down to pet the little fellow.

"I heard him cutting you down," Rachel said. "He ain't so proper as all that. Even if he was, he still wouldn't have no reason to be unkind. It ain't nothing wrong with you. It's him."

"All right," Caroline managed to say between sniffles and tears. Her chest was on the verge of an explosion.

"I got to tell you, child, since we're having this little talk. Part of your trouble *is* brought on 'cause you ain't acting right."

"What do you mean I ain't acting right?" Caroline asked.

"You've got to stop sniveling," Rachel said.

They sat on the secluded stone bench in the backyard. Caroline reached down and picked up Bruiser.

"And you got to be the lady you was meant to be," Rachel said. "Hold your head up high and look after yourself. Start thinking about what you want to do to please the Lord. Stop worrying about pleasing some man who ain't acting pleased with you when you been giving him your best."

"You don't think he's interested in me?"

"Stop sawing with that same old saw," Rachel said. "How could I know 'cause he don't know what he's interested in. I suspect he's mostly interested in hisself. Every time I think he's doing better he does worse. Maybe he'll grow up one of these days, and stop acting like a little boy. Some men do and some men don't."

"Like Brother George?" Caroline dried her tears. "He's a grown up man. He's kind to you."

"It wasn't always that way," Rachel said. "I had to train him not to be selfish."

"I could never train one, and I don't want one," Caroline said.

"Sure you can and you do."

*   *   *

Lydia and Millicent would need all sorts of clothes by September, when they were scheduled to go to finishing school. Caroline immersed herself in a project of making each girl two uniforms with long flowing navy skirts cinched at the waist and white blouses with hambone sleeves that were tight along the lower arms.

The high collars contained whalebones to keep them standing in place. She went to the Mercantile to talk to Mrs. Bently about ordering the whalebone. Jake was back at his desk conversing with a beautiful young woman who must have been new in town. Caroline pretended not to notice.

Back in her room, she removed her jewelry and put it in a little box. She was not in a mood for wearing it. She placed the jewelry box on the top shelf of her closet and locked the door.

*   *   *

To Caroline's surprise, Millicent helped her sew. She tried to learn as much as possible about sewing, even though she had frequent tantrums when things didn't go right. Lydia sat in the seat by the window and wrote poetry about her imagined love affair with Jacob MacGregor. She read her compositions to Millicent and Caroline.

Hortense wandered in and out of the sewing room. She had diffused her anger to include all three girls—Caroline, as always, for breathing air Hortense might not be able to spare and her daughters for going away.

One afternoon Jake came calling. Lydia rushed out to greet him, but Caroline and Millicent continued to sew. Hortense bustled into the sewing room. "Get up, Millicent. Go see Mr. MacGregor. Caroline, get the tea."

"I'm sorry, ma'am. I need to keep sewing. Also could Millicent stay and help? She's doing a great job. We don't have much more time. Lydia can serve the tea. She's been practicing."

Smack! Hortense slapped Caroline so hard that the noise could be heard throughout the house. Caroline shrank back, and Millicent stepped between them.

"Get out here," Hortense called as she went toward the parlor. Millicent, taking some hand sewing with her, went to the parlor.

Lydia was sitting on the couch facing Jake. She had a frozen smile on her face.

With the side of her face flaming red, Caroline brought the teapot to the parlor.

Rachel grumbled as Caroline went to the kitchen. "The devil's going to take that woman when her time comes to leave this earth."

Jake stood as Caroline entered the room. He couldn't fail to see the reddened side of her face.

"I have to be going," he said without staying for tea.

Lydia trailed after him, but he didn't look around as he reached for his hat and left. "Good day, ladies."

Crying in paroxysms, Lydia ran to her room and slammed her door.

"Apologize to Lydia," Hortense demanded of Caroline.

"I'm sorry, Lydia," Caroline yelled from the parlor. It was not a sincere-sounding apology.

Hortense fanned herself, "My nerves are getting the best of me. Caroline, you are driving me crazy."

To comfort herself. Caroline busied herself in the kitchen. Rachel told her, "You're being tested, honey. The Lord Jesus is taking you through the dark valley. You are going through midnight. Give yourself a little time and the midnight's going to meet the morning. The Lord will guide you."

*   *   *

Jake needed some fresh air. The five women in the Clemons house stifled his mind. Lately when he had seen Rachel, she had given him a sidelong glance that said, "I don't trust you."

He still believed Hortense was the key to his business success, but she was a bizarre piece of work. She injured poor Caroline with the slap. What he didn't understand was what

Caroline had done to provoke it. Was there something he was missing?

What was there about Caroline? Why did she submit to abuse? Could anybody do anything to help her? He was afraid he was falling in love with her; he had been wise to back away. Sometimes she was difficult to read. He wasn't sure whether she could care about him even if he made the sacrifice of courting her at the risk of offending the influential wife of the Senator.

Furthermore, he had too many issues of his own to solve. His mind was muddled with grief and confusion. The last thing he needed was to fall in love.

She's not so special anyway.

He tried to believe that she wasn't extraordinary, but every night when he drifted off to sleep her unforgettable face appeared in his dreams. Whenever he happened upon her, she was more beautiful than he had remembered. Underneath her warm smiles and polite glances, she showed unfathomable sadness. What was wrong?

He shook his head. *She's too much of a saint for me.*

He had sat in front of her and listened to her sing in her clear voice. She expressed enthusiasm and love for the Lord in every note she sang. He had sat across the aisle from the Clemons family. A sparkle lighted her eyes when she listened to the sermon. She seemed involved in the reading of the word and the prayers.

She's too dedicated to the Lord, and I'm mad at him. What would I need with a woman like Caroline Clemons?

He mulled over the thought.

I need her forever, but I'm not ready to make a commitment to anybody. I feel like such a jerk.

Lydia—he felt sorry for her because he had used her to give him some space from Caroline. The poor girl had started to think he loved her, and then she saw how upset he was about Caroline's slapped face.

Lydia knows I don't care for her. It would be best to stay away from the Clemons household.

Silly little Millicent—she was constantly toying with him for practice. She made flirty eyes at him, but she had no real interest in him

*   *   *

Sunday morning he sat in church beside Miss Victoria Robinson, who had recently moved to Taylorsburg with her family. They came from Atlanta. Hortense stood and announced, "There will be a box lunch affair next Saturday noon to raise money for the building program. If you are an eligible young lady, cook a box lunch. All you bachelors, be sure to attend and bid on them. Support this money-raising project and show off what a good cook you are sparking. If you bid high enough to get your girl's box lunch, you can share it with her on the grounds."

Chapter Seven

Mose Jefferson

Tuesday Caroline began her day early. She was in the kitchen making coffee by the time Rachel arrived.

"Morning, sweet girl," Rachel said.

"Good morning," Caroline said. "What in the world happened to your face?" Rachel had a swollen lump on her left cheek and a nasty gash over her left eye.

"Horsey got me."

"Are you all right?"

"Not really, but there ain't nothing to be done about it."

"This time she's gone too far."

"Just calm down, child. The Lord's going to stop her in his due time. We can't do nothing but make it worse."

"I'll get in touch with Papa."

"No, don't, honey," Rachel said. "We don't need no retaliation from that evil woman. Word tell is she's friends with some rough folks."

"Why did she hit you this time?"

"I was walking back to the kitchen yesterday while you were gone out. She'd made me clean what was done already cleaned. I must've got too hot. The next thing I knew I felt like

I was going to pass out, so I sits a spell in one of them dining room chairs."

"I can guess what happened, but go ahead and tell me," Caroline said.

"She says, 'Colored folk ain't supposed to sit in white folks' dining rooms.' She accused me of being uppity. I tried to get up but I couldn't. About that time she whaled the fire out of me. She had something sharp in her hand like keys."

"Madear, I'm so sorry." Caroline reached to hug her.

"Don't do that. Don't let her catch you touching me. There'll be hell to pay."

"Did it bleed much?" Caroline asked.

"Yes, it sure did. Here I was trying to stop the blood from getting on the chair and me feeling like I couldn't move."

"Wiping it on your apron?"

"Right. I don't remember much. Seems like I was on my hands and knees a little later cleaning that blood off the floor."

"Oh, Rachel."

"Check in the dining room and make sure I got all the stains up off the wood floor."

Caroline scrubbed up more blood and put fresh oil on the spot of discolored flooring. *Lord, show me how to protect Rachel from Hortense.*

*   *   *

Rachel had sat to rest more lately. With all the beans to be shelled and canned from the neighboring farms, she had sitting work to do. The shelling part of the process allowed her to rest. Caroline wanted to help her as she always did, but she had received an ultimatum from Hortense to finish the four uniforms and sew undergarments to wear with them.

"Lydia, please help Rachel shell butterbeans," Caroline said.

"No, I'll get stains on my hands," Lydia said. "Besides I don't even eat butterbeans. You know I don't like them."

Rachel shelled the beans and canned them. She struggled in the oppressive heat over the wood stove until she finished the job.

Friday afternoon not long before George was to arrive, Rachel lay down on the edge of the side porch. Caroline saw her through the window of the sewing room and ran out to check her. Millicent trailed behind.

"Can't get cool, baby girl."

"Millicent." Caroline spoke with urgency. "Get a pan of cool water and some washcloths." She knelt over Rachel to loosen the woman's blouse. As soon as Millicent returned, she placed cool cloths on her neck, face, and arms.

"Take her shoes and stockings off, Millie."

"Me?"

"Yes, you. Do it."

Caroline held Rachel's hand. Rachel squeezed tightly and suddenly went limp.

"Madear."

Rachel's eyes rolled back and closed. When she opened them, she had a vacant stare.

"Madear, can you hear me?"

Caroline hovered over Rachel until George arrived. When Rachel heard his voice, she surprised everyone by sitting up. "Must help me stand."

George on one side and Caroline on the other tried to bring her to an upright position but she collapsed.

"Bring me a blanket from inside now," Caroline snapped at Millicent.

"Which one?" Millicent asked.

"It doesn't matter. Hurry."

Millicent returned with a scratchy old wool blanket. "Madear," Caroline spoke in a tender slow tone, "we're going to roll you over onto this blanket. Help us."

George, Caroline, and Millicent positioned Rachel on the blanket.

"Come on, now," Caroline said. "Let's drag the blanket to the backside of the porch."

When they reached the edge, Rachel said, "Let me try to stand up now."

"Hold on till I get the back of the wagon close by," George said.

When the wagon was lined up, they raised Rachel to a sitting position. "Millie, spread the blanket in the bed of the wagon as quick as you can. Then come back over here."

They dangled Rachel's feet onto the ground.

"Brother George, you put your arm round her left side; I'll take the right; Millicent, as soon as we clear the porch, hop down and hold onto Rachel's belt in the back."

They managed to stand her up. "Now, Madear, please try to push one foot at a time forward."

They helped her into the wagon. "Get her shoes and socks, Millie, and put them next to her. Run get her bag out of the kitchen."

"Thanks, Miss Millicent. Mighty fine for you to help out," George said.

Caroline climbed into the wagon. Sitting with her legs spread on the floor of it, she cradled Rachel's head in her lap. "We're ready, Brother George."

He signaled for his team to pull the wagon home. When they arrived at the house, Caroline and George struggled to help her into bed.

They kept a vigil at her bedside.

Saturday morning Rachel awakened able to talk and move both arms. She seemed normal, but Caroline didn't want to take any chances. She spent the morning fussing over her dearest friend.

George, exhausted from being awake all night, tiptoed out to the porch with a pillow. He took a straight chair from the kitchen table and turned it over with the top down and the feet in the air. On the back of it, he placed the pillow. Reclining there he soon slept.

The loss of sleep had given Caroline a new burst of energy. "Rest. Whatever Rachel needs, I'll get for her," she told George.

George awakened and suggested they have a little lunch. He found some sausages and day-old biscuits. Rachel drank a few sips of buttermilk from the icebox.

"I'll take you back home in the wagon," George said.

"No, it's too dangerous to leave Rachel," Caroline said.

"You sure you feel like walking?"

"I'm fine. Keep your eyes and ears open for Rachel."

"Go on home then. Be careful," George said. "Don't worry about us. We'll be in the Lord's hands."

"If you need me, will you send for me?" Caroline asked.

"Yes, we'll send for you."

Rachel looked at Caroline with sad questioning eyes. They hugged and parted.

He walked out the door, down the steps, and into the yard with Caroline. He spoke in a hushed tone. "Tell your stepmother my Rachel is through working there. I'm going to keep her home with me and take care of her as best as I can."

"Okay, but I'll be down to check on you. I wish there was something more to do."

"It was a close call," George said. "I begged the Lord not to take her from me yet."

"I thought she was having a stroke, but she's almost back to normal today."

"There ain't nothing to be done for a stroke, but to take care of her. Like I said, her working days is over."

"I'll see y'all soon."

"Lord bless you, child. Don't forget to be careful. Go with God."

*   *   *

The time and day Hortense had announced for the box lunch party was harmful for Jake's business. He wished she had considered the prosperity of the town. Her favorite time to schedule the town's social events was in the middle of Saturday, when most of the folks shopped. He felt he had no choice except to show up, though; so he stood on the west side of Taylorsburg behind the little church during his best business hours.

*   *   *

Not far out of the city limits on the southeast side of Taylorsburg, Caroline made her way back home. She hadn't slept since she awakened at five o'clock Friday morning to sew the uniforms.

Trudging along she prayed.

Thank you, Lord, for Rachel. Please watch over her. She and Aunt Mahalia have been like mothers to me. You have taken care of every need I've ever known.

And please watch over George as he sees after Rachel. Bless Aunt Mahalia and Uncle Vester. And bless Papa.

It's so wonderful to see the way Millicent is growing up, Lord. I pray she will continue to mature and become sensitive to the needs of those around her. Bless her and Lydia as they go away to further their education. Bless Hortense. Please help me to forgive her for all the pain she's caused.

Please watch over Jake. He's so confused these days. Bring him back to the center of your will. Thank you.

The road led out of the neighborhood and took a sharp turn. The shade under the big oak tree in the bend invited her to sit a few minutes. If she had stopped, she would have fallen asleep and spent the day on the side of the treacherous Old Town Road. Still, the gentle breeze with its orchestra of birdsongs tempted her. Her bleary eyes failed to focus on the road as she stumbled along. No matter what was going on at the Clemons house, she'd need a long solid nap before she could sew school clothes or serve Hortense.

Mose Jefferson's house, a massive well-kept stone structure, sat on a sharp hill. A gravel drive connected his house to Old Town Road. Holly bushes lined the front edge of his deep yard. Mose was the source of alcoholic beverages for many of the residents of Taylorsburg, Mississippi. Not only was he the exclusive moonshiner for both sides of town; he was the number-one bully.

Caroline recalled . . . Hortense walked from the direction of his house early mornings. It astonished Caroline to think that her stepmother would bother to spend time with such a man—he had a bulbous nose and a flushed face. He wore soiled clothes and never seemed to comb his disheveled hair. Peculiar to see her carrying a croker sack with bumpy contents . . . her medicine, possibly. She suspected Hortense, like Mose, was nearly drunk most of the time.

She and Rachel talked it over once. She was glad she had not revealed this family secret to Jake. Her father would never divorce Hortense, but he couldn't take her with him to Jackson, where she would be invited to attend social functions. Besides, he needed to maintain a residence in the precinct he represented as senator.

Caroline had promised . . . .

Absorbed in her thoughts, she failed to notice Mose until it was too late. He staggered out from behind a bush and grabbed her. She gasped—too stunned to scream.

In no time he was squeezing her around the waist with one rough dirty hand and holding a knife pointing upward to her throat with the other. She froze.

*　　*　　*

On the other side of town behind Friendship Church stood an outdoor table long enough to hold all the dinners the women brought on Sundays when they celebrated dinner on the grounds. The boxed lunches sitting in a row on the church table dwindled. The auction progressed swiftly. Jacob thought the boxes were unmarked, but everybody seemed to know which box belonged to whom.

Observing the couples, he realized too late what the social was designed to do. It was another exercise in family formation. Hortense Clemons played a leading role in all such activities.

*   *   *

"Don't move, little filly." Mose growled. "Keep your mouth shut." He lowered the knife, closed the blade, and stuck it inside his pants pocket. "Just follow my lead, darling, and I won't need to carve you up."

She gulped.

"Understand?"

"Yes," she whispered.

His red-rimmed wild blue eyes glared at her. As he moved his face closer, his sour whiskey breath blew into her nose. When she thought she could stand no more, he forced his mouth onto hers. She tasted his sour vomit. He violated her lips with one hard kiss after another, and she resisted the urge to shriek. He filled her mouth with his regurgitated fermented grain and insulted her ears with the rotten fruit of his curses.

Hortense had introduced her to fear. As a result, she taught herself clever survival tactics. She needed a plan to outsmart Mose, but the horror flowing into her was beyond anything she had ever experienced. The revulsion made her sick.

He tied her hands behind her, tight and painful. She tried to cooperate in silence, but she couldn't stop herself from retching.

What if this is the last moment of my life? I'm not ready. Lord, you know I'm ready to meet you, but I still have my promise . . . cannot do . . . from up in heaven with you.

He pulled a red bandana out of his pocket. From the looks of the tarry exudate on it, she suspected he had blown his nose into the nasty cloth many times since it had been washed. He used the filthy rag to gag her. She couldn't suppress her cough.

Each second seemed an eternity. *Do you see me, Lord? Where are you?*

She didn't resist when he threw her onto the ground; she couldn't waste her efforts, with her hands fastened behind her and her skirt in the way; she had little chance of pushing the big strong man away from her, even if he was full of moonshine. Landing on her left side caused new pain to shoot through her left lower back.

The pain is more than . . . Lord, please just help me not to pass out. Then I won't be able to keep him from . . . I can't take any more.

She developed a plan: as soon as he tried to move close to her, she'd kick the masculinity out of him. Then she could outrun him.

He moved his body perilously close, his big hard belly pressed against her. She waited until he raised her skirts. With nothing to disable her efforts but her long pantaloons, she kicked with all her might.

He folded over with a hideous grunt.

Trying to stand with her hands tied proved to be more complicated than she had expected. She rolled down the yard to get away from him—each turn causing agonizing pain—until a prickly holly bush blocked her. Soon he was up and moving toward her. She couldn't stand.

"So you spent the night in the Settlement. You ain't nothing but white trash."

She thrashed about, but she didn't waste energy talking.

"I seen you going by here yesterday," Mose ranted. He was nearing her—she had no way to escape. "Teaching our white children. Daughter of the Senator. You cuss-ed little simpleton."

Reaching her, he was short of breath. "Don't be surprised . . . if . . . the Senator don't get his dues from the boys."

She seethed with anger.

"What business has a white girl like you got staying overnight in the colored community?"

He dropped to the ground. "You've done been ruined. You shouldn't mind what I'm getting ready to do."

In the meantime she rolled over, pulled her knees under her, and stood up. Grabbing and tearing her skirt, he pulled her down beside him.

He slapped the left side of her face. "What you get is what you need."

As soon as her skirts were out of the way, she rallied her remaining strength. She repelled his attack with a series of kicks. The more she kicked the more strength she had.

*   *   *

One box remained on the table. All of Jake's efforts had done nothing but raise the prices; yet he had failed to make a purchase. He looked at the girls standing nearby. Lydia seemed anxious. When he bought the lunch, she looked relieved.

The ladies went to the men holding their lunches. Lydia walked toward Jake. They found a place at the end of the low narrow picnic table. He placed the box on the table, and opened it.

"This smells awful," he said.

Lydia's smile faded.

"This food is spoiled. What happened?"

"It's not my fault. Rachel cooked it." She pooched out her lip.

"When?"

"I don't know," she said. "A few days ago."

He closed the box in disgust.

"I can't cook," she said. "I don't plan to ever have to."

"It's rank." He tossed it into the garbage drum.

She ran along behind him. "Rachel and Caroline didn't help me. Millicent didn't even bring a lunch."

"You shouldn't have," he said. "Why didn't Caroline help you?"

"She's gone," Lydia said.

"Why didn't Rachel help you?"

"She had a spell yesterday on the side porch."

"Really?"

"When George came to take her home, Caroline went with them, and I haven't seen her since," Lydia said. "She knew I needed her to cook for me, but she spent the night somewhere else."

"Later, Lydia."

He untied his horses and clucked to them. Rachel must have had a serious illness. He passed the Clemons home and turned right on Old Town Road toward the Settlement to look for the McBrides' home. He didn't know which house they lived in, but he would ask the neighbors if he needed to until he found it. Caroline had said it was the only painted house on the street. He thought he would have no trouble identirying it.

Why have I been such a fool?

He approached the curve in the road. Just before going into the Settlement he passed Mose Jefferson's house. "Whoa," he slowed his team so he could round the corner.

Mrs. Bently had talked about Mose, the town home brewer and moonshiner and Taylorsburg's worst drunk—also the town's worst outlaw. She told him the mayor liked the taste of Mose's spirits.

Glancing to his right, he noticed people scuffling in Mose's front yard beyond a big bush near the road. He didn't want to stop and become involved because he wanted to go check on Caroline and Rachel.

As he slowed his team of horses in preparation to round the sharp curve, he heard the muffled voice of a woman.

Caroline—it sounded like Caroline.

"Whoa." He brought the surrey to a halt and tied the horses to Mose's mailbox.

"Help me," the muffled voice cried. "Jake."

It *was* Caroline. His blood rushed to his head, his heart pounded, his muscles tightened. Jake bolted toward the sound of her voice. Mose held her pinned to the ground.

"She's a sassy filly, ain't she?" Mose said. "I like a woman with fight in her."

I wonder how he likes a man with fight in him.

"Yeaawwhh!" Jake bellowed as he charged into Mose with manly shoulders and tore Caroline loose from the monster. Again and again Jake pelted him with fists of iron in the face, on the side of the head, in the chest, the bloated gut. Sprawled on the ground, Mose didn't move.

Not checking to see whether Mose was alive, he scooped Caroline up and placed her over his shoulder without taking time to untie her. As fast as his legs would take him, he carried her to his surrey, where he loaded her onto the seat. He untied his horses and made a sharp turn back toward town. He used his whip—something he almost never did—to send the surrey flying.

As he reached his top speed, Caroline almost fell out of her seat because she couldn't balance herself with her hands tied. He reached with his right hand and held onto her tight until they were out of sight of the attacker's house.

"Whoa." He tried to untie her mouth and her hands, but the knot was tight. "Hold still." He used his pocketknife to cut the bandana and cords loose.

"Are you all right?"

"I will be," she told him.

"Let's go tell the sheriff," Jake said.

"It won't help."

"The mayor."

"It won't help," she said.

"Your father—will he help?"

"If I tell him what happened to me, he may help."

"What do you mean by 'may help'? What kind of man is he?"

"It depends on Mama Hortense," she said.

"Hortense?"

"We'll talk about it," she said.

Her eyelids fluttered, and she went limp. He took her to Dr. Woodley's house. As fast as he could, he tied his horses to the hitching post and went around to lift her down from the surrey. By the time he returned to her, she lay on the front seat with bloodstains on her clothes.

Again he laid her over his shoulder and took her to the door of the Woodleys' home. Mrs. Woodley met him at the door.

"In there," Mrs. Woodley said. "Leave her with me. I'll check her over and give her a bath. Can you get some clean clothes for her? Maybe something loose and comfortable."

"Sure, I'll be glad to," Jake said.

The Woodleys began examining Caroline.

Jake backed toward the door. "I'll go to her house and get her things. Then I'll take care of my horses. After that, I'll come back."

"Go ahead," Mrs. Woodley said. I need a few minutes. I'll dress her in one of my gowns for the moment."

*   *   *

Jake didn't want to waste a second returning to Caroline. He rode to the Clemons house and pulled up behind it. No one answered when he knocked and called. He found the back door unlocked. He knew the front rooms and another large bedroom near the front belonged to Lydia, Millicent, and Hortense. He tried a large room on the west side of the dining room. The lock prevented his entrance.

He wished someone would come and help him, but he was glad no one did. He looked into a sewing room, office, library, closets—where was Caroline's room? He bolted up the winding stairs. There he found a room the width of the house. It contained couches, tables, and chairs. At the far side, locked double doors stopped him He rushed back downstairs.

Running out of possibilities, he wandered into the pantry, where he saw a door on the left side. He started to turn around, but he needed to find her room and he had tried every other door. He unfastened a latch. The door sprang open to reveal a tiny cubicle containing Caroline's belongings. He snatched up an armload of her clothing. He hated to invade her privacy, but he had no choice.

He stuffed underwear into a bag from the pantry and threw clothing over his arm. Instead of seeing about the horses, he decided to rush Caroline's things over to Mrs. Woodley. He wanted to do all within his might to save her. Taking her a few clothes seemed such a little effort.

He tied the horses, grabbed what he had brought, and sprinted to the front door. Mrs. Woodley answered the door. "I'm sorry I was banging so hard. I didn't mean to disturb Caroline," he said.

"You didn't." She took him to the room where he had spent days after exchanging blows with Wilbur.

Caroline, clad in Mrs. Woodley's modest gown, sat propped up in the bed. She smiled at him. "You saved my life, not to mention my honor."

"Any man would have done the same," he said.

"No, that's not true. Some men attack women. Remember?"

"First I'll look in on Rachel. Then I need to go take care of the horses and check on Mrs. Bently. I shan't be gone any longer than I have to." He took her hand and squeezed it.

Looking exhausted, Caroline leaned her limp body back to rest.

*　　*　　*

He coaxed his horses to take the curve at a dangerous speed past the Jefferson home on the way to check on Rachel . . . . George assured him all was well.

As soon as he finished his chores and business details, he returned to her bedside and sat to wait until she opened her eyes. "Hello, beautiful one."

"I must look a mess," Caroline said.

"No, you're fine," he said. "The doctor said he wants you to stay here two nights. Monday he'll let you go home."

Caroline looked at him as he talked but didn't respond with so much as a nod. He sat near her. Maybe she would tell him more about what happened. To fill the awkward space of the moment he pulled out his new eyeglasses and reached for an old newspaper on the side table.

"Here's an interesting headline: Governor's Race Getting Hotter," he said.

"Jake, the Woodleys need to see about something for me. Could you step out a minute?" Caroline asked.

"Sure," he said.

"I'll call you back in a moment."

Jake was standing by Caroline's door when the doctor and his wife came out of the room where Caroline rested. The doctor turned toward Jake while his wife busied herself with disposing of some stained bandages.

"I'm not sure we should let her go Monday. I need more time to treat the injury on her left lower back. It's that old injury. She must have fallen and hurt herself again. Maybe she scraped it on the ground. So far she hasn't told me or my wife much about what happened."

The doctor looked long and hard at Jake.

"I doubt she'll rest or take care of herself at home, Doctor," Jake said. "She has tremendous responsibilities—lots of rigorous chores. I would hope she could stay here a few days."

"Jake?" Dr. Woodley's eyes pierced Jake.

"Yes, sir."

"How do you feel about men correcting their wives and girlfriends by striking them?"

Astonished to think Dr. Woodley suspected him of injuring Caroline, he said, "I think it's wrong."

"Do you ever think a man has a reason to do it?" Dr. Woodley asked. "What if a woman gets far out of line?"

"I'd never hit a woman. I've never done it." Jake fidgeted even though he realized he should have been steady during the interrogation.

"I see," the doctor said. "Let's go talk to her. Callie, could you come here a moment?"

Mrs. Callie Woodley, smiling and wiping her hands on her apron, appeared from the kitchen.

The doctor knocked on the door.

"Come in," Caroline said.

Jake walked behind the Woodleys to Caroline's bedside. The doctor told her, "We need you to stay a few days. Maybe by the end of the week, I'll discharge you."

She looked relieved. "Fine. I have one request though. Could you let me go down to MacGregor's Mercantile to use the telephone tomorrow afternoon?"

"Sure," Dr. Woodley said. "We can arrange for you to."

"Is that all right with you, Jacob?" Caroline asked. "Could you take me and let me use your telephone?"

"It would be my pleasure," Jake said.

The Woodleys left her resting. Jake sat beside her bed. Silent moments passed, and Jake decided he should go.

"I'll be at the back of the store tonight. Send for me if you need anything." He squeezed her hand. Then he raised it with tenderness. Bending forward, he kissed her fingers. "Goodnight."

He walked along the black street toward his store.

The way the doctor talked freely about Caroline's condition told me we must seem to be very close, and yet he implied I beat her. Should I tell him what really happened? Caroline doesn't want me to.

If he knew we haven't spent any time together lately, he'd have another reason to believe I hit her. What did I say while I was out of my head? I've always been afraid I'd do something foolish like that. My mind cannot control my heart in my sleep. Whatever I said wasn't real. The doctor should disregard it.

Heaven knows I tried to turn her out of my heart, but the Lord has brought us close for the present time at least. It's merely a temporary nearness because she needs me.

With most of my family gone and nothing but stinking plans for the future, I am going to guard myself from foolish mistakes, such as forming an attachment with this woman. She'd be sure to hurt me. I'll keep her out of my heart—no person and no event will ever affect me again. After I left Lydia with her rotten food and rushed to check on Caroline, a thought passed through my mind that I cared about her but I don't.

She has an old injury on her back. It's pain she's having, not some weird mannerism. I suppose it hurts worse whenever she becomes excited. The doctor must have thought she'd told me. If she ever does, I'll know she cares about me. How did I get back to that? I'm not going to love her or anybody else until I get myself together. I may need years. By then Caroline will be gone.

I wonder why she needs to make a telephone call tomorrow. She has so many concerns. I really wanted to help her. I can't help her sew for Lydia and Millicent, but I can check on Rachel.

What I want is to have Caroline laughing with me. I want to walk through the rain under an umbrella with her again. If I ever have a chance to walk with her, I won't cry. Why can't we simply have fun together? No, it won't happen because my emotions are getting tangled up. I can't allow this. I need to pray for her.

He made several starts to pray, but the words wouldn't come to his mind. Finally he made a simple request: "Dear God, please take care of Caroline and Rachel. Amen." It was impossible to petition God in detail while he was still angry.

*   *   *

Lying in the stillness Caroline felt the weight of the day. She had learned to pass through deep dark valleys with the encouragement the Lord sent her. Rachel was the one who sustained her, but now Rachel needed help. If Mahalia and Sylvester knew of Caroline's distress, they'd throw down whatever they were doing and run to her side, but she couldn't wait until they could come to her. She hated to rely on Jake. She didn't know how she felt about him or how he felt about her. She could neither stay focused on him long enough to think through their relationship nor asleep long enough to clear her mind with rest. Every creak in the floor frightened her.

Lord, I give my burdens to you. In the name of Jesus.

Sleep overtook her. In a dream she struggled to get her hands loose, she bit into the vile tasting handkerchief. Choking, she tried to stand up. Rolling, rolling, rolling, she fell onto the floor. The hard surface inflicted excruciating pain. Her screams caught in her throat. She pulled herself to a sitting position.

"Jake, were you here? Where did you go?'

She returned to bed and dozed, but she bolted to a sitting position. She held her breath so she could listen. Were there footsteps outside her window? The wind whistled under a loose board outside. The steps—they were steady and constant, not moving closer or farther away. She went first to the window by her bed to make sure it was locked. She checked the other two windows on the other outside wall. Upon her return to bed, the steps sounded closer.

Oh, it's my heartbeat.

She wanted to stop hearing it. She couldn't fall asleep . . . she visualized Mose's ugly eyes. She could hear his insane laugh. Mrs. Woodley had helped her rinse her mouth when she first came to their house, and now the taste of the nasty cloth filled her mouth again.

The attack was happening at that moment. Her heart thumped in skips. Out of breath and perspiring, she trembled as she sat up in the bed.

She put her feet on the floor. She would not sleep again if she had to sit there alert throughout eternity. She watched and listened. Outside the wind howled.

When she could resist sleep no longer, she fell over onto the bed into a tight ball. In her dream, Mose transformed into Hortense.

Awake again in her terror, with her chest feeling heavy, she choked. She shivered from the cold of her damp skin.

I can't go back home and spend the night until some time has passed. It's too scary right now. Besides real dangers lurk near that house. It's more than my imagination.

"Lord, help me. I will pray to you as long as I have breath."

She got up from her bed again. This time she lit a candle and sorted through the bag of items Jake had brought her. *I wonder whether he brought me my Bible. Yes.*

She turned to Psalm 18.

"I will love thee, O LORD, my strength. The LORD is my rock, and my fortress, and my deliverer; my God, my strength, in whom I will trust; my buckler, and the horn of my salvation, and my high tower. I will call upon the LORD, who is worthy to be praised: so shall I be saved from mine enemies." (Psalm 18:1-3)

She read all fifty verses and blew out the candle.

Chapter Eight

New Love's Agony

Jake arrived at two o'clock. "Are you ready to use the telephone?"

"Yes."

Dr. Woodley's eyes twinkled. "Go ahead and take the young lady for a ride in your surrey this afternoon. An outing in the fresh air will have healing powers."

"Good. I think so too," Jake said "How about it, Caroline?"

"Sounds pleasant."

The telephone was in a little booth near the back of the store. It seldom rang. Jake wondered whether it was really worth the space it took up. Hardly anyone else he knew had one.

"I've never used a telephone before, Jake."

"It's easy. Talk loud into the receiver and listen for a response."

"How do I place a call?"

"I'll get central for you, and then you can tell her what you need."

"Thanks."

Since she had not told him why she needed to make a telephone call, he concluded she wanted privacy. "I'll go check on the horses while you talk," he said.

"All right."

*   *   *

"Central, connect me with the home of Senator T. Chadwick Clemons in Jackson."

"Wait on the line."

"Yes, ma'am."

She hadn't planned to cry. She hoped her father couldn't hear her trouble. "Papa, it's good to hear your voice. How are you?"

"Carrie, hello. I'm fine," her papa said. "How about you?"

"Things aren't going so well here. Rachel had a spell. It first looked like a stroke, but she's better now. Brother George said he wouldn't let her work anymore. Hortense needs somebody else."

"How is she?"

"She is having some problems."

"What, baby?"

"We'll talk about it later." She knew that operators sometimes listened to the calls. With her father in public life, she understood the importance of being a private person.

"You sound upset," he said.

"I've been injured," Her voice cracked. "I had an accident involving someone who lives not too far from our home."

"Oh, no. Who?"

"I'll tell you when I see you."

"You're hurt?"

"Not too bad," she said. "I can't go back home. Some circumstances prevent it." She hoped he understood her vague remarks.

"I can't come back to Taylorsburg right now," he said. "What do you think you should do?"

"The doctor and his wife are keeping me in their home until the end of the week," she said. "Nothing's broken, but they are taking care of some things."

"Are you sure you're all right?"

"I am. I have to see about some business," she said. "Then I want to come and stay with you."

"Carrie, I'd love to have you. Will you be able to take a train by the end of the week?"

"Yes, sir."

"Is there anything you need me to do from here?"

"Yes, Papa. Please pray. Bye."

"I love you. Goodbye."

*   *   *

Jake came inside from checking the horses. "Ready to ride?" he asked.

"Yes. Let's check on Rachel."

"I want to."

"For your sake as well as mine, I don't want us to pass Mose Jefferson's house."

"Do we have a choice?" He didn't know all the roads around the community. "Do you know another way there?"

"Yes, but it's much farther."

"Let's go." He helped her gently into the surrey. She had massive bruises and scratches, and she moved her stiff body with difficulty.

"The road to get to the backside of Rachel's community goes through your farm and loops around. It comes up through the back way."

"Oh, we can make sure the farm is all right too," he said. "Are you sure you're up to this?"

"Yes," she said. "The doctor said it would do me good to breathe some fresh air."

Off they rode. Everything at the farm looked untouched.

"I worry about having this place out here and not being able to keep an eye on it. With the horses in town, there's not much left out here anyone could hurt."

"The house and the barn, but nobody's going to mess with those," she said.

They rode over the old creek bridge and then took a loop back toward town on the River Road.

"This is secluded," he said.

"It's all right though," she said. "At least it was the last time I came through here."

The road was deep between its banks with live oak trees spreading their branches draped with Spanish moss over the road. The River Road was a romantic place. Smoky and Firefly slowed to nibble the moss. It was a bad habit he shouldn't have allowed.

At the moment, however, he wasn't thinking about the discipline of his horses. He had a fervent desire to kiss Caroline, but he didn't want to make her uncomfortable. Maybe she would tolerate one little kiss. He slipped his arm around her.

He thought: *This secluded road is taking away my ability to guard the walls of my heart.*

Jake MacGregor, an athlete who had been a starting football player at Ole Miss, a man who could defend himself with his fists if an opponent forced him to do so, despite all his bravery sat helpless by the beautiful slight woman beside him, despite the fact that she was so sore she could barely move. He was conquered, even though he didn't want to be. He wondered whether she knew she had rendered him a willing subject to whatever she desired.

With all the courage he could muster, he lifted the brim of her bonnet. He took a deep noisy breath. His heart raced because he had no idea how she would react. Embarrassed, he moved his face toward her and gave her a little peck on her cheek. Kissing a girl he cared about required finesse—he had to do it right. He yearned to kiss her soft cheek; at the same time, it was as difficult as anything else he had ever done.

She looked at him and smiled. He tried to read her expression. She looked more compassionate than passionate. Why did she seem to feel sorry for him? He wished he could sit down and talk to his sister, who should be able to explain to him the way women think.

*   *   *

Only a few days ago, Jake had been indifferent toward her, but rescuing her had changed his entire attitude, Caroline supposed. She needed to check on Rachel and George, and he wanted to take her for a ride in his surrey. The whole idea, though, was a bad one.

It doesn't matter that the kiss was nothing but a little one. Whatever he did, I need to push him away. I'm less worthy of him or any other man than ever. I don't want to insult him, but I need to back away. After I leave, he'll get on with his life.

She shivered, even though the day was warm.

The new young lady in town, Victoria Robinson, will be perfect for him. He will court her as soon as I get out of the way. He already has a head start.

*   *   *

Jake felt ten feet tall after kissing Caroline's cheek. He tried to conceal his smile as he drove along the road. He realized what a treasure she was, and he intended to win her love.

When Jake drove his surrey into Rachel and George's yard, he and Caroline saw wagons tied to every spare spot on the fence between the yard and the garden. It was necessary to hitch his team far from the house.

"You feel like walking this far?"

Caroline nodded her head. "The walk will help me limber up."

Inside, guests were hovering around Rachel, propped up in the bed. Her smile was crooked, but she was giving it her best effort. George stood nearby.

He stepped outside with Jake and Caroline as they were leaving. "Remember, Rachel ain't coming back to work. Tell your pa what happened when you see him."

"I understand," Caroline said. "Don't worry. I don't know when I can come back. Something has happened, and I need to go to Jackson to spend some time. If I don't get to talk with Rachel before then, please tell her I love her. Brother George, it isn't something for you to have to worry about, but do you know of anyone who would be willing to cook for Hortense?"

"Let me think on it," he said. "If I do come up with somebody, I'll send her to the Clemons house to talk to Mrs. Hortense."

"That will be fine," Caroline said.

They rode in the surrey back down the River Road and to the farm again. "You're . . . . planning to go to Jackson to see your father?" Her failure to tell him ahead of time hurt.

"Yes," she said.

"I'll miss you," Jake said.

"I'm sorry, Jake. I realized last night that I cannot sleep at home until some time passes. It's too dangerous."

"That makes sense. As long as Mose is out there, you'll feel uncomfortable."

"That's part of the problem," she said. "Also I don't have Rachel."

"Rachel?"

"She protected me, and I've thought I could use her as a witness if I needed to."

"You make it sound as if someone besides Mose was a threat to your existence. I knew Hortense slapped you one day when I came for tea, but there's more to this, isn't there? Tell me more," he said.

"Maybe later. Let's not talk about that today. I want to thank you, Jake, for helping me and for being a good friend. I'm going to live with Papa all next year if I can find a job teaching in Jackson."

Hanging his head, he swallowed. "I wish you wouldn't go, but I understand."

"Jake, I want you to have a good time. The new young lady in town, Victoria Robinson, is very attractive and accomplished. I heard a rumor that she had her eyes on you. You've been sitting with her in church."

He decided it was best not to acknowledge her remark. He set his jaw hard.

"Victoria has met with the school board," she said. "She wants to teach here. If I go, she'll have a place."

"Oh, really?" Jake asked.

"Most of the eligible girls have their eyes on you."

"Hmm.'

"You don't seem to realize you are a great catch. You're very handsome. Intelligent. Considerate. You have a promising future. I hope you will find a great wife who'll take care of you."

"Right," he said.

"Yes," Caroline continued. "You seemed to be interested in Lydia. While she is pretty, she lacks the qualities you need in a wife. I don't believe she would be happy helping you with the store and the farm. She and Mama Hortense have frequent misunderstandings. Pardon me for saying so, but they have similar dispositions."

"I see." He was miffed.

"Millicent has a sweeter nature, but she is still a child. I'm elated to see the ways she is changing. By the time she grows up, you'll be an old married man. Besides, I don't believe you find her attractive."

"Miss Clemons, do you not think I have the common sense to make my decisions about these matters?" Jake asked.

"Of course you do, but as your friend I wanted to advise you."

"What do you think about yourself, Caroline?"

"I'm not in the picture."

Her remarks vexed him. They rode quietly back to the doctor's house.

"You seem tired," he said. "Thank you for a wonderful afternoon."

"Thank you for helping me," she told him.

He saw her to the Woodleys' door.

I had not realized she was so haughty.

He asked, "Would noon tomorrow be a good time to meet you? We could go to lunch, and then you probably need to attend to some other things. You probably need to make preparations for leaving."

"I need to have a talk with Mrs. Bently. Maybe she can help me find a seamstress to finish making the uniforms."

* * *

Caroline felt the doctor and his wife had taken her into their home as though she were their own. They asked no questions, but they tried to provide solutions. Mrs. Woodley cleansed the newly aggravated wound with a mixture of clean water and hydrogen peroxide twice a day. Then she applied ground ginger and garlic to it and covered it with a bandage. It was usually necessary to soak the bandage, which was sometimes stuck.

The doctor told her, "Go and come as you wish."

"Thanks. Just tell me how much my bill is. Papa and I will pay you." She didn't tell him about Mose Jefferson.

* * *

Over baked chicken at the Covington Monday Jake tried to make eye contact with Caroline.

He decided not to allow her attitude to provoke him. In four or five days she would leave. He couldn't waste time being mad. He was starting to regain his freedom to pray. *Heavenly Father, thank you for helping me curb my anger.*

"Do you know how much I'll miss you?" His voice pleaded with her.

"I'll miss you and everyone else around here." Her matter-of-fact response conveyed an atmosphere of forced coldness toward him. Why was she pushing him away?

"You'll be back in a week or two, I hope. Your students need you here." Although she had said otherwise, he wanted to let her know he didn't want to give up his pursuit. Her coldness whetted his desire.

Her smile looked coerced. It was her only answer.

He thought she was slipping away forever. "You'll have a good time in Jackson," he said.

"I hope so," she said. "And you'll have a good time here."

He had hoped for a different response. Although the lunch was well prepared, they picked at their food.

If I had tried harder to take care of her, things would have been different. If I had started really courting her, she wouldn't have been injured because I would have had her with me. She wouldn't be leaving town. I saw how Hortense hurt her. I should have done something. I'm still confused about that injury on her back.

He lost his appetite. She had also stopped eating. He thought about the lunch he had purchased Saturday. What a rancid meal that was. He pushed his plate away. In silence he lowered his head and closed his eyes.

What a price I paid . . . and Caroline paid . . . for a rotten reward. Lord, please forgive me for the mess I've made.

"Are you all right?" Caroline asked.

"I'm fine." He gazed at her with tender regret. They pushed the uneaten meal aside.

"Are you too sore to walk to the Mercantile?"

"As I told you yesterday, I need to walk.It will help me limber up my muscles," she said.

At the Mercantile she explained to Mrs. Bently her dilemma about the uniforms.

Mrs. Bently told her, "Don't worry. I'll find somebody. I can think of half a dozen women who are excellent seamstresses. Some of them will be glad to make a little money sewing."

Tuesday Jake brought Caroline a bouquet of zinnias.

"Thank you. Mrs. Woodley will love these." Caroline found a vase in the kitchen.

They walked to the Covington for lunch. As they finished he asked, "Are you ready to face Hortense?"

"Yes. Do you have time to go with me?"

"Of course," he said. "I'll try to distract her while you pack. Then I'll help you load your trunk into the surrey."

"Oh, a trunk—I do need one. Do you have one I can buy?"

"No, but I have one I'm giving you. It's loaded into the back seat of the surrey."

"How kind and generous."

"It's the least I could do," he said. "Don't try to lift it. I'll do that."

"This sounds like a workable plan," she said.

He grinned at her.

"Jake, you are a wonderful man."

"Aw."

"You'll make some girl a fine husband."

Her words pierced his heart.

A tall young woman wearing a starched white apron over a neat dress greeted them at the front door of the Clemons home. "I'm Frankie."

"Is Mrs. Clemons here?"

"No, sir, she and her girls have gone visiting."

"I'm Jacob MacGregor."

"I know who you are—the new man at the Mercantile."

"And this is Caroline Clemons. She has come to get some of her things."

"I know who you are too." Frankie's approach was both professional and matter-of-fact.

*   *   *

The week was passing fast. Caroline couldn't admit she cared. Tuesday night she faced more nightmares. Mose Jefferson was in her dream. She struggled to speak. Her hands were tied behind her. She fought to stand. Again she went rolling, rolling, rolling. Where was Jake? He was supposed to come and rescue her.

She climbed out of her bed, lit a candle, read Psalm 18 all the way through again and prayed. Then she blew out the candle and went back to bed.

Up early Wednesday, she shampooed and towel-dried her hair. She looked through her clothes Jake had brought. Since the trunk was full she would need to pack what she had at the Woodleys' in a satchel for the train ride. Among the dresses was the loose-fitting lingerie dress with the French lace. In the mirror she saw her face looking vibrant and rested again.

Jake arrived with sandwiches and two fruit jars of cool water. "This will be your last chance to see Rachel for a few days. I know you would love to go to her house. Last time too many people kept you from having a good visit."

"Jake, you are the most thoughtful man I've ever known." She didn't mean to say such a thing to him. Where he was concerned, she had taken a vow of indifference.

"Let's go around the long way," he said. "I like the pretty scenery. Besides we still don't need to ride by Mose's house. Someone told me he shoots at his enemies when they drive by. I believe you and I fit into that category."

They rode to Jake's farm and stopped at his little house for lunch.

"We can catch some cool air in the breezeway," he said.

"I call that a dogtrot," she said. They spread the tablecloth on the floor near the edge of the porch.

From the basket he pulled out two plates, sliced bread, a knife, and a cheese spread.

"Mrs. Bently make this?" Caroline asked.

"No." With a sheepish grin on his face he said, "She showed me how."

"Mmm. Pimento cheese. My favorite."

He winked at her.

"You're wowing me with all this food from your store—pickles, olives, sliced bologna, and iced cookies." Soon she was eating with a great appetite.

After lunch, they loaded up and traveled along the scenic River Road to see Rachel and George. Jake beamed at her and patted her arm from time to time as they drove along.

Caroline thought he would be the perfect husband some day except for two things. One was her disfigurement that left her a flawed person. Also she didn't like the thought of courting someone struggling in his relationship with God. She thought of a third problem. How was she to know he wouldn't go off chasing Victoria or Lydia or Geraldine—whatever pretty woman passed his way?

They crossed the romantic bridge without stopping.

George greeted Jake and Caroline in the front yard. "Do you know if Francesca Simons went to work for Mrs. Clemons?" George asked.

"Yes, we saw her at the house," Caroline told him.

"Great. She's a fine worker," he said. "She's my sister's daughter."

"Thank you for helping out," Caroline said. "I'm sure the family will be glad to have her. Please check to be sure she is paid properly."

"I'll look after her like she was my own. She's hoping to move on to something better. That's what our finest kids are doing. Moving on. They go to Chicago and Los Angeles. Places too far away. There ain't nothin' here for them."

He led them into the house. Caroline took Rachel's hand. "Have you been feeling all right?"

"I'm fine," Rachel said. "I ain't had no more trouble. You know having you go hurts me like you was one of my own young ones 'cause you are."

"Yes, Madear. You have been a mother to me."

"But a time comes when folks have to move on," Rachel said.

"Caroline echoed her. Yes'm, there comes a time."

"Somebody told me Mose Jefferson attacked you," Rachel said.

"I didn't want you to know," Caroline said.

"You can't keep secrets from your old friend Rachel."

Jake followed Brother George out to the porch. Rachel and Caroline continued their girl talk.

"I want to tell you one thing," Rachel said. "When you get up there to Jackson—well, I want to say two or three things. I say when you get up there to Jackson, don't forget to say your prayers to the Lord."

"I promise I won't."

"Make yourself look pretty every day."

"Aw, Madear." Caroline held her head down and blushed.

"Don't forget your old Rachel and Brother George back down here."

"You know I won't. I love you."

"And one more thing. I know you'll do all the other stuff, but you've got to promise me this."

Caroline waited.

"You got to promise me, sweet pea, that you don't let nobody treat you bad. I won't be back in the kitchen to take up for you. You're going to have to stand up for yourself."

"I've already started trying. Now it's my turn. Please give me your word that you'll take care of yourself. If you need me for any reason, send Brother George to the Mercantile to telephone me at Papa's house. Papa's got a telephone."

"I'll remember. Girl, go with God."

They hugged and parted.

Traveling back down the River Road, the horses moved at a snail's pace. Caroline said, "I hope I haven't taken too much of your time."

"You know I'm not very busy these days. The store can only do so much business. In the time ahead, I'll be busy farming and building a new house. Right now, I'm enjoying your company. I am thankful to God to have this time."

They slowed to a creep as they traveled across the narrow Lyon Creek Bridge, which they had crossed earlier without noticing the rising water. "Look. The beavers have dammed up the creek again," she said.

Leaving the bridge, the horses slowed to a stop so they could nibble the Spanish moss. She laughed. "They're continuing their bad habit."

She melted in the intensity of his gaze as he turned toward her. She delighted in the rugged masculinity of his face. She knew . . . she hoped . . . no romance would ever develop between them; yet she wanted to remember the moment's wonder. She wanted to treasure the way he looked at her with such tenderness. Thursday, the day of her departure, would come too soon.

She felt his breath on her cheek. The sweetness of his spicy *eau de toilette* intermingled with the aroma of his masculinity—how would she ever forget it if she lived to be one hundred? In that moment, her heart overshadowed her brain.

Lord, help me.

When he inhaled, she felt the essence of her life being absorbed into him. Such perfection Jacob MacGregor was, and for the moment he seemed to revere her. She knew it wouldn't last, couldn't last. Instead of backing away as her brain cautioned her, she sat close to him, lips tingling with longing.

He placed his hand on her bonnet. With her head tilted up to his face, she reveled in the sensation that he sought her lips, and she didn't turn away. When his mouth touched hers, she experienced a glorious emotion she had hoped she would never feel. His kisses, like his actions, were tender yet powerful. She trembled and her heart pounded. She needed to breathe. When she opened her eyes, the River Road was lovelier than ever before.

"I'd better stop the horses from misbehaving", he said. They rode back to town in dreamy silence.

Before returning to the doctor's house and clinic, they stopped by the Clemons home. Again Hortense and her daughters were out. "Frankie, please tell them I am staying at the doctor's house for treatment."

Leaving Jake talking to Frankie, Caroline went to her room and found her little jewelry box. Inside it her earrings and locket were as she had left them. She'd have Loretta Larson come over and get the school books for Victoria as soon as the school board hired the new teacher.

Thursday morning the benevolent doctor and his wife instructed her about the process of taking care of her injury. She paid them the amount they required, although she knew it was only a fraction of what their services were worth to her.

*   *   *

Jake's heart ached with sorrow. He hated to see her catch the train. He kissed her hand with gentleness and gave her a light hug.

He had a sweet memory . . . he wouldn't forget Wednesday, when she finally let down her guard enough for him to see she cared. He had tried to tell her he loved her, but he wasn't sure how she would react. Thursday, a sad day for him, came too soon.

From a window on the train she waved goodbye. His hand shook as he returned the wave. He stood and watched the train until it was out of sight.

Chapter Nine

A Fork in the Road

After Caroline's departure, Jake arrived at a divergence in his course. The low road would take him into despair. He could remain indignant at God for taking his family and now the precious one he wanted near him.

Traveling down that path, he could give up on winning her heart, which was encased in a thick fortress with only a rare light beam of her feelings escaping as it did when he kissed her on the River Road. Along the way he would encounter a plethora of young women who were either self-serving females with their own agendas or mysterious new ones requiring an expenditure of effort to learn their quirks. These exercises failed to fascinate him.

Caroline had taken his heart, and he had abandoned his plan not to fall in love with her. The only road that could ever reach her heart was the high one. Did she understand herself well enough to show him the path? It was a twisted trail he felt compelled to discover.

He needed help, but he had turned his back on the only Help available. He had taken a few baby steps back toward the Lord, but he required more. Abruptly he turned his surrey around and headed toward the McBride home. Brother George, the wise old preacher, would know what he should do.

"You got time to help a suffering man?" Jake asked.

"Pull up a chair, young man. I got all the time you need," Brother George said.

They sat on the porch and talked. Rachel wandered out when she grew interested in what they were saying and announced she'd go back inside to lie down when she grew tired.

"Brother George, I have a spiritual puzzle I need you to help me solve." He relived the story of how he had lost his family and dreams for the future.

"Like Job," Brother George nodded. "Yep, like Job."

"That's what Caroline said."

"Did she tell you how Job's life ended?"

"Yes, and she told me to read the book."

"The Lord restored more to Job as was taken away. Compare that to you, brother. The Lord is already restoring your blessings. It's true your family was taken from you. I pray they are with the Father in heaven and safe in the arms of Jesus. If they are, as hard as it is for you to accept, they are a thousand times better off than they were here treading their way through this pilgrim land."

Jake sniffled as he twirled his hat.

George didn't stop. "It's the truth you ain't going to get to go off and study in the next year or two to be a druggist or be a research scientist, but you've got a fine mercantile store. Wait a minute. You could sell it all, maybe, and leave out of here. Or you could hire a manager to take care of it long enough for you to go to school and come back. You don't want to though. If you did, you'd have done it already.

"So you are responsible to do your best with what you've got here. Excuse me for saying it. Stop your bellyaching. Are you doing all you can to make your blessings the best? In other words are you being a good steward?"

"I've failed to look at it that way." Jake hung his head.

"Sometimes we think we know what we need, but Jehovah has other ideas," George said. "He has plans for you."

"I'm ashamed I haven't been a good steward," Jake said. "I've been too busy thinking about what I wanted, what I thought I needed. The Lord has every right to be mad at me."

"The God we serve is longsuffering. That means patient." George gestured with his hands. "Slow to anger and tenderhearted. He'll give you a chance if you ask him."

"I've been too mad to pray much."

Rachel inserted a comment. "The dear Lord above done told us never to let the sun go down on our anger."

"Before you sleep tonight, you know what you've got to do." The aged preacher raised his voice.

"What about that fine farm?" Rachel inserted her question.

"I haven't been interested in raising cotton."

"You're smart, and you've been to college. You ought to be able to figure out how to cultivate that blessing in a way acceptable to you and to the Lord." George was moving into the chant of a sermon.

Taking up the chorus, Jake said, "Like Job, I lost my family."

"Uh huh. That's right," Rachel said.

Preacher George continued. "Job lost all of them but a nagging wife. She told him to curse God. In my opinion, he'd a been better off if he lost her. Me, I've been blessed with one fine woman. You ain't got a wife, but Caroline seems to like you a mighty lot."

"You better treat her good," Rachel said. "What you've got to understand is that she is a hurt child. She's smart and beautiful and loving, but she's like a delicate flower. It don't take much to hurt her because she's been hurt already."

"That's right," George said.

In a self-pitying tone, Jake said, "Caroline doesn't care about me."

"Women are hard to read sometimes," George said. "It took me a while to figure out Rachel back when we was young. You been figuring Caroline all wrong. You've got to *love* her. Love her enough that she will know it's safe to love you in return. You've got all a man needs. It ain't what you planned, but it never is. What you've got, you must use to the glory of God. You've got to let your woman know you'll provide for her."

"I love her with all my heart," Jake said. "I didn't mean to, but I do."

"Love for a man is a peculiar thing," George said. "He's like a honeybee with all the pretty flowers that smell sweet fluttering around him. It ain't natural to pick out one and forsake all the others. Then a man's got to love that one flower after it gets bruised from life. If he finds the right one and loves it enough, the nectar won't stop flowing. A man has to love his wife the way Jesus loves the church. In other words he has to love her enough to give his life for her. It's hard."

Jake lowered his head. "I plan to be a loving husband. You've shown me all kinds of goals I need to work toward."

"The plans that count are the ones that God makes," George said. "You got any paper in your pocket? And a pencil?"

Jake reached for his glasses, a small tablet, and a pencil.

"Take this down. For yourself to get back where you belong in the Lord's sheepfold instead of bumping into the back wall, read all the John books, all the ones named 'John.' That same John wrote Revelation, but you can read it a little later. For Caroline and you, read First Corinthians 13. It'll tell you how to win her over. Trust the Lord, and let him fix what ain't right."

"I've always known God was still there the way I knew him when I was a little boy," Jake said. "After the tornado, I thought I had to do everything myself. I didn't want to rely on God after he took my family."

"Like I told you, if your people knew him for their Savior, they're so much happier now up in heaven than down here on this troubled earth. Be thankful they are in the hands of the blessed Savior."

Jake scribbled on the notepad.

"Young man, write down a plan for your life with that pencil. Then give God the eraser."

On the way back to the Mercantile he rode through his farm, which looked different. What had been an old tumbled down double homestead, deserted before it had reached fruition, was a land flowing with milk and honey waiting for him to exercise possession.

He stopped to revel in the joy of walking in God's will. The grassy land dappled with scattered sunlight was the most beautiful location he had ever seen. He tied his horses and fell prone. He kissed the ground, and then he poured his heart out to the Lord. Bathed in his tears, he stood tall and resolute.

He began to see some changes he needed to make. On the high road where he chose to travel, the loneliness would come to an end. He was ill-suited for the life of a bachelor, but he would need to become proficient in his singleness to become suitable to join with Caroline.

As a university student, he'd learned to follow a plan. His pattern involved outlining a strategy based on thorough research followed by careful reasoning. Talking with George, he saw the need to consult his everlasting Father before each step.

The time had come to turn away from the weeks of floundering. George had convinced him. Although his inheritance of money and the store would supply his needs, he wanted to sense accomplishment as evidenced by the wise use of his resources. He dreamed of providing for a family.

Back in town after he put the horses up, he sat at his desk and munched cheddar cheese and soda crackers. While Mrs. Bently took a break from the store to attend to some personal business, he made a list of assets:

Farm: 320 acres, unfenced, timber ready to be harvested, four Tennessee walking horses, farmhouse needing repairs, stables in fair condition, garden plots.

Store: Excellent employee (overworked), hardware, dry goods, groceries, hodgepodge of outdated inventory, dingy appearance.

Self: Educated, accepted in community (after fight with Wilbur Mauldin), bored and uninformed about row-crop farming, interested in cattle, interested in horses.

Following the elderly pastor's advice, he returned to the sweet communion with the Lord that he had known as a child. At night he read his Bible. Saturday he tried harder to help Mrs. Bently in the store. After the store closed, he tried to call Caroline at the Senator's home in Jackson, but no one answered. He hoped she was having a lovely time, but he feared she would meet Mr. Wonderful.

When Caroline became more than a dream—more than a vision—nothing else mattered. Whatever was necessary to win her was what he would do. The McBrides had helped him spiritually, and they had served as the one possible link to the woman he thought about from the time he arose in the morning until he slept, when she invaded his dreams.

Sunday he enjoyed church and tried again to call Caroline.

Monday he bought lunch at the Covington for himself and Mrs. Bently and took it back to the store. When they finished eating, he told her, "Take an hour to do whatever you wish. It's a slow day." When she returned, he saddled his spirited mare Montana, who was in need of an outing. He rode to the Mauldin place, a mile southwest of his farm. *It's peculiar what I had to do to make friends with the Mauldins.*

By the time the afternoon sun began to set in the red sky, he had worked out an arrangement for Wilbur's brother, Monroe, to move into the farm cabin with his bride. Jake would supply paint and lumber. Monroe would renovate and enlarge it. When the Mauldins finished harvesting their corn and cotton, they would fence the MacGregor property for a contracted price. The old fence was in such poor repair it was worse than no fence at all.

That evening he wrote a letter to Caroline to bring her up-to-date. He supposed she would be surprised at all he was doing.

Every day he continued to help mind the store. He spent whatever spare time he had improving the neglected place. He began organizing and rearranging the displays. He wiped out bins that had not been cleaned in months. He washed and polished the woodwork, cleaned the windows, and scrubbed grime off the door. He spoke to everyone who entered. If he knew customers' names, he spoke them.

With Mrs. Bently's help he listed the name of each customer on a separate sheet of paper along with all the pertinent information he could obtain. He asked her for inventory ideas. "Let's find out from all our customers what they'd like for us to stock for them. We'll take their suggestions under advisement. If anybody requests a specific item, I'll do all within my power to get it. I want to make everyone who walks into the Mercantile feel special."

"What made you suddenly decide to improve the store?" Mrs. Bently asked.

He gave her a crooked grin. She smiled as she waited for an answer. "What was it?" she asked.

"Umm."

"I know," she said. "You're smitten. You have all the symptoms. You chased after a certain young lady with the hopes of winning her over, and now you are nesting. Good luck." She walked away laughing.

*   *   *

"How are you doing, baby girl? Are you happy here?'

"You know I am."

"How's the new piano?" Papa asked.

"I love it." A new Werlein upright piano occupied a prominent place in the living room.

"And I'm loving the music."

"But I'm out of practice," she said.

"Is there anything you want or need that you don't have?" The Senator hugged Caroline.

"There is one thing." She hesitated.

"What is it?"

"It's too expensive."

"Try me," he said in a reassuring tone.

"A sewing machine."

"You have not been pampered," he said. "Most young women I suppose would request money to purchase an elaborate wardrobe along with the services of a seamstress."

She smiled. She supposed that Mrs. Bently had helped her stepsisters find a seamstress to finish their sewing for school.

"We'll find you a sewing machine. I'll have it delivered here. Meanwhile here's some money to buy fabric."

He handed her a roll of bills without counting them.

She threw her arms around his neck. "Thank you. I won't waste it."

"If that's not enough, tell me."

"Okay. Papa, please let me stay with you this year. If I stay in Taylorsburg, I'll hurt your image. Conditions have changed. We can find me a teaching job here. I'll explain it all to you when you have time to spare."

She found pictures of the latest Paul Poiret dresses and designed similar ones for herself. She was too active to enjoy the clothing her stepsisters chose with the bodices requiring whalebone undergarments laced to miserable tightness. Such garments were painful on her injured back.

Lydia, who was pencil thin, liked the long slim look with plenty of ruffles in the fronts of her blouses and dresses. Millicent, who was chubby, suffered under the oppression of whalebone stays. Both of them loved contrasting sashes. Even in their day dresses when they went out in public they wore skirts that brushed the floor and had trains in the back. Caroline didn't want her dresses to drag on the floor.

I wonder what kind of fashions Jake likes. What is it to me? I have no right to care.

My dearest Caroline,

Everyone misses you. When I ride down the road, the birds ask me when you are coming back. They want to be close to you. The stars are not twinkling as bright because you are not here. The horses are in mourning for your pet pats.

And, my dear friend, I confess that I miss you terribly. I hope you are having a wonderful time, and I'm delighted that you are staying with your father. I pray you will be returning soon.

Here's an item of news: Hortense came complaining to Mrs. Bently because you had gone "who knows where?" Her girls' school uniforms, undergarments, and some more dresses were unfinished. "Where on earth has Caroline gone? It's hard to get reliable help." Precious friend, I had to restrain myself.

Mrs. Bently, expecting the tirade because you had warned her, told her she had already found some ladies who would be glad to finish the sewing. That was fine until Mrs. B. quoted their prices.

"It isn't worth it," Hortense said.

"That's the going rate," Mrs. B. told her. Then I had to contain myself to keep from laughing.

I remain

Your adoring friend,
Jake

He didn't wait for an answer. He was determined to woo her heart.

Dear sweet Caroline,

You will be thrilled to hear my exciting news. I went to a timber company in Laurel. On second thought you may be sad at the loss of some of the stately trees on the farm. I made arrangements to have some of the timber cut. I plan not to allow the woodmen to strip the place bare. Instead they will thin the forest. On some of the land I will maintain a thick forest.

Some parts will be pastureland. I'll keep a small pasture for the horses. By this time next year, we should have six horses. I know it's inappropriate to count the horses before the mares foal, but I'm a child at heart.

I've been riding Montana instead of driving the surrey. Both she and I need the exercise. I have been looking over the property. Plan to do that with me when you return.

The big pastures will be for cattle. While I was in Laurel, I went to the library and the stockyard to research different breeds. At the moment Herefords are my top preference. Please tell me which breed you prefer. Ask the Senator what he thinks.

I hope you are getting enough rest. I try to imagine what you must be doing. Sewing? Do you have a sewing machine? Are you sewing for yourself? Reading? Shopping? Making new friends? Have a good time, but don't fall for some smooth-talking Jackson lawyer.

I remain

Your loving friend,
Jacob

Every night he had something he wanted to tell her. One evening soon he would try again to telephone her, but he feared she would be out again. His imagination went rampant.

My precious Caroline,

You will be glad to know that I am in love with the Lord as I was in my childhood. Brother George has helped me, and so have you. I cannot get enough of the scripture. Every night I read the Bible. I need to discuss several matters with you.

I am gaining a peace over the losses in my family.

Lately the town has been quiet. When your stepsisters left, the social life went with them.

Hortense is not well. She seldom comes to the store. Instead she sends Jim for everything. The last time I saw Hortense she was in public without having combed her hair, and her dress was askew.

Could I call you some evening on the telephone? I crave hearing your sweet voice.

As always,
Jake

Letters from Taylorsburg packed her father's mailbox. Although she read every one of them until she could commit them to memory and although she pressed them with roses in her favorite book, she postponed answering him. She dared not encourage him. He would be disappointed if he knew what she really was, a damaged, flawed person. He wouldn't understand.

She pulled a thicker letter from the mailbox:

Dearest Caroline,

The money from the timber will go far toward paying for the fence around the farm and also building a new house. I've been trying to design a floor plan. Could you please give me some suggestions about same?

Your faithful friend,
Jake

P. S.
Study these and let me know which one you prefer. This house should last a very long time, and it needs to be well-planned.

In the envelope were two different floor plans.

She could not escape the realization that Jake deserved answers to his letters, but she knew she must not write him. He was dreaming about an imaginary Caroline, who was nothing like the real one. A part of her wanted to give up on him, another part didn't want to hurt him, and her heart wanted to be near him. She selected her best stationery to write her aunt.

My dear Aunt Mahalia,

Your letter gave me great joy. I am still delighting in the memories of the fun we had during your visit.

Papa and I are enjoying being together even though I seldom see him. He works all the time. His passion is to improve the educational opportunities of Mississippi. He is helping Edmond Noel, and he has several law cases. I try not to burden him with my problems.

What concerns me most now is Jacob. I fear that Uncle S. liked him too well to offer any objective advice. I must confess I think more kindly of him with each passing day. He tells me he has changed. Many of the aspects of his personality that I found trying have vanished. Most importantly, his anger at his Creator over his losses has vanished. He says he has a new love of the scripture.

He writes about something every day, even though I have not answered his letters. A week before coming to stay with Papa I had an accident, which caused new aggravation to my old injury on my back. I spent several nights in the home of the kind doctor and his wife. The treatments that they started are helping. I am able to relax here and avoid binding clothing.

The concern I have is that the hideous scar will repulse any man who would become my husband. I cannot bare the look of revulsion in his eyes. Marriage is not in my future.

I don't want to hurt Jacob's feelings. Ignoring him simply entices him to pursue me more vigorously. Also I fear that such a handsome, cultured, intelligent man would soon lose his fascination for me, even I didn't have this thorn in my flesh.

Thank you and Uncle Sylvester for your loving concern.

Hoping this letter finds you and Uncle well,

Your devoted niece who loves you,
Caroline

She penned the address on the envelope, applied a stamp, and inserted the letter into the mailbox on the porch. She pulled another sheet of her fine stationery from the box and stared at the blank page.

Dear Jacob,

The steps of the postman crossing the porch told her that she had twenty-four hours before she could mail Jake a letter—twenty-four hours to think what to say to him, twenty-four hours to pray about the man.

After the postman left, she collected the mail, including the usual, almost daily letter from Jake.

Chapter Ten

Home

Caroline couldn't resist. She used the letter opener so she wouldn't mutilate the treasure she had received. All Jake's letters were precious to her, but he didn't need to know. Her fingers caressed the envelope.

I'll press them with lavender inside another book. Until he marries, I'll keep these and read them when I wish. When the day of his marriage comes, I'll burn them. If I don't, there'll be a danger of my committing adultery in my heart. I will respect his wife.

She removed the letter from the envelope.

My cherished Caroline,

Hello. Could you please tell me what you think about the two house plans? Which one do you like better?

When you receive this note, I hope you will be having a wonderful day. I hope you are feeling well. I expect you to come back home in a few days.

In the meantime, I cannot resist helping you keep up with the news. First, Bruiser. He must have noticed a whiff of your perfume at the door of the Mercantile. I've been ignoring him, but he refuses to leave. Mrs. Bently and I decided to feed him. He misses you almost as much as I do.

Mostly today I have some details about things I've already told you. I took Firefly, Fancy, and Montana to visit the Mauldins' farm. Midnight, their stallion, will be the proud father of three colts next year, I hope. I'll give one of them to the Mauldins as payment.

Isn't it funny that they are my friends and business associates now?

Good news. The lumber company has agreed to plane enough lumber from the farm to build the house. I have enough fine virgin timber to cut all the long straight boards the builders will need. Expect a fine house.

I am

Your devoted admirer,
Jake

In the interest of being fair, she wrote to him.

Dear Jake,

Your letters are the highlight of every morning. You do an excellent job of telling me the news and I look forward to hearing what has happened lately.

You will need to decide which house plan you prefer. Think about what type of house would be more comfortable for you. I will be glad to discuss some specific details with you.

Some day when you meet the girl of your dreams you will wish you had had the opportunity to discuss the house with her in greater detail. Women have their preferences.

Personally I prefer Plan A, but I don't believe my opinion will matter much in the future.

Your grateful friend,
Caroline

*   *   *

When he received her letter, He crinkled it up and threw it in the trash basket. No letter at all was better than that one. He dashed off an angry response, which he also threw in the trash basket. Staring out the window he came upon a solution that would bide some time.

Dear Caroline,

The hot summer sun needed to make the cotton grow has slowed business. Every now and then ladies wonder in to buy fabric to make school clothes. I probably shouldn't but I'm extending credit to some of these poor ladies with the hopes of collecting after the cotton is ginned and sold.

I'm keeping a careful ledger, and I'm putting a very low ceiling on the amounts I allow on the credit bills.

Please look over the list of names attached to this letter. Tell me which ones you consider poor risks.

As always,
Jake

See attachment.

He knew she would not be able to resist helping him with a problem. As far as her letter was concerned, he would let her think he had not yet received it.

Walking to the post office, he couldn't stop grinning about what he considered a clever approach.

*   *   *

The telephone at the Senator's house on East Fortification Street rang.

"Hello?"

Caroline had a habit of raising her voice in such a way that everything sounded like a question. The finishing school and Aunt Haley had worked on it, but the habit soon returned when she left New Orleans.

"Hello. Can you hear me? It's Mahalia. We have a bad connection."

In a mixture of scratchy static, Caroline managed to hear, "Give him a chance. And give yourself a chance."

"Okay."

"What have you got to lose? As it is you're already losing everything."

"I'll do it for you, Tantaylee."

She started writing him a letter every day after her conversation with her aunt. The letters flowed in both directions. She remained reserved, but he poured out his heart.

She knew Papa would get the wrong impression. With his office in his house, the Senator, who sometimes brought the mail inside, was sure to notice the steady flow of correspondence from Jacob MacGregor. She tried not to let him see her savor Jake's letters; when she remembered, she waited until he was out of sight to go to the writing desk in the back of the parlor to write responses.

She wrote:

Dear Jake,

    You seem to be well and full of zest for life. I am happy that you have allowed the Lord to help you with the healing of your grief. Not on this earth will any of us ever understand sadness. I suppose when we reach heaven we can ask, but then we will have no need. We won't know sadness there, and we will be joined with our loved ones who have gone to be with God.

    You may wonder how I spend my time. I cook supper for Papa. Some days he works at the house here on Fortification, but I can never depend on him. He goes to the capitol often and to court. I never know when he will return in the evening.

    Did I tell you Papa bought me a piano? I practice every day. He bought me a sewing machine simply because I asked him. He is a generous man. I've been sewing clothes for myself. Thank you for having Mrs. Bently find a seamstress for my sisters.

    I am making other items too, such as tablecloths, napkins, place mats, pillowcases, and quilts. As a single woman, I will need these items eventually as much as a married woman would. Two high-quality stores with huge inventories are within walking distance of the house. I sort through the items on display to find the best bargains. I love to walk along the tree-lined streets of Jackson. It seems to be a very safe place.

    I remain

Your friend,
Caroline

    Even though she had started writing him, she couldn't resist every opportunity that presented itself to remind him they were merely friends. She wanted him to have a good life. She cared too much about him to see him build up his dreams about her with nothing but disappointment ahead.

No matter what Tantaylee tried to tell her; she was a person of little value. She thought back to the day of the revue when Tantaylee had seemed horrified by the appearance of the oozing scars on her back. After the scuffle with Mose Jefferson, it was much worse. She would never be able to let a husband see her shame.

Hello, Jake,

You may be amused to know that my father has purchased an automobile. It's a Thomas-Flyer like my aunt and uncle have. I drive it. Sometimes I take him to the capitol. Other times he drives to work. He has stayed there as much this summer as he would have if the legislature had been in session. He goes to court some days too.

Sometimes clients come to the house to confer with Papa in his law office here. I try to keep the house neat. With the constant onslaught of muddy or dusty shoes in and out the parlor to the office in the side room, it's a challenge.

We go out to restaurants with his political friends. Some of them are single. Others have their wives here in Jackson.

It is good to be here to help Papa entertain. He is lonely, but he is committed to his situation. I am sure you know what I mean. He will never invite H. to come here. Imagine how she would behave in the presence of the governor.

I am sorry, Jacob. My words were unkind.

Your friend,
C.

She continued to receive letters from Jake. He asked her whether she had been seeing any of the single politicians on a regular basis.

*   *   *

By observing her father, Caroline learned how to escape. Chad Clemons knew how to have the best of both worlds—Taylorsburg and Jackson. Not having the pleasure of spending time with a devoted spouse was a price he had to pay. Caroline would do the same.

Most people didn't bother to think about the fact that the Mississippi Legislature didn't have a session in 1907. Papa stayed busy though. He was getting ready to help Edmond Noel launch reforms in 1908. Also his law practice, mostly involved in the capital city, kept him busy. As far as his constituents back home were concerned, he was the Senator.

She had defended the family honor as long as she could. Like Papa, she escaped from Hortense. She hoped to find a place to teach in Jackson. As much as she tried to deny the truth, she missed Jake. Like Papa, she'd adjust to the idea of a life without romance.

*   *   *

Dear Jake,

I have been appointed to a teaching position in a new elementary school within walking distance of Papa's house. This is a wonderful opportunity.

Your friend,
Caroline

When Jake received this terse note, he lost control of his feelings. Tears flowed. "Mrs. Bently, I'll need to be out for a while." He saddled Smoky and rode to his farm.

I am a man. A football player. I'm not supposed to cry, but it seems lately I've had plenty to cry about. She told me she planned to stay in Jackson, but I thought I could persuade her to come home.

The old flames flared within him. *Why, Lord?* He didn't want to see anyone. "Come on, Smoky. Let's go. He rode into the deep woods of his land. Not going anywhere and not guiding his horse, he rode for two hours without touching the reins. After circling in loops, Smoky returned him to the farmhouse.

"Let's go back to town, Smoky."

Caroline's few words emptied his joy. She dashed his hopes aside. The aching of his heart left him feeling numb all over. Defeated, he took care of Smoky and checked the other horses. Seeing about them was a routine process that helped him through dark moments.

When he went inside the store, Mrs. Bently seemed excited. "There you are. You had a telephone call immediately after you left."

He didn't care about a telephone call.

Why must life go on when my dreams of a life have stopped?

He spoke in a monotone. "Was there a message?" He could not have been more unconcerned.

"No, except to call back."

"Who was it?"

"Caroline."

He must have heard wrong. "Caroline?"

"Caroline Clemons."

He rushed over to the telephone.

"Central, connect me with the home of Senator T. C. Clemons in Jackson."

"One moment," the operator told him.

He inhaled a slow breath.

"Hello, Caroline." He spoke her name with bittersweet excitement. "You called me?"

"Hello, Jake. He warmed to the sound of her voice. In only two words he heard a new confidence embodied in a sophisticated smoothness.

"How are you?"

"Fine. Papa needs to make a quick trip down to Taylorsburg. He is too busy to drive down."

Would she be coming with her father?

"He said he could work while he rides. So we're taking the train."

The blood rushed to his head.

"When?"

"Next week on Tuesday."

His spirits soared. "How long will you stay?"

"I'm not sure. I expect Papa to decide to come back to Jackson Friday."

It would be a quick visit, but he would make the most of the moment.

"Papa needs you to do something for him. He'll pay you. Jake, you don't have to do this if you don't have the time. I think it is an imposition."

"Anything he needs I'll try to do."

"He needs to canvass the farmers. He has never had any opposition, but he is working on some controversial laws. He wants to maintain the support of his voters. He wants you to drive him around from one farm to another in your surrey, and he wants me to go along too."

"I'd love to do that. Caroline, tell him no payment is required."

The line went dead.

I'll get to know the Senator, and I'll become more acquainted with my customers. The most important benefit is time with Caroline.

"Mrs. Bently, you need a break. Have I told you lately what a fine employee you are? Take the rest of the afternoon off. I'll watch the store."

"You sure?"

"Yes, I'll be fine."

"What if you can't find something?"

"I'll look for it."

"What if some lady needs fabric measured and cut?'

"If she can't do it herself, I'll tell her to come back tomorrow."

As soon as she left, he swept and dusted the store. He made the displays neat. After he closed the store, he curry-combed all four horses until their coats were shiny.

My heart is running away like a fast train. I'm making a fool out of myself over that girl.

At bedtime, despite his exhaustion, he had difficulty sleeping. After spending hours trying to fall asleep, he sat up and made lists.

Tomorrow. Get a haircut. Polish boots. Pick up laundry from Mrs. Carson's house. Find someone to work in the store on Saturdays. Clean and polish the surrey.

Top priority. Call Caroline to find out which train they will take.

To discuss with Caroline. The house plan. The house site. What kind of big dog she likes. Bruiser. The horses. The next time she will come home. Rachel and George.

To discuss with Senator C. Mose Jefferson. Hortense. Intentions regarding Caroline. Politics. Cattle breeds. Horses. Automobiles.

Thank you, Lord, for bringing Caroline home.

Finally relaxing, he remained motionless, taking in the delicious air and staring into the black velvet of the darkness. Life was good. No, better than that—life was superb.

Mrs. Bently's voice followed a knock.

What is she doing here in the middle of the night?

"Wake up, sleepy head."

He scrambled out of bed and proceeded to study the list marked "Tomorrow."

As soon as he made himself presentable, he called Caroline. He could not contain his elation. "I'm happy you're coming home even if you are going back soon."

The delayed response on the other end of the line told him he needed to try to curb his enthusiasm. "I forgot to ask you what time the train will be arriving. Do you know yet?"

"Some time after one o'clock."

"Thanks. Goodbye."

"Goodbye."

Men aren't supposed to let ladies know how they feel. I am impractical. I need to develop some technique.

Driving back from collecting his laundry, he decided to check on Hortense. Frankie met him at the door.

"Miss Hortense is resting."

"Is she ill?"

"She's resting." Frankie gave him a vague look.

"I wanted to make sure she is aware that the Senator and his daughter will be coming home Monday. They will stay here for a few days. I wanted to be sure you knew."

"Thank you. Everything is clean. I don't need to cook much these days; so I clean to stay busy."

"The house looks nice. Maybe you will want to plan to cook more next week."

He went to the Covington at lunch. He doubted that the Senator would want his visit announced, but he wanted to make sure the cook was having a good menu next week.

Every day he cleaned the store more. For the first time he saw the spider webs in the high ceiling. It was necessary to climb up a ladder to sweep them away. Then he had to dust again. He made sure all the details in the store were in good order.

He rode out to the farm to select some possible house sites. He'd begin building the house for Caroline before she would be ready to accept his proposal. He made a mental note to ask the Senator about house builders.

Pleasurable eagerness rose from the depths of his heart. When he looked in the mirror to comb his hair, he could not escape the elated look that lit up his face. His eyes sparkled. He seemed to stand straighter with his chin jutted forward with the anticipation he felt. He would have falsified the obvious if he had not realized he looked attractive; yet he had no arrogance.

Lord, thank you for the look of love on my face. I pray Caroline will see. I know I'm a clumsy guy, but please let her see in me what other young women seem to see. Please change her heart. I praise you for all the ways you've changed mine.

* * *

Caroline dreaded the trip back home. She felt her father was taking unfair advantage of Jake, but she didn't want to discuss the problem with Papa.

Since Jake is a lonely man with news to share, he stuffs our mailbox. He always seems to be available. I thought by now he would have something going on with Victoria Robinson. She is petite, sophisticated, and delicate—the perfect woman for him.

The thought made her shiver. She didn't know why since she knew she was not in love with Jake.

She felt numb about the tedious string of young attorneys who ate with her and her father at the Seafood Grill. She couldn't remember their names from one time to the next.

Papa thinks Jake and I have a special closeness. I try to tell him we're nothing more than friends. When Papa gets an idea in his head, it's impossible to change his mind. Sometimes I think he is as stubborn as I am.

* * *

While her father worked on papers as the train jerked along, she held *Great Expectations* open in her lap. She never looked at the words. Instead, she stared out the window.

She wore a white dress with a long bright blue jacket and a matching blue hat. She had copied the ensemble from a picture of a Paul Poiret original. The neck was open. She wore her locket with her mother's daguerreotype inside it and a belt with a hanging chain. She had tucked her blonde hair in a roll along the nape of her neck. She wore her mother's diamond earrings. She dressed up because she wanted to maintain her father's image and because it was fun to wear a new fashion she had created.

Papa looked up long enough to inspect her. "You are a lovely sight. You look sophisticated in the latest fashion."

The train jerked to a halt. She couldn't help noticing that Jake was even more handsome than she remembered. When she had left, he had a look of disturbed preoccupation. Now he seemed to glow.

Lord, you know I promised Aunt Haley I'd give him and me a chance, but don't let me go overboard. I don't want to be hurt. I don't want to see him hurt either.

Chewing her lips, she stood and started slowly to the door.

"Come on, Carrie. Let's get going. This train will be leaving soon. If you don't get off, we'll end up in Soso."

"I'm sorry, Papa."

"You seem to be having trouble walking. Are you all right?" He bumped into her to keep her moving.

She looked back at him with a nervous giggle and started rushing down the aisle to the door. She carried her hatbox, book, and bag. The porter carried her dress bag and soft-sided suitcase.

Her father carried his bulky briefcase and received his bags from the porter.

"You are more radiant than ever, Caroline," Jake told her as he reached to help with her luggage.

"Carrie was frazzled from all the physical trauma and emotional turmoil when she first arrived in Jackson. But now she is radiant. I'm glad you noticed."

Smoky and Firefly bobbed their heads up and down with snorts of recognition. Caroline walked over to them to give them a pat. They nuzzled her. Firefly tucked her muzzle in the hollow of Caroline's arm.

"Looks like the horses are glad to see you," her father observed.

The men shared a hardy handshake; Jake and Carrie shared a light sideways hug.

Jake loaded her bags as the Senator tossed his luggage into the back of the surrey and climbed in. Taking her hand, Jake guided her into the front seat of the surrey. When he closed her door, his wide smile that crinkled his eyes evoked a sweet smile from her.

Her efforts to close him out of her heart had failed. His face, which reflected anew the glory of the Lord, illuminated the little windows of her stronghold. She couldn't control her smile. His romantic behavior made her sparkle.

The shiny horses pranced with a showy walk. They were halfway up the short hill when Bruiser came running from the direction of the Mercantile. His bouncing gait made Caroline delirious with happiness.

As they approached the house, her thoughts turned to Hortense. With dread chilling her bones, she felt her face droop. Her back hurt.

Chapter Eleven

Max

The relief caused by being away from Hortense a few weeks vanished. Jake's gaze showed her he was concerned. By the time he parked his surrey in the back driveway, she was trying to force her hands not to tremble. Frankie met them at the kitchen door. "I'm Chad Clemons. You must be Francesca Simons?"

"I like to be called 'Frankie.' Pleased to meet you."

Jake unloaded Caroline's bags in her tiny room, and her father took his bags to the second bedroom on the west side of the house.

In his usual sophisticated manner, which seemed appropriate in the presence of legislators, clients, and the governor, but out of character in his home, he walked to the center of the parlor. "Where's Mrs. Clemons?" he asked Frankie, who stood looking at him and wiping her hands on her crisp white ruffled apron.

"She's resting in her bedroom, sir."

"Go in, please, and tell her I am here." His voice was soft but masterful. While he waited, he whistled softly. Jake stood near Caroline, and Caroline bounced her hand against her left lower back.

"Do you feel well, Carrie?" Papa asked.

"Sure. I'm fine."

"Your back hurts?"

"No, Papa." She didn't like to lie, but she liked less to complain.

Frankie cracked the door open and slipped out of the room, her head down.

"What did she say, young lady?"

"I don't utter curse words, even to quote them," Frankie said.

Papa walked to Hortense's door. First, he knocked lightly and then he entered without waiting for an answer.

"Let's sit for a few minutes," Jake said, "Frankie, do you have any tea?"

"Do you want some cold sweet tea or hot tea?"

"Cold will be fine," he said.

Caroline realized: *He's the host here now.*

She looked into his misty eyes. He brushed back a lock of hair that had fallen from her coiffure.

"It's quiet here," he said. "I've come by a few times to check on Hortense, but she is never available."

"I haven't heard from Millicent and Lydia," she said. "They may still be miffed at me for deserting them."

"Millicent wrote me. They are enjoying school. Lydia is scouting for beaux."

"I suppose they'll be home for Christmas break."

"I hope you and your father will come home too."

"If I don't?"

"I'll go to Princeton," he said. "I won't be able to tolerate Christmas without you."

"You shouldn't flatter me that way." She couldn't help herself. A little grin crossed her face as she thought: *What about Victoria?*

"I know you visit Rachel and George often. Are they well?"

"Yes. Rachel hasn't had any more problems."

The door to Hortense's room opened; the Senator stepped out and closed it gently. "What do you think, Jacob? We can make a visit or two before supper."

"That's fine. Could we stop by the Mercantile? You can visit Mrs. Bently if she isn't busy."

Caroline smiled. "She is a woman of influence, not only on the way her husband votes but over most of the shoppers in Taylorsburg. The Mercantile is a good starting place."

All the hitching posts in front of the store were occupied. "I don't know when I've seen so many buggies here on Monday," Caroline said. She concluded that Mrs. Bently had mustered a welcoming committee for the Senator. Jake's face, which was easy for her to read, appeared surprised.

"We'll park in the back," he said.

"Let's look at your horses," Papa said.

Caroline rushed to see her old friends. "All of them look wonderful, Jake. You've been grooming them often, haven't you? And you've repaired the stable gates."

Jake grinned.

"Fine horseflesh," the Senator said. He smoothed his clothes. "Let's go in the back door." They walked down the short hall and into the store, which was brimming with noisy customers. It was obvious that they were there to shake the Senator's hand.

"Jake, everything looks wonderful, and so do you." Her eyes skimmed the interior of the building. "Complete renovation."

He smiled at her. "I've been busy."

T. Chadwick Clemons went from person to person. He called each shopper by name, shook the hands of all the gentlemen, nodded toward the ladies, kissed the babies, and joked with the children.

Men lined up along the aisles with their lists of hardware needs. Some had sample screws and washers so they could be sure to select the correct sizes; others had an assortment of implements needing repair parts; some brought leaking pots and pans to select the correct sizes of washers and screws to fill the holes. Jake rolled up his sleeves and went to work.

"I'm glad we stopped by here," Jake said.

"You seem surprised," Caroline said.

"I am."

She helped Mrs. Bently measure and cut fabric.

When the store closed at six, Jake said, "Let's go to the Covington for supper." He didn't want to witness a scene with Hortense.

Eating was a slow process. As soon as they placed their knives in their hands, other diners approached the Clemons table to speak to the Senator.

"Harold, charge this meal to my account," Jake told the waiter.

"Oh, no you don't." Chad Clemons pulled out a roll of money and paid the bill.

They walked home. "I'm sure you two want to walk some more. I need to go inside and get to work," the Senator said.

Caroline blushed and patted her back. It was clear that Papa had selected the man he wanted for his son-in-law.

Does he have to be so obvious?

"Great idea. Let's take a little stroll," Jake said. It was a dark night with clouds covering the stars. The moon was new. Patches of fog loomed low in the gas streetlights.

He offered her his arm to hold onto. When they were out of her father's sight, he slipped his hand into hers. She enjoyed the touch of his hand against hers—she hungered for the feel of it.

Too much—I like holding his hand more than I should.

He squeezed her hand. She felt herself melting like hot caramelized sugar.

I can't let this happen. I want to give him a chance, but only a small chance to be my friend. I don't want to prevent his happiness. He is wasting his time with me.

With her heart aching from ambivalence, she withdrew her hand and slipped it inside his arm again. He looked at her with a look she considered sad and confused. She returned the look showing the same emotions.

Several moments into their walk, he broke the silence by bringing up a neutral subject. "You know, Caroline, I've been trying to get men to come to the store for months. They all came back today."

"Your store was a major success this afternoon. I can think of several reasons besides Papa. The word has gotten around, I suspect, that you have become serious about operating a good store. Also you've made friends with the Mauldins and Brother George."

"I hate it that this community will not allow people of color to enter the front door," he said.

"It's that way all over. Probably most of them would be afraid of the white folks if they did walk in the front."

"I've cleaned up the side door and moved stuff around to make it spacious and inviting. I don't like to demean anybody."

"Me neither. Rachel is a mother to me."

"And now Brother George is *my* closest friend. It's all silly. Once they step inside the store, all the customers treat each other well and receive the same service, but some of them cannot walk through certain doors."

While she was thinking about the problem, she noticed that he had straightened his arm. Maybe he was distracted. No, his hand reached again for hers. This time he laced her fingers with his. She could not prevent her feelings from pouring into her fingertips.

They turned back toward the Clemons house. "How does it feel to be here? You haven't spent the night in this house since Mose Jefferson attacked you."

"I'm scared, Jake."

"Do you think Mose brings whiskey to Hortense?"

"If he does, it's during the night when people won't see him. I don't have Rachel to protect me anymore."

"She's never been here at night. Protect you from what?"

"Oh, nothing. I'm sorry. That didn't make sense did it?" She emitted a nervous laugh to try to cover what she didn't mean to say.

"I've tried to ask you about this before." He held her in a gentle hug the way a man hugs his sister. "Something sinister goes on in your house you'd rather not talk about." He pulled back the locks of hair that the wind blew into her face.

"It seems you've been gone for years. I've missed you so." He held her head inside his two strong hands and gently brought her mouth up to his. He brushed his lips across hers.

Her heart was beating so loud she could hear it. She expected it to jump out of her chest.

"Jake."

He crushed her lips into his. Lingering close, he prolonged the kiss with a gentle but firm insistence. They kissed until she pulled away to catch her breath.

"What were you saying?" he asked.

"I don't know."

"Your papa calls you Carrie. I like that."

"Okay."

"Goodnight, Carrie." He opened the door and walked away.

"Goodnight, dear Jake."

"See you tomorrow, sweetheart," he called softly over his shoulder.

Having crossed the threshold and secured the door, she depended on the wall to keep her from falling to the floor. The afterglow continued to cause her heart to pound even when the sound of his footsteps had faded. She tingled in the wake of emotion.

She tiptoed through the dark house. The floors creaked. She felt the palpable threats to her safety. When she reached the kitchen, she delved into the cabinets until she found three iron cooking pots and pans with lids and set them on top of the kitchen work table. Since everything in the house was as she remembered, she didn't trip as she moved about in the dark.

The sewing room was as she had left it. Scissors waited in the drawer of the cabinet. The spool of twine used for tying packages was on the shelf.

So the pots wouldn't clang, she made three trips to her room from the kitchen as she carried them separately. She closed her door and latched it.

It was impossible to continue in the dark. A big candle waited, and so did the matches. In the flickering light she saw something reflected in the glass. Whiskey in fruit jars. Evidently her room with its insignificant entrance was the storage room for the stash.

All the fear of Mose Jefferson returned. She knew she couldn't sleep in her clothes; so she removed her dress and pulled her gown over her head. As she had done every night for the last few weeks, she applied cocoa butter to her back. The drainage had subsided with the passage of time.

Because she felt she would suffocate from the humid heat if she kept the windows closed, she turned the latches so she could open them. She removed the thick dowel rods wedged to keep the windows shut. She raised the windows and used the dowels to prop them open.

Caroline examined the dark yard with its back driveway, where people turned off the street to make deliveries. With its big open windows, the room seemed to be no safer than the outdoors from Mose Jefferson, but she needed the windows raised to get a breath of air. She hoped no one would notice the windows were open, since they probably stayed closed most nights.

The pots, pans, and lids tied together on a string would protect her in case someone broke the flimsy door latch. She strung them above the door.

Lying in the bed seemed too dangerous. If the wind blew, the curtains would blow open. Anyone passing in the yard would see her. Until Mose Jefferson assaulted her, she had not considered the danger. Now that her room had become the storage place for Hortense's medicine, she feared he would deliver whiskey to her room at some point in time. She pulled the bed sheets and quilt onto the floor to make a pallet.

She sorted through the few objects in the top drawer of her bureau until she found the key to a box built into her table drawer. She took her Colt revolver from the box. It was loaded as she had left it. She placed it under the bed on the floor. She blew out the candle, found her way to her makeshift pallet and put the gun by her pillow.

I should take my gun back to Jackson when we go.

It had been a long day. She and her father had taken a taxi to the train station in Jackson before daylight. She needed to rest.

She prayed for God's protection as she curled into a tight ball on the floor. Despite her resistance, sleep came fast; hours passed.

While the sky was still black, she heard the familiar clump-clump of a team of large horses followed by squeaking wheels on the brick pavement. Bottles placed on the back doorstep sloshed and clanked. She crawled over to the window in time to peek out and see the milkman.

Back on the pallet, she closed her sleepy eyes again. She wasn't sure how much time passed. The sky was still dark. Clump-clump. Clump-clump. It was not the milkman. He never doubled back. The horses and the wagon sounded different.

The wagon pulled into the back driveway. Caroline scrambled for the gun. "I always take it inside and put it in a little room on the far side of the pantry," a thick tongued loud voice said. She sat up on her pillow and pulled back the hammer on her Colt .45.

"She leaves a key under the second step tied on a string. She hangs it on a nail under there. We'll get this done quicker tonight with you driving, Malone." She recognized Mose Jefferson's voice without doubt.

Malone unlocked the door. His thudding steps came closer. Closer. Closer! He pushed against her door. "Stuck—this door won't open." He crashed into it. She thought he must have backed up and slammed it with his body to pry it open.

The heavy iron pots and pans with their lids fell onto the floor and made a horrible racket. He dropped the whiskey in the floor and ran like a frightened mouse, cutting and dodging in case something was being aimed at him.

Pulling his pants on, Papa came running to the direction of the noise. "What on earth?"

Hortense, in her gown and cap, stumbled along behind him. "Caroline, what have you done now? You are trying to expose me." In a low menacing tone, she said, "I'll kill you."

"What is going on?" Papa stumbled into the whiskey supply and caught himself in time to keep from falling. Aromatic liquid poured from broken jars.

"Ask her," Caroline said in a nonchalant tone.

"In the first place, what were you doing back here, Carrie?" Papa asked.

"This is my bedroom."

"No, it can't be." Senator Clemons was incredulous.

"Ask her," Caroline said.

Hortense, trying to walk toward Caroline, slid on the wet floor. She spit out her words. "Sloven little wench, clean up this mess. Wait till I get my hands on you." She reached for Caroline, tripped on a cooking pan, and took a dive to the floor.

"I guess I need to light a candle." Caroline spoke in deadpan voice.

"Somebody's bleeding," Hortense said. Blood dripped from Hortense's arm.

"You must have cut yourself on a piece of glass," Caroline said, rushing to apply a clean face towel from the rack by her washbowl.

"Let's see if you can stand up," he said. Caroline and the Senator rolled Hortense over, guided her to crawl to the side of Caroline's bed, and helped her first to sit and then to stand. They supported her as she managed to walk back to bed.

"It's all your fault," Hortense accused Caroline. "You're nothing but a trouble maker. Now you've scared Mose off. How will I get my medicine?"

"Do you feel all right, Mama Hortense?" Caroline asked.

"Keep your hands off me." The Senator and Caroline led her back to bed. Hortense slung her uninjured hand at Caroline.

Too little of the night remained to spend it cleaning up the mess. Caroline picked up the big pieces of glass and threw some old cleaning rags from the kitchen on the blood and the spilled whiskey. She crept to the parlor to finish what was left of the night.

With the coming of the morning, she sent Jim to fetch Dr. and Mrs. Woodley to make a house call to check Hortense.

Meanwhile Caroline found an old housedress to wear. She carefully removed the bullets from her revolver and placed it in her reticule.

The good doctor dressed the cut. "No bones appear to be broken," he told the Senator. "We're glad to see you looking well, Caroline."

"How's your injury?" Mrs. Woodley asked.

"Much better. Thank you."

After breakfast Caroline went upstairs. The huge upstairs party room had a full-length mirror with a gilded frame on the wall. Caroline noticed she had dark circles under her eyes brought on by losing sleep.

As usual the double doors to the room her father planned for her were locked.

*   *   *

Jake rushed through his morning routine of caring for the horses and opening the store so he could go to the Clemons house as soon as Mrs. Bently came to work. He hoped Caroline's fears were unfounded, but he was anxious to know whether she had enjoyed a night of restful sleep.

As usual, Frankie answered the door. "Come on back," she said. He followed her to Caroline's tiny room on the other side of the pantry. From one of the side rooms, he heard a heated discussion between Mr. and Mrs. Clemons.

Caroline and Frankie were busy packing the items left in Caroline's room before she went to Jackson. Wearing the worn housedress and some old slippers, she looked up but didn't stop working. In a pleasant voice she said, "Good morning, Jake. You have perfect timing. Would you mind helping us take these boxes upstairs?"

"I'm glad to help." When they reached the second floor, Jake asked, "Now where?"

"To the double doors."

"We'll have to get the key from Hortense," Caroline said.

At the moment they went back downstairs, Senator Clemons, well groomed and fully dressed, emerged cheerfully from his room. "Carrie, while you finish getting ready, I'll drink a cup of coffee with this fine young man. Frankie, you have some coffee ready, don't you?"

"Papa, could you coerce your wife into giving me the key to the upstairs bedroom? I'll dress in there."

His demeanor darkened. "Give me one moment," he said in a low controlled tone. He walked over to Hortense's room, knocked, and entered. Seconds later he emerged with a key in his hand. Caroline and Jake followed him upstairs.

He tried the key in the door. "Here you go." With the door open he turned to face Caroline. "How long ago did she lock you out of your room?"

"This has never been my room."

"Carrie!"

"We'll talk about later, okay, Papa?"

The three of them moved her boxes and clothes on hangers

*   *   *

Caroline wanted to look her best for Papa. She buttoned her Vici kid shoes and selected her sheer white batiste embroidered middy blouse. It had a fitted waist, pouter pigeon front sailor collar, and lace edged cuffs. She slipped into her navy blue trumpet skirt. Its almost straight cut hugged her figure flowing into a hem flounce softly bouncing away from her body. She swept most of her wavy blonde hair to the top of her head, left a few curling tendrils flowing past her shoulders, and plopped her white had with a red scarf on her head.

*   *   *

Jake was popping to know more about what had happened. With no mention of the obvious problems in the household, Senator Clemons showed Jake an outline of what he wanted to do that day.

"First, let's drive by and look at your farm. Carrie said you were planning to build a house on your property. I know you are eager to show her what you have in mind, and I'd like to see too."

After going over the list and planning the day, the men went to the parlor to wait for Caroline. Holding her skirt in one hand to keep from tripping and her reticule in the other, she descended the stairs. Jake stood gazing at her in wonder. He observed a rapt expression on her father's face.

Jake swallowed hard. His heart longed for her. He hoped the day would come when she would have feelings for him as he had for her. He regretted the way he had treated her earlier. Even though she was the refined daughter of a prominent man, she was so much more. Only a moment ago, she had helped carry boxes from a tiny room, where she had lived. He sensed her servant's heart. Most of all she had a heart that loved her Creator.

He had never seen a lovelier creature. Her face looked tired, but he looked beyond that to see perfection.

Standing there holding his hat, he resolved to treasure every moment. Sooner than he would like, the time with her and her amazing father would be a memory to which he would cling in the gray days ahead.

But what about the kiss last night?

*   *   *

She gazed at the two men as she descended the stairs.

Papa. Jacob. I am blessed.

Frankie told them, "If you'd like, I'll be glad to leave you a hot supper on the stove this evening."

The Senator stopped a minute and gave her an appreciative look. "Never mind, Frankie. You'll have your hands full with Mrs. Clemons. She is in a difficult state of mind. Eating here would add to her confusion. We'll go to the Covington."

When they reached the surrey, Carrie climbed into the back seat with Jake's assistance. "Don't be surprised if I doze."

The soothing sound of her father's conversation with her friend accompanied by the gentle movement of the surrey lulled her to sleep. She was surprised when they stopped at the farmhouse a few minutes later.

"You had a bad night?" Jake asked.

"We'll talk about it later. Right now show us the possible locations for your house." She smiled brightly although her eyes were bleary.

What was I thinking last night? Why did I allow this man to kiss me goodnight?

"If I were you, son, I'd put it on this little knoll, where you will have adequate drainage."

"You have a good point. What do you think, Carrie?"

"I agree, but I think that you need to drill another well first. Try to arrange it so that the water can be pumped with a windmill somewhere in the backyard."

Both men agreed.

"What about the view?" Jake asked.

"Not a bad view out here," she said. "I'm sure that you and the bride you select someday will landscape the yard so you'll have a picture-perfect view."

Jake rolled his eyes.

They visited the McBrides. The men sat on the porch while Caroline and Rachel strolled through the yard. I'm thankful to see you looking good, Madear."

"You might say both of us are healthier away from Miss Horsey, but I miss you so."

"I've accepted a teaching position in Jackson next year."

"Jacob told me. I thank the Lord, but oh I'm going to miss you. It's worth the sacrifice to get you away from Horsey's meanness though."

They traveled to farms throughout the area. Samuel Benton promised to support the Senator. William and Zoe Cameron served tea to Senator Clemons, Jake, and Caroline. Stuart and Melva Cameron smiled and chatted.

At noon Jake took the three of them to drop in on the Mauldins. Mrs. Mauldin was serving lunch to fifteen people. "Come on. Pull up some chairs. Three more won't be no problem."

"We're honored to have you as our guests," Mr. Mauldin said.

Throughout the afternoon they visited farmers near Taylorsburg. As they rode from one house to another, Papa talked about state politics, farming, and timber management. "Tennessee Walkers are the best horses . . . Hereford cattle, the best beef cows we've got . . . Jake, you've picked the best lumber company."

She knew nothing would ever come from her friendship with Jake, but she supposed it wouldn't hurt to dream. She tried to follow her aunt's suggestions, but she was ashamed because she seemed to be playing a game.

After checking on the store, which was much less busy than it was on Monday, and eating dinner at the hotel, the three of them walked back to the house. Again the Senator went inside and suggested they take a walk.

"What happened last night?" Jake asked.

"I'm sorry," she said. "You've waited all day to hear. You'll never believe this. I guess you can see Papa is a private person when his personal life and his family are involved. He wouldn't object to my telling you, but he would be uncomfortable if he had to listen. I don't think he realized how miserable life has been in that house until last night. He escaped before things got unbearable. If he divorced Mama Hortense, his political career would be over."

"So he leads a separate life, but you said he remains loyal to her."

"His morality would prevent any other behavior." She gave him a play-by-play account of the previous night.

"Why doesn't your father do something?"

"He will. I really believe he will. Right now he's weighing all the ramifications of his actions."

"Hortense threatened to kill you. I had no idea she would do such a thing."

"You are already losing respect for my family, aren't you? Not just me but Papa too."

He didn't say anything.

"I shouldn't have told you," she said. "I knew I was making a mistake."

"No, that's not true. I'm so shocked I don't know what to think, what to do. Give me a chance like you are giving your father. He doesn't know what to do, and neither do I."

She fumed. "How could I expect you to understand?"

"Let's talk about all of it. What is he going to do about Mose Jefferson?"

"I don't know. But I do know this, Jake. Mose Jefferson is nothing but a symptom of a disease. If we do away with him, his buddies will take over his illicit business. I realized that last night when I sat there with my gun in my hand and heard him talking to his driver. He doesn't operate alone. It's a network. The mayor and the sheriff allow him to do business. Nobody is powerful enough to stop them."

"Caroline, listen to me. I don't disrespect you. The more I get to know you the more I admire your strong character. Underneath your incredible beauty is a bastion of strength—physical, spiritual, and emotional. I've never known anyone quite like you. Sometimes I simply haven't understood your motivation. Don't get puffed up at me. Try to help me know what is going on."

They walked along a dark part of the street nowhere near a gaslight. She was not at all expecting what happened next. He stopped and took her hand. Then he pushed her hat out of the way. He reached under her hat and the wavy blonde hair hanging down until his hand touched the back of her neck. His other hand he placed upon the back of her head to tilt her toward him.

"Please let me kiss you, my darling."

She was surprised at herself. He had given her an opportunity to resist. What about that strength he had just mentioned? Her heart raced as her face met his. Her eyes closed with a flutter of her eyelids. Softly his mouth met her tender lips. The kiss was for her a token of his approval. She was beginning to think he might be able to accept her at some future time if he knew more about her, but with the fear of what he would think, she stiffened. Pulling away from him, she patted her back with the back of her hand.

"It's time to go home," she told him.

Wednesday and Thursday passed the same way. The three of them continued to go from house to house. Not once did they tell the truth about Hortense to any of the voters.

*   *   *

Jake knew his heart, but he also knew that he understood little of Caroline's heart. Tuesday night she had bared a little of her soul, but then she pulled away. In spite of her obvious ability to resist evil forces, she suffered from something within that he would have to share before she could accept his love.

Until he could help her resolve her inner conflict he would never move to the place where he hoped to be some day.

He wanted to be her betrothed, her confidante, her husband, her spiritual leader, her lover. Before he could move to that glorious island where a man and a woman have their own existence separate from the world and sacred between the two of them and the Lord, he would have to swim through a murky sea of mysterious pain.

Every time he tried to wade into the waters, she pushed him back. During their walks Wednesday and Thursday night, they exchanged small talk about light subjects. Each night he kissed her cheek at the door.

The Senator offered to pay him a generous amount for his trouble, but Jake explained that the week had been a great pleasure for him, as well as a business benefit.

Friday morning, he took her and her father to catch the train. Loading into the surrey took more time than they had anticipated. On the way Bruiser kept running in front of the horses and slowing them down. They barely had time to board. As they stepped into the train, a tall handsome blond young man dressed in the height of fashion and carrying a brief case called, "Caroline."

She turned toward him. "Max. This is a wonderful surprise." She let go of Jake's arms and ran to hug the man. He threw his arm around her shoulders and kissed her cheek. It was obvious they were delighted to see one another. The train whistle blew. She looked back at Jake and said something, but he couldn't read her lips. The Senator, Caroline, and Max rushed to board. She sat with Max on the train. Jake, with his mouth gaping, glared into the little train window. As they pulled away, she waved goodbye.

Chapter Twelve

Unopened Letters

A few days later, Caroline sat embroidering a dresser scarf. Losing Jake hurt. She couldn't concentrate on reading, but needlework helped.

Papa sat reading his newspaper beside her in the parlor. "I'm taking Hortense to a treatment center in New Orleans. They'll keep her four to six weeks or even longer, depending on how it goes."

"I see. Taking her out of the state is a good idea."

"Yes."

"Papa, you know I've tried to keep my promise."

"You've done a beautiful job. Stop worrying about it."

"How do you plan to take her there?"

"I'll go down to get her on the train," he said. "I don't want her to know ahead of time that she's going to stay in a hospital."

"You are wise."

"Jim can take us to catch the train, and I'll go with her. Then I'll return to Taylorsburg to make arrangements at the house. I'll cancel deliveries and services but I'll retain Frankie. Maybe Brother George will know some more people who can help keep an eye on things while Hortense is gone."

"Good."

"Carrie, I don't think you should go. Your presence would give her a reason to act worse. She has a demented mind. It is impossible to reason with her."

"You're right. Besides it's time to start teacher training. I can't leave right now."

"Do you think your friend Jacob could drive by the house occasionally and see if everything is all right?"

"I suppose so, but I haven't heard from him since we came back to Jackson."

"Really?"

"I am not sure why. I told him about that bad night I had. Maybe I shouldn't have."

"He's a better man than that. Try to work it out with him. He's a great fellow."

"Papa, you seem to have your mind made up, but as I told you I'll never marry. Maybe the time has come for Jake and me to part ways." Unbidden tears flowed down her cheeks.

"Baby." He placed a strong arm around her and wiped her tears with his handkerchief.

"It's okay, Papa."

"We'll talk about it some more soon. In the meantime try to work it out with him."

"It's for the best. He can get on with his life now."

"You're wrong, Carrie. Men like him come along rarely in a woman's lifetime. I believe the Lord sent him to you. I see something special between you and him. It reminds me of the way things were with your mother and me."

*   *   *

Unopened letters from Caroline formed a growing pile on Jake's desk. He said little to Mrs. Bently. All his food tasted like the pith of bad sugar cane. It took only two weeks for his clothes to hang loosely on his frame. The horses were irritable, and Bruiser lost his appetite.

The men of Taylorsburg started coming to the store on a regular basis. When they tried to talk to him, he made an effort to respond, but he had trouble thinking about what they were saying.

It isn't simply that she has a flame for this Max. What's worse is that she is deceptive. I thought we were starting to develop a close bond. I know she has secrets I don't understand, but I had no idea she had other suitors. Maybe she would have told me if I had only asked her. Maybe she had her reasons to be distant at times.

For whatever purpose, she's trying to patch things up with me. If I open these letters, I'll read some phony explanations. I can't face the letters now. I'll get around to reading them eventually I suppose.

His telephone rang.

What if it's Caroline? Would she be so brazen to call me?

Central said, "This is a call for Jacob MacGregor from Caroline Clemons."

"Yes? What do you want, Caroline?"

"Papa will be coming to town tomorrow on important business, but I can't come with him."

"Why not?" He thought: *She can't leave Max.*

"I can't leave my job."

"Has school started?"

"No, but we have meetings for training."

Sounds phony. Since when did schools have meetings for training?

Also because of the nature of his visit, it's best I stay away. I hope you understand what I'm saying. It's a personal family situation."

"Oh." Her father was a nice man. It would be unfair to blame him for her actions.

"Are you still on the line?"

"Yes, ma'am. How can I help?"

"Papa will come by and talk to you."

"Is that all?"

"Yes. Goodbye, Jake."

"Goodbye."

*　　*　　*

Caroline took a nap late every afternoon. The anticipation about starting a new job, the concern over her father's trip to New Orleans with Hortense, and most of all the distance that had suddenly sprung up between her and Jake left her exhausted.

I have to get myself together. It isn't the schoolchildren's fault my life is in shambles. I have to work hard to prepare for the school year. I knew the time would come when Jake would become sick of me. He doesn't really know me. He thought he cared, but now he has abruptly stopped.

*　　*　　*

Senator Clemons walked from the Taylorsburg depot to the Mercantile. "Jake, I need to speak with you in private."

"All right. Mrs. Bently, I'll be away for a while." Jake hitched his horses to the surrey. "Let's take a ride."

"Good. I'm sorry to show up unceremoniously. Carrie called you, didn't she?"

"Yes, but she didn't say much. She seems not to trust Central."

"Smart girl."

They rode toward Jake's farm. "I've come to take Hortense to New Orleans. We'll leave early tomorrow morning. She doesn't know. It may be difficult, but I'll get her down there any way I can. I've made arrangements for her to spend as long as necessary, perhaps four, six, or eight weeks, in a treatment center for alcoholism. Son, I trust that you will mention this to no one. It's the kind of thing that could destroy my career."

"You have my word."

"Jacob, I want you to understand. I have worked in government long enough. I could retire from it and live a comfortable life as an attorney. My law practice is sufficient to provide for my family and me nicely. I continue to work as a lawmaker because this is my calling. I hope to help the state to progress. Right now we sit at the bottom of all the states in the Union as far as income and literacy are concerned. If my career is ended by rumors of my wife's conduct, children throughout the state of Mississippi will suffer."

"I admire you," Jake said.

"I have to get Hortense ready for her trip. This will be a difficult process."

They rode along quietly.

"I want to talk to you about another matter," the Senator said.

"Whatever you wish."

"It seemed to me that you and my daughter had a wonderful friendship. I hope you know I approved. What went wrong between you?"

This man is direct. I'll approach him the same way.

"Max."

"What? You're upset because she was excited by a surprise encounter with Max? They grew up like sister and brother."

"Really?"

"He is Mahalia and Sylvester's son, her dear cousin."

"I didn't know. She didn't tell me."

"I suppose the subject didn't come up." The Senator gave him a hardy slap on his back. "I shouldn't tell you this, but she's been sick over not hearing from you. She thinks she has lost you. By the way, you don't look so good either."

"I haven't been eating."

"Make it up with her. Now."

"Yes, sir."

"If you don't mind, would you let me off at my house?"

"Sure. I'll keep you and Hortense in my prayers," Jake said.

"Thank you."

*　　*　　*

Jake studied the pile of letters. He restacked them with the earliest date first.

Dearest Jake,

It was wonderful visiting with you. Thank you for your kindness to my father and for helping me move upstairs. I will always remember the days the three of us spent together.

Seeing Max was serendipity. It had been two years since I saw him last. We talked all the way to Jackson, and then he had to continue his travels to Memphis. You do remember that he is Aunt Mahalia and Uncle Sylvester's younger son. The older one is Will.

I spent years in their home after Mama died. They have been as close as brothers to me. It's a shame we never get to visit. Will and Max send me post cards as they travel, but writing them doesn't work. They never stay in one place long enough to get my mail.

My aunt is ready for them to settle down, marry, and give her some grandchildren. She hopes for girls.

Whew, we almost missed the train. I was yelling to you to introduce Max, but I suppose you didn't hear me.

I remain

Your admiring friend,
Caroline

He worked through the entire stack. Then he went to the barber for a shave since it had been two weeks and it would be difficult to remove the growth. Also the barber cut his hair.

When he returned, he apologized to Mrs. Bently for being such a grouch. "Thank you for putting up with me, Mrs. B."

"You are a little more temperamental than the old Mac, but that's okay. The younger generation is like that."

He walked up to the Covington and requested the cook to prepare the best supper in the house for him. Then he went back and called Caroline, who should have been home from her meetings by then.

"Caroline."

"Yes, Jake."

"I'm sorry."

"Sorry for what?"

"For distrusting you. For not reading your letters. I read them today. Are you all right?"

"I'm fine."

"Your dad made it here. We'll talk later, okay?"

"Goodbye, Jake."

"Goodbye, beautiful."

*   *   *

Making up with Jake, Caroline was as lightheaded as if she were whirling on a flying jinny. She needed to but the brakes on the runaway relationship. She could not afford to fall in love, but the most wonderful man in the world was falling in love with her.

Sometimes Jake was clueless. He didn't understand her at all during those times. If the day should ever come when they would marry, his revulsion would result in an annulment. She couldn't let it happen.

No man would ever accept her, especially the handsome, emotionally labile Jacob MacGregor. No man would love her.

She was glad she brought her gun back. Spending the night alone anywhere had become frightening. She kept it in her bedside table. It would be good to have her father return. A time would come when she would spend every night alone. This practice in adjusting to it was good.

Although she prayed about the problem, she didn't expect much. It was her thorn in her flesh, and she knew she had to bear it. No man would accept her.

When the letters from Jake started flowing into the mailbox again, she reminded herself that she would treasure them until Jake found a wife. Then she would burn them. She would bury the embers of this tender attachment deep within her heart in cold ashes. She would grow old alone. No fly-by breeze of memory would ever ignite the relationship again.

When Papa returned, she turned her thoughts to him and all he told her about his trip to New Orleans. "I'm glad to have you home," she said.

Chapter Thirteen

Courage

As he often did, Jake visited Rachel and George. "Young man, we need to talk serious tonight. Let's precede our talk to each other by talking to the Lord." Preacher George said. Rather than the contemplative counselor, George was a man spring-loaded for action.

"Sure," Jake said.

"Our most gracious and dear precious heavenly Father, we come to thee with humble hearts. We adore thee, and we thank thee for sending thy beloved Son to minister to the lowly outcast of the world."

"Yes, Lord. Hallelujah," Rachel chanted.

"We thank thee for sending the Holy Ghost to live in our hearts. I thank thee for this good woman you gave me. I thank thee for my children and grandchildren in Chicago, Lord. I thank thee for this fine young white man. Bless him and watch over him. Send thy angels to keep evil men away from him."

Rachel was crying. "Yes, Almighty Lord. Protect this fine man."

Jake had no idea what was behind this prayer, but he followed along.

"Dear Lord God, bless our little girl, Caroline. Keep her from all harm. Thank thee for her ministry to Miss Hortense. Thou, O Lord, hast taught us to bless those who misuse us and to turn the other cheek to those who strike us."

"Do a work on Miss Hortense's heart, O Lord, we beg." George said.

"Heal the child, Lord. *Heal* her," George prayed. "She is like our own."

"Yes, Lord," Rachel cried so hard she shook. Jake cried too. What did he not know? After all, the woman had threatened to kill Caroline, but she was out of her head with drunkenness.

Maybe the abuse had gone on a long time. Maybe the scars were deeper than he realized. If he could lead Caroline to trust him, she would let down her guard. As he learned more about her, he saw she reacted to people the way an abused dog would. She was starving for affection but refusing it.

George continued his prayer. "About Mose, Lord. When he comes before your great white throne, please judge him according to his actions. Thank you for sending this young man to save our girl's life. I petition you on her behalf. How long must she suffer at the hands of those who spitefully use her?"

Jacob didn't hear much forgiveness toward those who abused Caroline. When he thought of the ways she had been hurt, his blood sizzled through his arteries.

"We come to thee, O most high and holy King of all the earth and heaven, and we beg for changes in our government. We beg for the bloodshed to cease. Bless our Senator. We know he is a kind man with a heart for thee. He would do more to help us if he could. Send thy angels to watch over him. Keep evil people from hurting him and his sweet child. And if hatemongers come near my wife or me, send your angels to strike them dead in their tracks. After you strike them dead, give Rachel and me forgiving hearts." George chuckled.

"Amen. Yes, Lord Jesus." Rachel sobbed.

Jake jerked to attention when the Reverend George McBride said, "Let this young man do what thou hast shown me to request of him. Help him to go with a brave heart. To thee, O Father be all the glory. We beseech thee in the precious name of thy Son."

A long pause followed. "Lord, we pray thou wilt remove any evil now from our hearts." In the long silence, Jake understood he was to pray in his own mind while they did the same. Then there were inaudible mumblings and groaning. Jake prayed as he had never prayed before.

The preacher said, "In the blessed holy name of Jesus."

All three of them said, "Amen."

Tears flowed. For the first time in his life, Jake tingled as the result of praying. They had gripped each other's hands until perspiration covered them. "Could I have a glass of water? My mouth feels a little dry," Jake said.

"Me too, Mother," the Preacher said.

"It ought to after *that* prayer," she said.

"What is my mission?"

The old man got up and walked around in his front yard. He looked every direction. "My dogs are on the front porch, and they ain't barking. Nobody's fed 'em neither. We can talk."

Jake made a mental note to get a dog soon.

"Forty-nine men. Forty-nine God-fearing voters, from this area, have signed a petition to be presented to Senator Clemons."

"You signed it?" Jake asked.

"Yep. They let me vote. I have enough money to pay my poll tax, and I can outread most of them."

"Amazing," Jake said.

"They let a few of us colored reverends vote in Mississippi," George said.

"I don't expect they'll ever let us women folk vote," Rachel said.

"You are the man the Lord has put on my heart to deliver the petition to the Senator in Jackson. I don't think you understand you are in danger coming to a colored man's house way too often. People will cold-shoulder your business. They may even burn your store. If they find out you are delivering the petition, they may hang you."

Jake was incredulous. "Do you really mean that?"

"You know I do. But something's going to throw them off their tracks. Since you've taken a shine to Miss Caroline, they ain't going to suspect nothing when you show up at the Senator's house in Jackson."

"Remember the angels," Jake said. "But wait a minute. What does the petition say?"

"Oh, we did leave out that little detail."

"Is it about the poll tax?" Jake couldn't believe how much his thinking had changed.

"No, Son, we know nobody up to the governor himself can revoke the poll tax and all them silly rules."

"But, if all the men could vote . . ."

"Next thing you know, the white women would expect to vote." George laughed. "And then the colored women."

"I done told you it ain't going to happen," Rachel said.

"My wife is smarter than most of the men that vote, but she's scared for folks to know she can read."

"Free, white, male, and twenty-one," Jake said.

"It's awful tempting for this preacher to cuss." George shook his head. "We've got to choose our battles. Here, read it."

"We, the undersigned, request . . . for the Senate to pass a resolution to build a training school for the colored children in each county of the great sovereign state of Mississippi." Jake read aloud.

"They ought to begin, of course, in the town of Taylorsburg. Some counties already have schools for our people, but most of them don't. This is a pitiful step, but it *is* a step. Even the white folks don't have enough in the way of schools. The state of Mississippi spends four dollars per student a year on buildings and textbooks for each white child. Nothing much is left over for our little ones. Northern states spend a hundred dollars or more per student no matter what color. I know Mississippi ain't got no money to spend. It's the poorest state in the union, but we got to start somewhere. We must educate our children. Did you know that a white schoolteacher in Mississippi has on the average thirty to thirty-five pupils in her room but a Negro school teacher has seventy-five pupils in her room on the average? That is, if they have schools at all."

"I'll sign it. Number fifty."

"You paid your poll tax in Schmidt County yet?"

"Sure." Jake fumbled in his wallet. "Here's my receipt."

"I expected you had. And I know you'll deliver this petition to the Senator too."

"I'll tuck it in my shirt, and I'd best be going," Jake said. "I won't come around here at night for a while."

"You see the danger now."

"I'll go to Jackson as soon as I can."

"Let me say one more thing. Rachel and I have talked it over. Nobody can take our lives—and that means you too—till our Father is ready to call us home."

"Okay," Jake said.

"If they kill us, they can't hurt us. All they'll do is send us to the presence of the glorious Lord."

Jake realized he faced a danger that Senator Clemons would be angry or feel trapped, but what he had seen in the Senator's behavior led him to think the petition would be all right. He didn't want to take advantage of their relationship though.

He knew Caroline wouldn't object. He believed if it affected her at all she would move closer to him. She was dedicated to education, and she loved the McBrides.

He looked first at Rachel and then at George. Then he gave them a bright smile. "Go with God," Jake said.

"And the Lord be with you," George said.

They shook hands, and Jake hugged Rachel. Leaving the McBrides' house, he knew he would be a foolish man if he did not admit his life was in danger. All he could do was pray. His horses knew the way home along the back way, the River Road, which he always took.

*   *   *

"Papa, Jacob plans to visit us." Caroline went into her father's office with the latest letter.

"You will have a splendid time, I'm sure," he said.

"He's actually coming to see you about business."

"What is that?"

"He didn't say."

"How convenient," the Senator said as he looked up at her over his glasses.

"No, I think this is really serious. It's something about Brother George."

"Oh." The smile on his face changed to a contemplative frown. "The Lord's will be done."

*   *   *

Caroline threw herself into a frenzy. She vowed to cook ahead of time and scrub the house until it was immaculate. She shopped at the Jones-Kennington Dry Good Store for tablecloths, napkins, couch pillows, and pictures. With cosmetic changes she gave Papa's house a fresh look.

*   *   *

Jake said he would arrive on Saturday. That day the Senator drove the auto somewhere, maybe to the Edwards House. Since the general election was a few days away, Mr. Noel was living there with his family. Caroline wasn't sure where Papa had gone.

Staying away for long periods was not unusual, but she couldn't understand why he didn't wait at home for Jake. She was sure he remembered Jake was coming that day. She had reminded him again over breakfast.

Jake arrived at their house on East Fortification in a taxi at noon. She was sitting on the front porch. "I'm sorry we didn't meet you. Papa has business going on today."

"Hi, Caroline," Jake said.

"Oh, hi. I'm sorry. I didn't say hello before I started telling you stuff. I regret that Papa isn't here to meet you."

"It's all right. I'm glad to see you." He handed her a bouquet of bronze and yellow chrysanthemums.

She felt awkward having him there. She showed him a vacant room so he could set his bags down, and she hurried into the kitchen to find a vase.

While he was out of sight, she rushed to the kitchen to get some food she had prepared—stuffed eggs, slices of a baked ham, sliced bread, pickles, mustard, and horseradish. She took it to the porch. She went back and brought two Biedenharn bottles of Coca-Cola and a German can opener. Also she brought slices of a yellow cake with thick chocolate fudge frosting.

"You know it won't be long until it's too cool to eat outside. Let's sit on the porch and enjoy the fall air while we can."

He leaned toward her and stole a quick peck. "Girl, am I glad to see you. It's been way too long."

"Good to see you too." His presence swept over her with a pleasant sensation.

They sat in the gliding chairs. He took her hand and asked a blessing of the food. With a short table between them, they made sandwiches. Since all the food wouldn't fit, they placed items on the floor and reached for them as needed.

"You must have an excellent cook here."

She laughed. "Thank you. I'm the cook. I've had to learn to prepare meals that can be eaten cold. I never know when Papa is going to show up. Sometimes he has already eaten. Other times he is famished."

He gazed at her with glistening eyes.

"What are you grinning about?" she asked. He seemed to have some secret.

"Nothing except I'm thrilled to see you." He reached across the table to pat her shoulder.

After the meal she said, "Let me take you on a little tour. We're close enough to walk downtown. I do it all the time. Give me a minute to put these dishes up."

He helped her. While she went to get a light jacket and scarf, he went to the guest room. When he came out, he said, "I wanted to place my papers in a secure place. I hid them under the quilt. I'd feel foolish if I misplaced them after coming to deliver them to your dad."

She asked no questions, and he gave no information. She took him down the street and showed him the Manship House. "This is one of the few houses in town that survived Sherman's march. It's a Gothic Revival cottage villa."

"Thanks for showing me." He gave her hand a playful squeeze. "You remember bits and pieces of facts. I can believe you are an excellent teacher."

She rolled her eyes at him as she continued. "People called this town Chimneyville because Sherman left hardly anything but chimneys standing, but this house survived."

They walked toward town. At the top of Capitol Street she pointed out the old state house. Then they walked by the governor's dilapidated mansion.

"Let's go down to the Edwards House," he said. "I need to rent a room."

She was relieved to know he didn't plan to stay at Papa's house. She never wanted to do anything that someone might frown on. Papa constantly guarded his reputation. "Would you wait a second while I run upstairs to look at the room and make sure it's okay?" She sat in the lobby and looked at magazines until he returned.

"How was it?"

"Marvelous. Now could I interest you in some hot tea?"

"I'd be delighted."

They sat across from each other in the cozy tearoom with its flickering lights and dark shiny paneled walls. He talked about the Mercantile and the way the business was growing. He told her that the Mauldins were working on the fence around the property and painting the farmhouse. She listened with interest.

"How are the horses?"

"The mares are filling out nicely."

"How is Bruiser?"

"Cute as ever. He said to tell you he misses you. I still plan to get a puppy soon. It will take time to train her."

She told him about her new teaching position. He listened and commented on her stories.

She caught him gazing at her again. "I'm so glad to see you," he said.

She blushed. She needed to cool the relationship. For weeks she had lain awake trying to think how she could. Then she would dream about him, see his handsome face, relive the times he had kissed her, smell his *eau de toilette* mingled with the smell of his manly skin.

She knew, even without asking God, she had no right to a man such as Jake. She had always prayed about everything else, but this was something she knew without prayer. When she did talk to the Lord about him, her prayer was always a question about the way to end the courtship and remain friends without breaking his heart or hers.

They walked by the new capitol and back up to State Street. She had been hoping to see her father's Flyer, but he didn't seem to be anywhere around. When they returned home, the Senator was still not there. She didn't think she could guard her heart or his hands inside if they waited in the parlor. Even if they behaved, it would be inappropriate for him to be inside the house with her.

"Would you like to sit on the porch swing and watch the sunset?"

"Thank you," he said.

Leaving the swing for him, she stationed herself on a rocking chair.

"Won't you come sit on the swing with me? You can enjoy the view better from here." He patted the seat of the swing and motioned toward her. With his chin down and his big blue eyes focused on her, he gave her an invitation she couldn't resist.

With the lowering of the sun in the late autumn, the temperature dropped. "Wait here a minute. I'll be right back."

She went inside and found two throw quilts that she had made. Also she layered a big bulky sweater over her jacket. As the temperature went down with the sun, she faced a dilemma. She was frustrated that her father had failed to come home. Sometimes he got tied up in meetings and was hours later than he had planned.

She suspected her father of arranging times she could spend with Jake. Papa's pointed maneuvers embarrassed her. The more she tried to explain to him she planned to be a maiden lady all her life, the harder he tried to marry her off. His nucleus of concentration was Jake.

She returned to the porch with the throw quilts. As she handed one to Jake, she said, "It's getting chilly." He accepted the quilt and threw it over his lap without a comment. She returned to her spot next to him and threw the quilt over her legs.

Minutes passed before either spoke again. She folded her hands in her lap. With hesitation, he dared to place his arm on the back of the swing behind her. She gave him the beginning of a smile.

She repeated her apology. "I'm sorry Papa is late. He gets tied up with people. I know you need to see him so you can get back to your hotel and catch the train early in the morning."

"It's all right. If he doesn't have time to talk to me tonight, I'll spend another day."

"At any rate, I'm sorry you are having to wait."

"Believe me, Caroline. I'm enjoying the wait. It's a joy to have a chance to visit with an old friend."

His remark startled her. "Oh," she said. Before she realized what she was doing, she jumped back.

An old friend? Maybe he realizes our relationship is nothing more than friendship. I've tried to show him many times. Or maybe he's playing me like an accordion.

"I have an idea. Let's go to a restaurant. We can enjoy the city some more," Jake said.

"I like your suggestion. Let me write a note to Papa and leave it in his chair." She went inside and scribbled a quick explanation. She rushed into the downstairs powder room, smoothed her hair, and placed a hat on her head.

When she returned, Jake had stepped inside the living room and placed the quilts on a chair.

"I'm ready," she said. "How about you? Have you found the powder room yet? It's down the hall to the left."

"Thanks."

She stepped back onto the porch to wait for him. She told him, "It's a mile to a restaurant. Do you feel like walking again?"

"Yes, let's walk," he said.

She took off the sweater and put on a cloak. He threw on his coat that had been hanging on the rack in the foyer.

"We'll probably get warm walking down there, but we'd better plan for a cooler walk back home," she said.

She locked the door and placed the key inside her reticule. He offered his arm and she took it as they began a pleasant stroll. The full moon came up wide and golden.

"The Pearl River is not too far from here. The moon must be beautiful rising over it. Imagine all the snakes though."

"And bobcats."

She suspected he was teasing her. She shivered and held onto him tighter. "The river makes it cooler here I suppose," she said.

They walked along underneath the honey golden moon and an occasional streetlight shining through the soft darkness.

"We should have worn gloves." She released her arm from his and rubbed her hands together.

He reached for her. "You're as cold as frost."

"We're almost there." She tried to sound matter-of-fact, but she couldn't remain unaffected when the warm pressure of his hand on hers was causing her heart to pound.

"Am I walking too fast? You sound out of breath."

"No, I'm fine." She dared not tell him she found his touch exciting. She needed to pat her tender scars. Since he was holding her left hand, she placed her right hand on her back. The pain seemed to have a way of nagging her at the most inconvenient times, such as this moment when she was going on a moonlit walk with the most handsome man she had ever seen. He had come to see her father, but he seemed not to be in a hurry to go back to Taylorsburg.

Her feelings were in an upheaval. Her mind wanted him to go away forever. Her fears told her she should have sent him to the Edwards House the minute he arrived, but her heart kept leaping for joy when he was near.

"The restaurant is just up ahead," she said.

He didn't respond. Where was his mind? When they reached a dark spot on the street less than a block from the lighted entrance, he simply spoke her name.

"Yes, Jake."

He spoke in a husky whisper. "I want to kiss you." He placed his hand on her arm to pull her close. She could feel his breath on her face.

"Okay," she spoke brightly and turned her right cheek up to him, but nothing happened. She turned toward him. His soulful stare embraced her, and he encircled her with his arms. She placed her hands on his broad shoulders.

In the intense moment, two words came to her mind—tender and sacred. He reached for her chin. Involuntarily she closed her eyes and tilted her face upward. Her lips puckered slightly. She delighted in his warm sweet breath on her cold face. Her heart was racing so fast she gasped for air.

Slowly he moved his face closer to hers as he held her waist firmly. She could hear a moaning noise in his throat.

She reveled in the anticipation. When his lips touched hers, she felt tingling warmth even more pleasant than she had known when he kissed her weeks before. For a few seconds he communicated with her in a new way she had never experienced. She didn't want the kiss to end, ever.

But she knew it needed to stop. When he moved away releasing her, she tried to speak. To her surprise, her voice was throaty when she spoke his name. She finally managed a giggly laugh. "I guess we need to go eat."

She sped up the pace and he followed silently. She realized he must have thought she chastised him. Perhaps he would cool his expressions of affection.

They ordered salad with Jackson's famous Comeback Sauce and an assortment of broiled seafood with scalloped potatoes. When the waiter brought the salad and a basket of large buttered rolls, Jake reached across the table for her hand and asked the blessing.

All through the meal he made starts to say something, but she always cut him off and changed the subject. She was afraid of what he might say.

When they finished, he asked, "Would you like to walk back or would you prefer to take a taxi?

She had to make a decision. Perhaps Papa wouldn't be home. Walking would take more time, but they had walked enough. Besides, Jake would need a way to get back to the hotel.

"How would you like to take a horse-drawn taxi?" she asked.

"That's a great suggestion."

Soon they were loaded into the buggy and tucked under a blanket. The big horse clopped along the brick street. In the moonlight, she studied his handsome face. He turned and smiled at her.

I have to stop. This poor man deserves so much more than I can ever give him.

He leaned over to her and whispered into her ear the words she dreaded to hear but longed for: "I love you, Caroline."

She lowered her eyes. Her lips quivered.

"I will always love you with all my heart," he said.

She didn't know what to say.

When they reached Fortification Street, she could see light through the windows. He asked the buggy driver to wait for him. They went inside. Her father must have gone to bed. Jake rushed back to the guest room to fetch his bags and papers.

"Do you want to go to church with us tomorrow?"

"Yes, I do," he said.

"I'm sure it will be all right with Papa. We'll drive to the hotel and give you a ride."

"What time?"

"Look for us around nine o'clock," she said. "We'll pick you up on the Capitol Street side."

"Good night, my darling." He brushed a kiss across her lips.

"Good night, Jake." Her voice faltered.

*   *   *

In his hotel room, Jake opened the curtain and gazed at Capitol Street below. He placed his palms on his forehead and massaged his aching head. He was perplexed. Had he not reached the place where he could tell Caroline how he felt?

He wasn't sure how she would react. He only knew when she looked at him she had a look of love in her eyes. Each time he kissed her, she trembled. Maybe he moved too fast. He had taken a chance, a gamble he considered a safe one, but she said nothing. She wasn't ready. What held her back?

He asked the Lord to help him with his problem. Then he settled into the hotel bed. A moment later he slept. Bringing intense longing she visited him in his dreams as she did most nights.

The following morning he waited in front of the hotel. He was amused to see Caroline driving the auto. She pulled into the circle that went under the covered loading area. Senator Clemons opened the door for him and moved to the back seat. "Good morning, Jacob. Great to see you."

Jacob moved into the front passenger's seat and closed the door. After church the Senator drove, Caroline sat in the back, and Jake kept his seat in the front. At the house she scurried into the kitchen. As soon as the oven heated, she popped a pan of angel biscuits into it. In a jiffy the lunch of hearty beef and vegetable stew was hot.

"The stew is tasty, Caroline." Jake focused his blue eyes on her. "Do you have any more cake?"

"More than half of it. How about a cup of coffee too?"

"You are an amazing cook," Papa told her.

"I had amazing teachers," she said.

"Son, let's go to my office and talk.

*   *   *

Caroline sat and waited. She had filled her two favorite novels with his letters. *Pride and Prejudice,* packed with rose petals, contained his earlier letters. She had overfilled *Jane Eyre,* packed with lavender. She hoped to select another book with another fragrance soon. She shuddered at the thought of burning the letters when Jake found someone worthy of his love.

It is not only the scar. I've been abused so much I'm not sure I can . . . Lord, please heal my heart and body. Last night when Jake said he loved me, he had good intentions, but he doesn't know me well enough. Once he sees my back, he will despise me.

The present pain coupled with the remembered horror overwhelmed her as she sat in the parlor next to a lamp. In her humanity she had to re-forgive. It was time to embroider because reading didn't help her sooth the pain.

Jake had zest for life, especially when things were going his way. She recognized his faults, such as this anger with God. At least he had admitted the problem and dealt with it. She had a much more even temperament than he did.

In some ways I think I would be good for him. I could help him even out his emotions. I have my highs and lows, but I think I could help him not to overreact to situations.

She loved the looks of his handsome face and his powerful physique. More than these, she loved his relationship to God. It was apparent to her that he had fallen in love with the Lord anew as he said he had.

Brother George has helped him along the way in his spiritual walk. If it were not for what has happened to me, we could have a glorious future together. After I tell him how hideous it is, he'll lose interest in me and move on. No man is strong enough to cope with my scars, physical and emotional.

* * *

"I believe you have a document for me, Jacob. The Senator sat beside his desk in a chair near Jake.

"Yes."

"Show me the petition."

"You knew about it?" Jacob asked.

"I did. The world of politics contains few real surprises."

Jacob handed it to him. The little speech based on what Brother George had said became unnecessary. George's words had been for him, not the Senator.

"Son, it's an exciting time to be alive. We're still trying to rebuild our economy. I hope to right some wrongs. We have dirigibles, the airplane, trains connecting our towns, gas stoves, ever increasing telephone lines, improved fashions for the ladies, new fashions for men, the new Mississippi capitol building, and automobiles. All those things make life a great adventure.

"What excites me more than all of these is the way our future governor is planning with us to improve the education of all our children. He has limits as to what the people will allow. Cowards hiding behind bandanas thwart us on every turn. Personally, I'm not afraid of them. They can take my life here on earth, but they cannot take my soul.

"For my family though I have concerns. Also if they take my life, they will silence me. Then I won't be able to help anybody. I have to choose my battles carefully and move discreetly. Do you understand?"

"Yes, sir." Jake gulped.

"You're a dear friend to my daughter and me. Young men like you are the hope of the future of our state. All this brings me to another question. Please forgive me for being indelicate, but what are your intentions toward my precious daughter?"

"Ur uh!" Jake was more than a little surprised. He wanted to make a good impression. Had not Senator Clemons seen that he had risked his personal safety to deliver the petition? Had he already forgotten how hard he worked in the house-to-house canvass?

He hesitated. He didn't want to say more to Caroline's father until she accepted him, but something stood in her way.

"It's all right, Jacob. Actions speak louder than words. God bless you."

"Thank you."

"I want you and Carrie to be good to each other. Right now I can see you adore her. She is like a magnificent flower, such as an amaryllis that has opened into a gorgeous bloom. What will you do when you see her faults?"

Swallowing hard, Jake sat facing the man. "She will always be perfection in my eyes."

"Enough of this." Chad Clemons stood. He hid the petition underneath his desk pad. Would you like a Sunday afternoon ride?"

"Oh, sure."

"Let's see if we can talk a certain young lady into accompanying us."

A few minutes later the three of them loaded into the Thomas-Flyer for a sightseeing tour of the capital city. They drove across the Pearl River and back.

Papa took them to a secluded road. "Jacob, have you driven an automobile before?"

"No, I haven't."

"There's no time like the present to learn."

Jake jerked the car off. Caroline laughed at his bungling efforts. The engine died from the rough bucks. Senator Clemons gave him a lesson in starting it. "Don't let it get you down. Driving this thing is not as easy as it looks. We'll have you doing it in no time though."

Jake pulled his handkerchief from his pocket to wipe the perspiration from his face on a cool day. "I'm going to master this. One of these days I plan to buy one of these."

After a tedious lesson and a ride back to the house on Fortification, the Senator said, "You did fine. Precious, do you have any more angel biscuit dough?

"Yep," she said.

"Now, Jacob. I have something for you to do that you have had more practice with. I know you cut meat at the store. Would you do us the honor of carving some slices off that ham bone Carrie has in the kitchen?"

"It sounds like you're putting us to work, Papa. What's your job?"

"Who, me? I'll open a can of that Schmidt County molasses a fellow gave me when we stopped by his place."

"Don't strain yourself working too hard."

"You know it's hard to pop one of those lids off the can," the Senator said.

"I thought maybe you could scramble some eggs. You know you had to cook for yourself before I moved up here. You want to pretend you don't know how."

"Who wants eggs?"

"We all do," she said.

After a pleasant visit, they snuffed out all the candles and turned down the wicks of the lamps.

"We'll give you a ride back to the Edwards House," the Senator said. "Monday morning will begin early for all of us."

A dim street light sent a glow through the window. Jake kissed her face and shook the Senator's hand. "Both of you have given me a weekend to remember." The three of them started to leave.

"I left my magazine on the writing desk in the guest room," Jake said.

"Wait a minute. I'll light a candle," Caroline said.

"Not necessary, but come help me find it." The two walked down the hall to the room and left the Senator in the parlor.

After they rounded the corner of the doorway he placed a hand on each of her arms and pulled her to him. Holding her, he let his mouth find her lips in the darkness. They kissed until it was time to breathe. He pulled away for an instant and returned with more insistence. And again. He released his passionate hug with gentleness.

"Fire!" He took her hand and they rushed back to the parlor. The light of flames came through the windows.

"I'm over here." Papa spoke in a hushed tone.

"Shh," Caroline said.

"Take this." He handed Jake a rifle. "It's loaded. Guard the office windows."

'You staying in here?" Jake asked in his softest voice.

"Yeah, by the window farthest from the door. Don't fire unless they do or unless they get inside the house. Carrie, here's your reticule. Call the police and station yourself across from Jake."

In the front yard a bonfire sizzled its angry flames. Twenty or more men wearing bandanas over their mouths milled around. Jake stood in his position and aimed his weapon.

Making as little noise as possible, Caroline called central and talked to the police. Jake saw her shadow as she moved to the opposite side of the office window. "I've got my pistol," she said.

"They ain't home," a man yelled in the yard.

"Good," a familiar voice responded. "That's what we'll tell the boss."

"We can't lynch him tonight then."

"Cowards." Carrie breathed the word in a barely audible voice.

The men left. They rushed into the street and loaded into a fleet of buggies. The police didn't arrive. Neither did the firemen. The Senator, Jake, and Carrie sat quietly in the dark parlor for more than an hour. Jake held her hand.

"They did their job and the police aren't coming," the Senator said.

"That's it?" Jake asked.

"Yes."

"Papa, you need to hire body guards."

"Tomorrow I'll do that. Right now we need to get Jake to the Edwards House."

*   *   *

Monday before daylight Jake took a taxi to the west end of Capitol Street so he would reach the train station on time . . . .

The train took him farther from the one he loved and his dear friend, her father. He'd never loved anyone the way he loved Caroline. He was ready to become as one with her. He wanted to build a house and make it a home for them. He'd share everything, including an abiding love for Christ. Both he and Caroline had survived adversity. Together they could build a strong fortress that would endure the way the Manship House had. Having tasted the danger of the previous night, he found it especially difficult to go back to Taylorsburg.

Lord, thank you for giving me happiness in my life. I'm sorry I was angry at you. I understand now that you have a plan for me. Thank you for blessing me with such great parents. Thank you for my uncle. I'm grateful for the time I had with them.

Send angels to watch over my beloved. Keep her safe.

Now please, if it is your will, give Caroline a love for me that is not reserved. Help me to be patient with her and to understand whatever problems she has. I'm sorry for the times when I could have treated her better. She says she is less than I deserve but she is more. In Christ's name.

Ideas flew around in his mind about ways he could win her love. He wanted her to see he was preparing a place for her as his bride. But he didn't want her to accept his love if she didn't have true feelings for him. Women were complicated.

*   *   *

Someday Caroline would no longer dream of him, but until then she would hold his sweet memory in her heart.

Chapter Fourteen

Papa

"Not safe to be out after dark with hoodlums after us," Papa said Monday over breakfast.

"I've been grading papers and making lesson plans at school before walking home," Carrie as her father and now Jake loved to call her said.

"The days are growing shorter," he said.

"Okay, I'll be home before dark."

He drummed his hand on the table. "Carrie, either take your pistol to school or I'll have the guard walk with you."

"I have to go to school today, and I cannot take a gun. You haven't had a chance to contact a guard service."

"I'll drop you off at school this morning," he said.

"And after school?"

"A guard will meet you. I'll give him a note to present to you so you won't have any doubts."

*   *   *

It was Monday evening after Jake left. Next to a crackling fire, she sat reading the children's work so she could mark errors and write notes of encouragement.

With the *Clarion Ledger* in his hands, Papa sat across from her. "Nothing in the paper about last night," he said.

"Papa."

"Yes?"

"You have *not* made many mistakes in your life, but what about Hortense?"

"When I married her, she was a beautiful woman. She knew how to behave in cultured social settings. She needed help with her two daughters. I thought she would be good to you. I thought she was a woman who honored God."

"You didn't love her though."

"Not really. I thought I would learn to love her. Many times throughout the history of mankind men have made decisions to love women or women have decided to love men. Passion was not a factor. Everything seemed to work out fine in most of those arrangements. I suspect though that those marriages had a gray sky most days and dull nights. But the dullness provided a comfortable productive relationship."

"And it was like that with Hortense?"

"Yes. She was an attractive woman with an appealing name. It means *gardener*. I was mesmerized by her charm, but I was not in love with her."

"You didn't think it mattered." Caroline bit her lower lip.

"She had a hidden drinking problem I failed to see. Added to it was her testy temperament she managed to curb until she gained a ring on her finger and a roof over her head. We started pulling away from each other before we became close. We needed to be friends before we became husband and wife. We needed to have three in our marriage, not simply two self-serving people."

"Three?"

"Yes, we needed to form a circle of love. We needed to hold one another's hands, and we needed to hold on tight to the unchanging hand of God. Inside that circle we needed to place our girls in loving protection. I am sorry I failed. I never got around to what was important. I was looking at the bigger picture of what I could do to help enact child labor laws and build schools. I didn't realize that my wife was overworking my own daughter. Ironically. I was here in Jackson fighting for prohibition while my wife was the local moonshiner combination home brewer's best customer. It seems now that prohibition is making the alcohol problem worse in our state."

"You're blaming yourself for everything." She stood behind him and wrapped her arms around his shoulders. "She had faults you failed to notice. I didn't mind working hard. I was trying to support your causes by helping her. What I resented was the way she talked to me. Remember, I made a secret promise to you to help preserve our family reputation and to take care of Hortense and her girls."

He laid his glasses down and placed his hands on hers. "Too much to ask of a young girl . . . with a sweet tender heart." Tears slipped down his cheeks. Again he said, "I'm sorry."

Again she bit her trembling lip. "She hit me."

"Oh, how I hate that," Papa whispered.

While he stoked the fire, she looked for her handkerchief.

"I was too busy. I was married to my work, and I confess I didn't know how to take care of my wonderful daughter."

"Tantaylee and Uncle Vester gave me a blessed childhood when I lived with them," she said.

"But after we married, I got the stupid notion that you could live with your new stepmother. I sensed some friction. When the town moved to the new location, I thought the beautiful new home with plenty of space for everyone would make life better for you, Hortense, and her girls. I hoped to get to see you more. She seemed a little eccentric. I depended on you to bring some normalcy into her life and set a good example for Lydia and Millicent."

"I wanted to help you," she said. "I tried to make things look good

"Carrie, I thought too much about appearances."

"I was proud of you, and I wanted to be a perfect daughter."

"You were my most important responsibility. I turned a blind eye toward this woman who was abusing the dearest person in my life."

Carrie was quiet for a moment. "Papa, I have no hard feelings toward you, and I pray every night for Mama Hortense. Forgiving her is an ongoing process."

"I had no idea she had abused you the way she did. It was criminal."

"She beat me within an inch of my life. Look, Papa." She stood in front of him so she could pull her blouse and camisole up in the back to show him. She lowered her skirt and petticoat enough to expose the flesh below her waistline in the back. She removed the soft dressing to expose the wound.

"Oh, Lord. It's my fault too," he wailed. "Child."

"It is a huge scar. It goes down farther. As you know, I recently re-injured it. That's another matter. As she talked she righted her clothing.

"You heard her threaten to kill me. I don't think you understand that she almost succeeded a few months ago."

"I—uh—it's hideous." His face failed to belie his revulsion. His words pierced into her self-esteem.

"You, too, Papa." She raised her voice. "Aunt Mahalia acted the same way. Now, you think I'm hideous but you expect me to have a courtship with Jake. If he saw this, he . . ."

He reached for her but she turned her back. "Don't touch me."

She paced away and stood sobbing. "While we're talking," she said as she turned to face him, "let me tell you—she said things to me that were calculated to destroy me."

She pressed on. "I realize she was under the influence, but what she said hurt me more than the way she hit me. All I knew to do was smile and take it. I was trying to protect you. I promised *you* I would take care of her and Lydia and Millie." She flashed her eyes at him.

"Unbelievable."

"Can't you see?" Anger burst from her.

"I didn't realize she had you sleeping in that little hole of a room on the back side of the pantry."

"She begrudged me *that.*"

"Why?"

"She wanted to place a live-in servant next to the kitchen. She really didn't know what she wanted. To her, providing a bed for me in a tiny room and my meals meant she was paying me a big wage I didn't deserve. In her convoluted thought processes, I was a burden on her."

"You were to be mother and daughter."

"She ignored the fact that I was family. I was in her sick mind a teacher, a designated public servant, who didn't deserve a decent wage. She felt she was helping pay my wage by providing for me. She wouldn't have tolerated a woman of color as a live-in servant. I think she wanted to find another teacher not related to her. She is ashamed of me because I work in a job."

He started to speak but she ignored him.

"I know it sounds crazy, but she is criminally insane. Now she probably thinks I am a run-away slave. She has not written me once since I was attacked by her friend. All she has done is write me a threatening note that she placed on her bedroom door. She is serious about wanting to kill me."

He walked over to her, placed his arms around her, and wept violently. "Girl, I'm so sorry."

She pulled away from him, this time not in rejection—she was softening—but she had more to say. She realized he had not heard all she said. "I want to be fair with her."

"You've been more than fair."

"Excuse me, Papa. Listen to me. She didn't do *all* this to my back. Rachel and I had it getting better, but it was still draining pus. Then he re-injured it."

"You stayed at the doctor's clinic for several days. It all is starting to fit together now. I'm sorry. Since you've moved in with me, I've been caught up in my work more than ever."

"Mose Jefferson."

"What about him?"

"When Rachel had that sick spell, I went to stay with her. Brother George and I stayed awake seeing about her through the night. On my way back home, I was like I was walking in my sleep. I should have paid closer attention." The hardness in her voice melted into frightened paroxysms of words mixed with tears. She pulled away from him and sat in a ball on the edge of her chair.

"Oh, Carrie."

He reached for her hand, but she refused to hold his. With wild eyes she looked out into the room. She pointed with her hand at nowhere in particular.

"I walk past his house. He has a big yard. Bushes near the road. You know where he lives. Hid behind the bushes." She had to stop.

"Can you go on? Tell me."

"He is behind a big bush. Jumps out at me."

The Senator's face was crimson. He paced and slung his fists. He attacked the burning log in the fireplace with the poker.

"Jumps on me. Knocks me down . . . kicks me across his gravel driveway . . . ties my hands behind me . . . makes me hit my sore back with my own hands because of the way I'm tied." She returned her psyche to the safe warm room in Jackson. "Give me a minute, Papa."

He sat across from her and leaned forward. They held onto each other as the angry tears flowed.

Returning, she continued to recount the atrocity. "Pulls out a nasty handkerchief. Dried mucus and vomit all over it." She heaved. "Ties a gag around my mouth." She ran to the powder room because she felt sick.

When she returned she continued, "He . . ."

She stood in front of the fireplace.

"Try to tell me. Get it all out."

"He—I have a plan to get away. I wait until he pulls up my skirt. I'm lying there in my pantaloons with my skirt and petticoat out of the way. I kick the blazes out of him. Hard. Hard." She shouted and stomped her feet. Her fists were flailing.

"He falls back. I try to get up so I can run, but I can't. I roll, roll, roll down the side of the hill toward the ditch." Her hands demonstrated her rolling motion.

"What next?"

"It hurt, Papa. My back!"

"Did he?"

"No, Jacob came by and saved me."

"You're just now telling me."

"Jake and I talked it over. Nobody was going to help me. The sheriff and Mayor Samson weren't going to do anything. The Senator's wife is Mose's best friend. Think about it, Papa. I wanted to protect you." Her sardonic smile goaded him.

Papa heaved a sigh.

"I kept my promise," she said.

Papa shook his head. From his face he wiped tears and sweat.

"Dr. and Mrs. Woodley put me back together. Jacob MacGregor saved my life."

"Fine man, that Jake."

"I never told the Woodleys what happened to me."

"They may think Jake beat you and brought you for help. People do that sort of thing."

"Thanks for letting me know. I'll have to clarify that the next time we go back to Taylorsburg. I don't want anybody to think ill of Jacob."

Papa disappeared into the kitchen. When he returned, he had two frosty bottles of Coca-Cola. He wrapped napkins around them and handed her one.

"If Jake had not come along and saved me, there's no telling what Mose would have done. Papa, Jake is a very strong man. He was an outstanding athlete at Ole Miss. He can fight when he has to."

"Is that the problem?"

"What do you mean? You think I'm afraid of him." She shook her head. "No . . ."

"Daughter, are you unsure whether you love him or feel grateful because he saved your life?"

"No, Papa, "she wailed. Vehement tears spouted from her eyes in torrents. She quivered. "Why can't you understand?"

She went to him and threw her head onto his strong shoulder. "He won't love me. No man will, not even somebody hideous like Mose Jefferson."

"Why do you say that?"

"I showed you." She had an accusing tone. "No man will be able to look at my body." She broke into screams.

"Calm down, Sweetheart." He stroked her shoulders.

"I'm never going to marry anybody. I want to break it off with Jacob, but he has his problems. Life has been so hard for him. Nobody ever gets over something like what he went through. Losing his family in a tornado."

"True," he said.

"He's doing much better. He tried to turn his back on God, but God wouldn't let him. Now that he is doing better, I don't want to hurt him."

"Moreover, Carrie, you cannot deny the truth." Papa smiled in the midst of all the upset. "You love him and you know he loves you."

"That's what makes it so hard." She whimpered like a hurt puppy. Sometimes I feel desperate. Trapped."

"Do you pray about it?"

"Yes, but . . ."

"Yes, but?" He chuckled at her as they sipped their sodas.

"I don't ever ask the Lord what to do. I just tell him what I'm going to do—help Jacob find somebody worthy of him."

"He already has."

"I can't Papa."

"Shh." He reached toward her, patted her, and let her cry it out in his arms.

"I told you I can't be a man's wife."

"Oh, honey. I am so sorry, but you're wrong."

"You did the best you could," she said. "You didn't know."

"I want to make it up to you." He hesitated. "Somehow."

"It's okay. I need to live the life of a maiden lady. How can I love somebody if I can't love myself? I can barely tolerate looking at my own body. The place is getting better, but it hurts."

"That's why you pat it."

"Right."

"Do you have any chocolate pie?"

Usually the tingling sweet brown drink helped her through difficulties, but the novel taste had failed to distract her.

"Yes, there's pie," she said.

"Let's have some. Then we'll talk some more."

She stood.

"Keep your seat," he said. "I'll get it." She followed him into the kitchen and sat down. He pulled the pie from the icebox and cut two generous wedges. They returned to the parlor with her walking behind him, puppy-like.

"We all have to take some chance in life. I say, 'Go ahead and tell him.' If Jacob MacGregor is the man I think he is, he will love you, scars and all."

"At least I don't have any warts." She smiled at her lame attempt to quote an old joke.

"If he's not the man he should be, find out now. Then you can move on."

"I don't want to lose him, but I know I need to give him up. I'll never be able to keep him."

"Carrie, we lose people all our lives. The only hand you can hold onto is the nail-scarred hand of Jesus. We all have our thorns in our flesh—even Jesus. He kept his scars to remind us of the price he paid for our sinfulness."

She sipped the last of her drink and savored each drop.

"Maybe the worst thing that happened to you was that you decided you had to be perfect. To win my approval, promote my political career, and stay out of trouble with Hortense. To measure up to some idea you have about your mother."

"All that." She placed her hand on her locket.

"When you realized you weren't and never could be, it broke your heart."

"You're right. So I'll keep trying to be all I can be, but I won't share myself with anybody. I'll be the best daughter and the best school teacher I can."

"You're still not accepting yourself for who you are. Where do you get all these ideas about being perfect?" Papa smirked.

"Look in the mirror, Papa. Listen to yourself. You think *you* have to be perfect."

"What we all need to do is turn our eyes onto the perfection of Christ. I haven't thought about this until now. When we expect perfection in ourselves, we are manifesting pride. As long as we miss the joy of relying on the perfect one, we miss some of the pleasure of our fellowship with him."

"Pride is a very big sin, Papa. You've always said that."

*   *   *

Friday afternoon after school, she found Papa perched behind piles of papers on his desk. He looked up at her over his bifocals. "Did you have a good day, Carrie?"

"Great day. I enjoy my job."

"Did the guard walk you home?"

"Yes, that's working out fine."

"I'm sorry. I have to draft a bill this weekend. Our plan is to have all the bills ready ahead of time when legislature goes into session so we can present them before the opposition has time to organize."

She didn't object to his staying in his office and working. It was good to have his company, even when he was quiet. She had her own activities planned. "That's fine."

He flipped through the day's mail. "Here's what I was looking for. You have a letter from Jacob."

She had started packing his letters pressed in sweet olive blossoms between the pages of *Great Expectations.*

"Let me use your letter opener."

"Mm. Uh huh." He was already absorbed in his work again.

Her face beamed as she enjoyed the sweetness of the letter. She thought she must have looked silly, but she didn't care. No one noticed. Life was good. As she turned to the second page, her countenance changed.

"Listen, Papa. I know you're busy, but you have to hear this. Jake wrote:

"Everybody in Taylorsburg is all abuzz about the news of a shootout between the Jefferson clan and the state police. The police went to their house to talk to them and, the Jeffersons started shooting from the windows. One of them shot an officer in the arm."

Papa removed his glasses. Rubbing his eyes, he listened. "Go on."

"Mose and his brother Malone were killed, but all the officers survived. The checker and domino players have been debating over who will take Mose's place as the town's top manufacturer and purveyor of illegal spirits."

Papa looked sheepish. Without a comment he placed his spectacles back on and continued writing.

*   *   *

Tuesday, November 5, Papa took Caroline to the Edwards House to celebrate. The final election results would take weeks, but from all indications Mr. Noel was the newly elected governor. He had no serious opposition, and the prospects of a written-in candidate were nil.

"The inauguration will be on New Year's Day in 1908," Papa told her.

Chapter Fifteen

Christmas Coming

Caroline idealized a Thanksgiving with all the family around the long table back at home. In her fantasy she saw turkey, ham, and all the fixings.

The others who would have joined her and her father at the Taylorsburg table were out of town. Jake went to Princeton to visit his sister and her family. Hortense and her daughters were in New Orleans during the holiday. With occasional letters, Millicent and Lydia kept the Senator up to date about Hortense's condition, but they ignored Caroline's correspondence. After Hortense was dried out, the administrator at the treatment center recommended she spend some time in a spa, where her activities would be monitored. Chad Clemons asked the administrator to make the necessary arrangements.

Caroline's dreams of Thanksgiving passed into reality. Senator Clemons had too much business to leave town. He took her with him to have lunch at the Edwards House with Edmond Noel, his wife Alice, and all their family.

Men destined to hold key positions in the new administration, along with a few prominent legislators entertained at the Edwards House Friday evening. Eligible young men swarmed around Caroline.

The first week in December Papa caught a train to New Orleans, fetched Hortense, and took her back to Taylorsburg. He promptly returned to Jackson. Busier than ever with the plans for the new administration and two controversial lawsuits, he worked late every night.

The Christmas vacation, consisting of a few days before Christmas and more than a week afterwards, approached. "We'll have to come back to Jackson as soon after Christmas as possible," Papa reminded Caroline.

She sang with her students: "Christmas is coming. The goose is getting fat." Every child in the school participated in a festive program.

*   *   *

Jacob called on Mrs. Hortense Clemons two weeks before the Christmas break. He drove into the front circle driveway and tied his horses to the hitching post. He rang the bell and knocked on the door until Frankie came to the front. Hat in hand, he stood at the door. "Is Mrs. Clemons resting?"

"Not this time." Motioning her hands, she invited him to come sit in the parlor. "I'll tell her you're here."

He waited on the sofa. The cuckoo clock and the grandfather clock announced he had waited thirty minutes. He organized the contents of his pockets: reading glasses, note pads, pocket watch, crumpled dollar bills.

I wonder what Caroline is doing this minute. She loves teaching. It must be a blessing to enjoy a career as much as she does. Thank you, Lord, for guiding me to enjoy the store and the farm.

Hortense's doorknob shook, and Frankie appeared from the kitchen to help her open it. Her posture was distinctly worse than he had remembered. She leaned forward while she held onto her door facing for several seconds and then she took little running steps in his direction. He jumped up in time to help her walk. In a soft slurred voice he could barely hear, she said, "Hello."

"How are you, Miss Hortense?"

She shuffled toward him. Fearing she would fall, he extended his hand toward her. She stared at him without reaching for the hand. He held onto her waist and assisted her to the chair where she used to sit.

She gave him a blank look. "I know you, don't I?"

"Yes, I'm Jacob MacGregor."

"Jake." Her face had a mask-like quality.

"The Mercantile." He tried to reorient her.

"Lydia's boyfriend."

"No. Just a friend of Lydia's."

He noticed she wore a dressing gown, robe, and slippers, even though it was late in the day. Night cream smeared on her face was not absorbed. Her disheveled hair slipped from the hairpins.

"Caroline, bring tea." She looked into space. "Hard to get good help these days."

Frankie brought hot tea with liver paté on crusts of bread. From the selection of sliced lemons, cream, honey, and cane sugar, he flavored his tea. Frankie pulled a chair close to Hortense to feed her because of the extreme palsy. In a matter-of-fact way, Frankie wiped her employer's chin often to clean off the drool and the bread Hortense chewed and spit out.

"What are you planning for Christmas?" he asked.

"I—I don't know," she said in a dismissive way.

"Lydia and Millicent will be home soon, won't they?"

She looked muddled. He could see an *L* forming in her mouth in the middle of wasted motions of her tongue. He barely heard her say, "Lydia this weekend."

"Good. That's good."

"See them," Hortense said.

"Yes, it will be good to see them. Frankie, this is a marvelous snack."

When he finished, he caught Frankie's eye when Hortense wasn't looking. "I have to be going. Good to see you, Mrs. Clemons." He bowed to his hostess and motioned with a sharp nod of his head to Frankie. She followed him outside the door.

He talked fast so Frankie could return to her Hortense. "Mr. Clemons and Caroline will come in Friday, December 20. I want to have everything nice for them. If you could work late Friday the twentieth and come in on Saturday, the twenty-first, to fix and serve supper, I will pay you for the extra time. Send Jim to the Mercantile with a list of groceries you will need to cook supper those nights. I'll put it on the Senator's ticket. Plan to serve eight people."

Frankie said, "I'll be glad to help. It will be good to make extra money for Christmas."

"Evidently Lydia and Millicent will be coming home sometimes around the thirteenth or fourteenth."

"Okay."

*   *   *

Saturday Mrs. Bently had yards of fabric to cut. Teenaged girls in buoyant moods rushed into the store to select their Christmas gifts. Having settled their accounts with Jacob, their farmer fathers unleashed the women to buy some goods for the holidays. The girls received their Christmas dresses early so they could wear them at any appropriate opportunities. Mrs. Bently was sagging under the pressure.

Jacob felt helpless. "I'll never understand about fabric, Mrs. B. You're a genius."

He hired her sister-in-law, who required constant supervision.

"I wish I had Caroline here to help me," she told Jake.

Everything made him think of her. She was, in his estimation, perfection. He knew if she had been in town she would have gone to work at the Mercantile to help them through the Christmas rush.

Customers were in two lines. The women formed one. The men were waiting too. They formed a line that extended outside past all his hitching posts. With his glasses in place, Jacob was manning the frequently ringing cash register.

He looked up in time to see the two rows extending their heads in unison like cranes on the side of a river. Their faces turned in the direction of the front door.

Two young women lugging heavy bags burst into the doors as the men held them open. Coarse black nets hanging from their black felt hat brims covered their faces. As much as possible the hats were identical. They had wide floppy brims lavished with dried flowers and multicolored ribbons. Peacock feathers extended in tails down the backs of the hats. The left side of each hat displayed a *pièce de résistance :* a bird nest on each hat complete with a stuffed male humming bird.

The ladies wore capes with abundant cashmere scarves. High-heeled boots caused them to drag their feet in pain. They polished their outfits off with elbow length kid gloves. Their provincial acquaintances, scarcely acknowledged, tried to exchange greetings with them. Jake had little patience with their parade. Their old friends snickered behind their backs.

As they processed toward Jake, who remained behind the cash register, the lines parted like waters opening for the children of Israel. Ears extended toward them. but Jake, who was too busy to greet them properly, barely looked up.

"Jacob, we need a ride to the depot to get the rest of our bags. Then take us to the house."

He realized Lydia would not dare to lower herself enough to ask one of her old friends to give her a ride. She would not obligate herself in such a manner.

He called over his shoulder. "Hi, Lydia and Millicent." Between customers he added, "Welcome home. You look stylish."

They set their heavy bags down against the wall behind a counter. When he continued to pay more attention to his customers than to them, Lydia placed her hands on her hips with her elbows stuck out, and Millicent blew her net away from her face.

"I'll be glad to help you, but I can't leave now."

"Our *clothes* are at the depot." Lydia paced back and forth wherever she could find room to step. When customers tried to engage her, she seemed not to remember who most of them were.

"They'll be all right if you checked them with the agent."

Fifteen minutes later a drizzle began. The men moved closer in line.

"Please do something." Her demands went ignored.

"You could walk to your house. I don't know if Jim is there or not." He was too busy to talk to them further. Instead, he smiled at the customers.

"Need an umbrella?" he asked after several minutes passed.

"We can't go out there. Our hats will be ruined."

"You can leave them here."

"And go bareheaded? No."

Millicent added, "My feet hurt."

Jake admonished them. "Stop complaining. This is a place of business."

The crowd thinned enough three hours later for him to go hitch his horses and give them a ride. By then the blowing rain forced them to leave their hats inside the store.

*   *   *

Monday morning he called at the Clemons house to return the hats. "You know what would be fun, Jake?" Millicent, now in a brighter mood, said, "We ought to have a party. I'm sure plenty of people will attend."

He considered the possibilities.

"A party at church? Maybe Saturday after caroling time," he said.

"It's fine to do it then, but I was thinking about a party upstairs," she said.

"Be sure to invite me," Jake said.

"We need you to help with the preparations," she said.

"Okay." Although he had other plans, such as minding the store and planning for Caroline's return, he submitted to Millicent's demands.

After the store closed and he fed the horses, he went to the Clemons house to help arrange chairs and tables. He pulled a tablet and his glasses out of his pocket.

"Let's make some lists to get organized."

*   *   *

Caroline shopped for Christmas presents in Jackson. She mailed a box to Mahalia and Sylvester with gifts included for Max and Will. Instead of wrapping what she bought to take home, she packed the gifts unwrapped.

It was the busiest time of the year. In her spare time, she replayed the conversation she had with her father. Never had she thought her feelings for Jake were mere gratitude as he had suggested. It was a relief to know she could possibly be feeling nothing more than thankfulness because he saved her life. She wasn't really in love with him.

Every time I remember how he kissed me, why do I tingle all over? I really should forget about it . . . I won't let it happen again.

She dwelled inside a fortress built around herself. Jacob MacGregor was on the outside. She would never allow him to enter. She couldn't afford to be defenseless.

Occasionally she would allow part of herself to step out of her fortified place to interact with Jake. Most of the time though, she kept her inner being inside her stronghold. When she did let part of herself go where he was, she viewed him from inside while the public part of her went out to relate to him. The public Caroline could manage quite well, but the private Caroline avoided any opportunity to be wounded.

Papa wanted her to give Jake a chance. Doing so would involve letting her guard down. That could be her New Year's resolution. Beginning in 1908 she would resolve to be totally honest with Jake, even though she would risk being vulnerable.

For the time being, it was almost Christmas. For the moment she wanted everyone to have a joyous celebration. She would act cool toward him. She's warn him about the unsightly scars on her back, and he'd be gone.

After the inauguration on January 1, she would write him and explain. That way she could choose her words with care. He wouldn't have to see her face. She fully intended to give him a chance but not while she was in the same town with him. He would reject her. Then he would pity her. The last thing she wanted was his compassion.

The conversation with Papa had many benefits. Thoughts came into her private stronghold the way furniture, clothes, supplies, groceries, and magazines entered a house. Faulty thinking filled her fortress up the same way stuff cluttered a house.

After an emotional cleansing, which felt like a spring housecleaning, she didn't have anything else to share with anyone. She had told Papa everything. Wasn't telling him and listening to him talk from his heart enough for the moment? Clearly, some time would have to pass. She was in a refractory period. She wanted to enjoy Christmas with Jake but not open the doors of her heart to him.

She recalled the beaver dam she and Jake saw when they crossed the bridge over Lyon Creek on the River Road. For months she had dammed up whatever feelings and memories she had until they burst through like water that evening when she talked with Papa. With her emotions drained, Christmas vacation would pass lightly.

She made her resolution for the next year. She promised herself she would let him see her abused soul and know about her pulverized body in 1908. With that resolve she boarded the train with her father on December 20, to begin their vacation. Papa worked on items from his briefcase while she looked at a magazine.

When they arrived at one o'clock, Jacob was waiting, his horses and surrey tied to the first hitching post. He held Bruiser in one arm. In his other hand was a red rose. He looked like a model out of an Edwardian fashion plate.

How can I hold onto my heart if he is going to stand there looking like that? I have missed him every day. Lord, please keep me strong. Let us have a sweet Christmas honoring the birthday of your Son since it will be our only one together.

Dressed in a new blue and black striped slim dress she had designed by copying a picture of a Poiret original, she looked elegant and relaxed. Since the day was not chilly, she carried her cape on her arm. She had arranged her hair simply with its waves and curls streaming behind her.

She barely touched him with a light hug, and the Senator gave him a hearty handshake.

At the Clemons house, Papa went to his room, Hortense was nowhere in sight, and her stepsisters were out somewhere. Jacob helped her take her things to her room upstairs. On the way across the big room, she noticed it looked ready for a celebration. A tree not yet decorated stood waiting. The chairs and tables were polished and rearranged. Garlands and wreaths hung everywhere imaginable. Berry-sprinkled holly and ivy bedecked the stairs.

"Lydia and Millicent want to have a party tomorrow night. They've invited the young people to come here after caroling. They have been working, and so have two fellows." He looked amused. "Oh, let me tell you about that. Lydia seems to think both of them are coming around to see her, but one of them can't keep his eyes off Millie."

"This is supposed to be a surprise for you, but now you know about it. We need your help. Frankie's been working hard cooking, cleaning, and decorating."

"Good. Tonight we can decorate the tree. Was that your plan?"

"We do need to decorate it tonight."

"Jacob MacGregor, you'll make some woman a wonderful husband one of these days. You'll make her very happy. I have you in training for a real girlfriend." She bit her lip. She shouldn't have blurted out those remarks. She didn't mean to bring up the subject.

He seemed to be hurt. "Is that really the way you feel about me? I don't think so."

He didn't wait for her as he went downstairs. She followed him. She remembered her resolution not to discuss relationships. Why had she already started talking about the forbidden subject?

On the way down, he turned around at the landing six steps from the top and beamed at her. He reached toward her where she stood on the step above him and laced his hands into her golden strands of hair. "Welcome back to Taylorsburg." He kissed her lips with persistence before she was able to turn her cheek to receive the kiss.

She wished she could deny what she felt. She looked at him with her sad half smile.

"Girl, sometimes you irritate me."

Standing with his hands grasping her arms, she teased him. "I'm sorry. How can I make it up to you?"

She made a puppy-dog face. She looked overhead just in time to see several ample sprigs of mistletoe tied in a bundle to a red ribbon. It dangled above their heads.

She wondered: *How did all that mistletoe get up there? Who did it?*

She dared not let him know she saw it. If she had seen it before he kissed her, she would have tried harder to dodge his kiss.

He probably thinks he has succeeded in a major conquest.

"Invite me to breakfast tomorrow morning at seven."

"All right. Are you leaving now?"

"Not so fast. Your father has invited me to dinner here tonight. I'll be back as soon as I close the store and feed the horses. It's really busy this close to Christmas. I have to help down there. And we have the tree to trim."

"It's quite a tree. I don't know how you got it upstairs."

"I was planning for you to tell us what to do. Lydia and Millicent have promised to help."

"What should I cook for supper?

"It's all taken care of. Enjoy your break from school."

"I'll go see Rachel then."

"Good. Jim can drive you there."

*   *   *

She took Madear and Brother George their Christmas presents early. "Place these where you can see them every day, but don't dare open them ahead of time."

Then Jim took her to the Mercantile. "Here's something for you and your family." She handed Jim a card with a voucher for credit at the Mercantile from her and Papa. Jake accepted her offer to help work in the store until closing time.

*   *   *

That evening the family and a few guests gathered around the massive dining table. Frankie served roast pork, dressing, Rachel's vintage canned pear relish, field peas, and hot water cornbread. Senator Clemons sat at the head of the table with Hortense next to him. Millicent helped feed her mother. The entire time Millicent answered to the name "Caroline." Lydia stationed herself between two suitors. Jacob sat at the other end of the table with Caroline between him and Millicent.

The family had changed within a short time. In a few months she had watched Jacob mature into a radiant Christian young man who enjoyed his relationship of trust in the Lord. Glad to have him as her friend, she resolved not to mess anything up. Christmas time was coming.

Saturday night's party was a success. Caroline thought it was the beginning of a pleasant Christmas vacation.

Chapter Sixteen

Promise

December 23, which was Monday, Jacob was able to spend some time away from the store. He asked Caroline to ride with him to look over the farm.

"God blessed the day He showed you to me," he said. "You were posing as the maid for your family, even though you are the beloved daughter of the Senator."

"I had no choice."

"So you thought. We're like that sometimes. We think we have no choice, but we are children of the King. Sometimes it's scary to step up and claim what is ours, but we don't have to be. We're royalty."

I'm losing my resolve. It isn't 1908. I don't plan to tell him now. If I look at him and explain to him that I merely want to be his friend, Christmas will be ruined for all of us. Lord, please help me wait until next year to tell him. Why did I let him bring me here?

"You look beautiful today, Carrie."

"Thanks. And you look quite handsome."

When I am with Jake, everything we do is amazing. Everything we see along the side of the road is awesome. This is the way I always hoped to feel if I ever fell in love, but I cannot.

"You're too quiet. What's on your mind?"

"Not much."

I wish I could go back to Jackson, but it would be a selfish thing. I have to wait. We all need to enjoy this Christmas.

"Caroline." He spoke her name with a degree of sternness he had never used with her. "You aren't giving me a chance."

He is making it difficult. I wish he wouldn't use those words.

"What is going on with you?" he demanded.

She forced a smile. "Not much."

"Sometimes I wonder whether you are seeing someone else in Jackson. You are such a kind and loving person. We have no commitment to one another. I wouldn't blame you. I just need to know if you are."

"I don't have anyone else. Can't we enjoy the Christmas holidays? Papa loves having you around. So do Lydia and Millicent. I enjoy your company too."

The blood rose to his face, and he appeared to struggle for control. She didn't want to see him that way. He gave her a look that said he was bewildered.

"Aunt Mahalia and Papa and Rachel—all of them said I should give you a chance."

"Okay. What else?"

"After I tell you, Jacob, you're not going to want to be around me."

"Am I such a bad person as that?"

"It's not a problem concerning anything you have done or said. It's about me. Rachel said I should let you try to understand. I've been totally against the idea of trusting you or any other man to accept me ever."

"More riddles, woman."

"It's my appearance, Jake."

Now I've gone too far. I wish I could suck my words back into my mouth.

"You're beautiful. I don't think I've ever seen a more attractive woman. To me you are perfection."

"I have flaws."

"I don't see them in your physical appearance, but I do see flaws in your attitude."

Her bottom lip quivered, and she couldn't stop her chin. She stared away. She didn't want to cry, but the tears persisted. She didn't wish to manipulate him with tears. Instead, she wanted him to be objective about what she would say; she knew, however, that he wouldn't be. She regretted her failure to keep her resolution.

"Could we talk about this later? I promise I'll tell you about it after Christmas."

"No, Caroline. If you will be honest with me, I'll be fine."

"I'm trying," she said.

"This sounds like something you have imagined to be a problem."

"What I have to tell you is real. It has to do with something you have never seen."

"I'm trying to get you to understand. I think that by now you should know how I feel about you."

"After I tell you, I'm sure you'll change your mind about me. I have a huge hideous scar over my left lower back."

He looked stunned. "Go on," he said.

She couldn't read his response. Was he thinking how unattractive it must be? Or was he simply waiting to gather more information? She decided to try with all her might to be adult about the situation. The two women she loved more than many love their mothers had convinced her to give him a chance. The time had come.

"So that's what the doctor was talking about."

"I've been thinking that you'd lose interest in me when I tell you this. I have been pushing you away because I wanted you to go before we hurt each other. I didn't want you to reject me. As a result, I've kept you at arm's length much of the time. Aunt Haley asked me, 'What have you got to lose?' She explained that I can go on pushing you away or I can give you a chance to accept me as I am. It would be better to be honest with you. I had planned to tell you about it in a letter in early January."

Jake said, "Whoa, Smoky. Whoa, Firefly." He hopped out and tied the horse to a sapling next to a red oak tree dripping with Spanish moss. "Do you want to get out and walk or sit while we talk?"

"Let's sit."

He hopped back in. "What are you talking about? You don't have to give me specifics if you don't feel like it. I don't want to embarrass you." She noticed his mood had changed. Was it concern or fear? She couldn't read him.

"My scar is taking forever to heal. It hurts sometimes especially when I get upset or stretch my back too tight."

"Like when you ride a horse?"

"Right."

"I wonder if the pain will ever go away. I re-injured it when I rolled down the hill in gravel that day Mose Jefferson attacked me. I don't know what can be done."

"Let me make one thing clear to you now," Jake spoke with a deep serious tone. "I want whatever problem you have to be my problem." Emotion wailed up as he choked out his words. He clasped her hands in his firmly. "When I told you I loved you I meant it. I *love* you."

She was shaking as she looked down and away.

The way you love your sister.

"Now, trust me enough to explain to me what *our* problem is."

No matter how much she willed to maintain her composure, she was losing it. "I will."

"How long have you had the scar?"

"Since last February."

"And still not healed?"

"It's improving. I'm doing what the Woodleys said."

"Start from the beginning and tell me what happened."

"It was Friday. Most of my students had stayed home with sniffles. They had been coming down with chills and fever all week at school. I remember feeling so bad that Friday I had trouble walking home."

"You were getting it too, whatever it was."

"I dragged into the house late. Rachel had already left. I supposed Lydia and Millicent had gone to spend the night with some of their friends. That was their plan.

"When I went inside, I heard Mama Hortense back in her room. I put my things down in my room and went back to the kitchen. The supper was still on the stove. I had failed to serve her supper on time.

"It didn't matter that I had worked while she lounged all day. She always had impromptu assignments for me, and I didn't mind helping her when I could.

"Something happened to me. I went over to the wood box and collapsed on top of it. Evidently I had a fever. I don't know if I fainted or simply fell asleep. All I remember is that I couldn't make it back to my room.

"From somewhere far away I thought I heard Hortense grumbling. She sounded like she was talking to me from the other end of a tunnel. She cursed me as usual. I didn't know whether it was happening or not. I could have been dreaming. Then I woke up with a terrible pain. I felt the warm blood oozing out onto my back. I don't know what she hit me with that time."

"That time?"

"She has always whipped me with the leather strap used to sharpen Papa's straight razor."

"Why?"

"I needed it," she said simply. She could see his jaw working while his face reddened. She observed his intense anger, but she admired his extreme control.

A powerful man.

She pitied him for having to endure what she told him. They sat silently. Smoky and Firefly nibbled Spanish moss.

"I'm sorry I interrupted. Go ahead."

"The next time she hit me. I saw her. She picked up the first thing she saw and staggered over to me. I think she meant to hit me broadsided, but she stabbed me with a meat cleaver. It didn't go in deep, but she kept hitting me with it. It pulverized my skin. I had some gashes too." She couldn't talk any more.

Jake held her in his arms and placed her head with tenderness on one of his powerful shoulders. "It's okay, my darling. Go ahead and cry." He stroked her hair and patted her softly.

Minutes passed. She said, "I wanted to tell you without crying. I wanted you to know about the scar. I'm damaged goods. I wanted to wait until after Christmas. To make matters worse, I re-injured that place."

"Mose Jefferson," he said.

"When I tried to get up, I couldn't. So I rolled."

She watched him. More time passed.

"I remember something else too. This is the first time I've thought about it. I guess I blocked it out. He dragged me up his gravel driveway."

His jaw set in a firm line, he stared into the distance.

"It's revolting, Jake. You don't want a woman like me."

He kissed her fingertips.

"No matter what kind of scars you have on your body, you have deeper ones in your heart. I have scars too. We've talked about them. Both of us have lost so much this year. Together with God's all powerful healing love we can build back. He will heal you and me too."

"Oh, Jake, you are so wonderful. You have changed completely since I've known you."

"The Lord has changed me. The Holy Spirit has redesigned my heart. He wasn't comfortable with all the pride I had in there. He rearranged things so it wouldn't be so crowded."

"Oh, is that what happened?" She smiled.

"Tell me the rest of it."

"I managed to get away from her."

"She yelled, 'I'll go ahead and finish killing you. I've got a good start,' she said. You won't believe what she told me. 'You need killing.' She must have gone to look for her pistol. In my foggy state I knew I had to move out of her way. I dragged myself back to my room. On the way, I locked the pantry from the inside. I latched my door and collapsed on my floor in case she decided to shoot at my bed through the window.

"I'll never know whether I was dreaming or not. I thought I heard gunshots.

"I stayed there until Monday morning without going out. When Rachel came to work, I told her to send Brother George over to the school and tell the headmistress I was sick so she could make arrangements for the children."

"Did you clean your wound?"

"When my fever broke, I took some of the water from my wash table and cleaned it the best I could."

"What did Rachel do?"

"She dressed it the best she could with what she had. She was afraid to get the doctor."

He encircled her hands again.

"Jake, do you want to hear the unbelievable part?"

"Sure. Tell me."

"Until the last few months when Rachel's health failed, she didn't take much off Hortense. If Hortense pushed her too far, she would resist. When Rachel asked her what happened, Hortense didn't remember. To this day she still thinks I inflicted the injury on myself to make her look bad."

"Incredible. I realized you had no choice but to leave when you did because your life was in danger, but I didn't want to let you go. At times I've behaved like a stubborn mule."

"I've never noticed that you did. Papa decided to let me come stay with him a school year. Also I had the opportunity to teach in a city school. I've learned so much this semester. My contract goes through April."

"Did you tell your father about Hortense?"

"Yes, I finally told him."

Anger showed in his face. He let go of her hands and tightened his fists. Then he struck his left palm with his right fist. "You protected her. That went on a long time, didn't it?"

"Yes. You see, I was protecting Papa. She would have ruined his career. I had to be sure he wouldn't do anything foolish. I should have realized he wouldn't, but I made a promise to him to protect his position."

"Does his career mean that much to you, Miss Clemons?"

"Not for the reasons you think. Remember what I told you? Papa and Hortense do not live as man and wife. Listen to me. Papa can't change some things, but he does have influence in the state. With *your* help, he's leading other people in positions of leadership in Jackson to start doing something about the schools."

"I didn't do anything."

"Oh, yes you did. You were a brave man."

"Thank you."

"Papa is brave. He doesn't care if thugs kill him, but he's tired of those cowards running the state. He is a gentleman, and he gives all of himself to improve the living conditions of all the people. He's trying to put a stop to organized crime."

"So what about Hortense?"

"We can pray for her and try to keep her out of sight."

"Even though she isn't drinking, she is disoriented. You've noticed she is in a terrible state, haven't you?" Jacob asked.

"Probably not as much as you've noticed."

"What will become of her?"

"Papa will see the problem. He can get Brother George to find people to nurse her around the clock. That palsy she has now is bad. The time has come. Let Papa handle it. I know though you'll help keep an eye on her. I appreciate the fact you've been checking on her.

Smoky and Firefly grew restless.

"I want you to know that when I look into your heart I see the most wonderful person I've ever known," he said.

"Shh."

"I mean it, and I love you, scars and all."

Like a sister. He loves me the way he loves his sister. That will be the only way he will be able to love me. Men love through their eyes.

Looking ahead in silence, they rode along. "Caroline, my precious friend, let's go back to the hotel and take a little break."

Several moments later she sat across from him in a booth against the wall of the warm Covington dining room.

"Would you prefer coffee or hot tea?" Jake asked.

"Tea, please, with lemon and honey."

After she told him, she sensed it wasn't as bad as she had feared. She felt as though they were fast becoming the best of friends. He said he loved her but she knew he could no longer feel romantic love for her. They would have a comfortable relationship. Why had she not trusted him enough to tell him before? She knew he would immediately stop all the romantic moves. She sensed that she truly was his sister in the Lord. She had not ruined his Christmas after all; yet she knew it would be a bittersweet time.

"Jake, I realize this must be a difficult Christmas for you. It's the first one without your family."

"It hurts, but I'm better. They are in a new home, and so am I. Families change. The pain is hard to bear when our loved ones step through the veil of death to the presence of the Lord."

She reached over and patted his arm. "God had a purpose."

"I don't know what it was, but I see now that he did. My life is working out better."

Soon he will begin to enjoy life more when he finds somebody worthy. I am glad he is handling it so well. It doesn't seem to matter much to him that we are breaking off our courtship. I think he understands it's time for him to move on. He has accepted what I told him.

She gave him a Mona Lisa smile.

It's sad and sweet at the same time. If only I were normal . . . I'd have enjoyed what we could have had. It's time to start falling out of love with him. He is a sweet-natured, intelligent, man. It has been fun to be with him. Our friendship has been good.

The melancholy mood swept over her. *Bidding farewell brings sweet sadness.*

Victoria Robinson walked into the Covington with some handsome man who must have been new in town. They were openly affectionate. Jake didn't look their way.

*   *   *

After he drank coffee and she drank tea, he said, "I want to take you on another ride. Let's start over on this little excursion."

He left a tip on the table. While he signed a ticket for the warm drinks, she went to the powder room and splashed cool water on her face to wash away the residual salt from her tears. She smoothed her disheveled hair before she rushed out to meet the man who had filled all her pleasant dreams, that way keeping away the nightmares, for months—Jacob Nathaniel MacGregor. The time when she would have to stop dreaming about him had arrived.

Smoky nudged Caroline as they passed him when Jake escorted her to her side of the surrey. When they were situated, Jake said, "Hang on." He coaxed Smoky and Firefly to cover ground fast.

This time they rode to the front yard of Jake's farmhouse. "You will soon see a fine country house not far from this spot. With an automobile, this won't be any distance at all from town. I was foolish to think this was a bad location. The Mauldins will be moving in here any time. They've been working on the inside of the house." He tied the horses to the hitching post and assisted her as she jumped from the surrey.

With her arm inside his, they strolled along the cedar-lined lane on the edge of the sweeping grounds in front of the farmhouse.

"Are you warm enough?"

"Yes, I'm fine."

He had never mentioned marriage. She had merely assumed he had that in mind before he knew about the scar.

When I return to Jackson, I'll reread his letters one last time. I can't remember the exact words in them. Maybe I've been jumping to conclusions, or maybe he has changed his mind about things since I told him about the mess on my back

He is a practical man. He has been very polite to pretend it was not a big deal. I want to enjoy Christmas, and then next year things will be different. I know he loves me, but I was probably imagining it was the kind of exclusive love a man feels for a fiancée or a wife.

As far as I'm concerned, it has been more blessed to have felt this way and lost Jake than never to have known how love could be. Nobody will know my heart is breaking. I have experience covering my feelings.

She enjoyed the stroll down the lane with him. Sometimes he did erratic things. For example, he had wanted to—how had he said it? He wanted to start the excursion over.

He withdrew his arm from hers and fumbled with his clothing. Their walk halted as he reached into his shirt pocket and unpinned a little pouch. "I've been carrying this around for months. I pin it in my shirt every day, afraid of losing it."

He pulled out an ornate gold ring with a large luminescent sapphire, beautifully cut and exquisitely mounted with surrounding diamonds. "It was my grandmother's, and I've been saving it for you." He took her left hand and slipped it on her ring finger. It fit perfectly. He brought her hand to his lips and kissed her fingertips. Then he bowed deeply and gently kissed her hand.

I'm confused. Could I have been wrong?

He took her into his arms, and she raised her eyes to meet his. He gazed tenderly at her for several seconds.

I can't believe this is happening. Jacob loves me.

He brushed a lock of her golden hair back from her face. She ran her fingers through his dark hair. They nuzzled each other's faces with their cold noses. The temperature had dropped. At the hitching post, the horses snorted.

"My darling Caroline, I love to look at the sweetness of your smile." With his gentle fingers he traced all the features of her face. He started at her forehead and finished by tracing the outer edges of her lips. Then he placed his hand behind her head and drew her face up to his.

In anticipation she closed her eyes. Her heart was pounding. She felt herself immersed in the happiness of Jake's precious love. Breathless, she drew in the chilly air, held it, and slowly released it.

As if he had the rest of their lives to kiss her, he paused. She quivered when she realized he was savoring the moment. His lips brushed hers back and forth before he vanquished her tender mouth. The eager insistence of his kiss captivated her senses. His moist lips remained on hers until both of them required time to catch a breath.

Arm in arm they walked back toward Smoky and Firefly "Whatever challenges we face in life, we can work through them with joy because we have God's promise he'll be with us."

She believed him.

"Someday youth will fade, but what we have will last forever. As long as the two of us live, you will be my unblemished bride, no matter how many scars befall you."

Again he kissed her. Tenderly but insistently he caressed her until they lost track of time. The horses snorted and shook their heads.

"Jake."

"Yes, Caroline?"

"I love you."

"I love you," he said.

They strolled back to the surrey. The MacGregor homestead was the most beautiful place in the world.

"I'll have a man-to-man talk with your father at the first opportunity. I'm sure he'll say yes. First, let's seal our relationship with a talk to our heavenly Father—oh, I forgot something. Caroline, will you marry me?"

About the Author

Mary Lou Gregg Cheatham grew up in Mississippi. She now divides her time between north Louisiana and the Texas Panhandle. She has had careers as a teacher and registered nurse. The mother of one daughter, Christie Cheatham Stanley, Mary Lou loves visiting with her friends, reading inspiring books, writing in a variety of genres, and spending time with pet dogs and horses. Her deceased husband, Robert Cheatham, was a well-loved trumpet teacher and band director at Louisiana Tech University.

As Jane Riley she has written a novel, *Solomon's Porch,* noted for its presentation of Guillain-Barré-Syndrome and a Southern story cookbook, *Flavored with Love.* With Dr. Paul Elliott, she has co-authored a story cookbook about collards and cornbread, *The Collard Patch.* She has also written a daily devotional book, *Do You Know How God Loves You?*

In 2011 Panhandle Professional Writers awarded first Honorable Mention in the Inspirational Novel Category for her novel *Abi of Cyrene.*

Visit Mary Cooke on Facebook.

Read more at Mary Lou Cheatham's author page on Amazon and Collard Patch blog (http://collardpatch.blogspot.com/)

Thank you . . .

My sister Ruth Ishee is a beautiful encourager. She listened to me read the first draft of the entire manuscript. After every scene she stopped me and said, "That reminds me of something." She provided a wealth of ideas.

Paul Elliott, M. D., a good friend who values my writing, read *Secret Promise* in its early stages and made several suggestions. Also he served as a professional consultant regarding the characters' medical conditions.

The Panhandle Professional Writers critique group hosted by Laura Stephens provided valuable help: Mike Akins, an expert in combat, helped me make the fighting scenes real; Deryl Stephens pointed out the need for me to put more of my heart into the story, along with appeals to the sense of smell; Karina Ohmes breathed new life into the manuscript; and Patsy Rae Dawson has mentored me every step of the way.

At Patsy's small critique group, she and I discussed the book with Paula Taylor, a talented novelist, who provided inspiration. Also the Inspirational Writers Alive! Amarillo chapter offered insights. John Schmidt, a member of the group, showed me ways to portray Lydia and Millicent effectively.

Thanks to my daughter Christie Cheatham Stanley for appreciating what I do, to acclaimed author DiAnn Mills for professional help and motivation, and to Jon Lineback of WestBow Press for not only assisting me but also for promising to pray for this book every step along the way. Special thanks to some of the most fun loving and genuine people I know, my classmates who graduated from Taylorsville High School in 1961. They gave me moral support.

Most of all I thank the Lord for placing in my heart a mission to write and share.

Don't you love a good story?

Robert, my father born in 1898, and Myrtle, my mother born in 1907, lived their entire lives in the south Mississippi piney woods country. My sister Ruth and I share a wonderful legacy of recollections from our parents about life in the early twentieth century as they experienced it.

It was a challenging time and place to live. While the industrial areas of the nation were reaching the end of the Golden Age and the West was emerging from a pioneer status, the South was coming out of dismal years of Reconstruction. Poverty and social upheaval gave way to a unique mindset, sometimes less than kind. Of all the qualities my red-blooded hard-working forebearers had, the saving one was their sense of hope, fortified by a palpable relationship with the Almighty Creator of heaven and earth.

Growing up listening to the two best storytellers I have ever known inspired me to write the *Covington Chronicles*. Please accept my invitation to enjoy this series of historical novels depicting in a realistic manner the hardships and delights of life in the first decade of the twentieth century in south Mississippi.

Although some of the places mentioned appear on the map, they are presented as fiction. Except for the governor of Mississippi, all characters are fictional with no intentional resemblance to those who lived at the time. While some events may resemble actual historical occurrences, please do not expect the *Covington Chronicles* to be an accurate account of actual events.

Come look at this unique time and place
in a fresh new way.

Book One: Secret Promise

A Village Love Story

The year is 1907. A mammoth tornado passing through Princeton, Mississippi, takes away Jake MacGregor's parents and their home, his beloved uncle, and his sister's home. He inherits a Mercantile store in Taylorsburg, Mississippi, and an underdeveloped farm nearby. With his hopes of attending the new school of pharmacy scheduled to open at Ole Miss dashed, how can Jake overcome his frustration?

Three years prior, a new railroad, which bypassed old Taylorsburg, caused the town to dry up and move five miles to the southwest, where the railroad crossed the Hastabucha River. Caroline Clemons, a teacher in the lower elementary grades, has her dream fulfilled—a new school constructed in the new town.

But in the year 1907 Caroline receives a wound that refuses to heal. Will she have enough resilience to embrace life? Caroline suffers hideous attacks on her physical and emotional integrity. At the expense of losing all that can bring her happiness, she guards her family's secrets.

Social issues of racial discord, abuse, inadequate education, and prohibition dominate the scene of Mississippi in the early 1900's. Come shop at the Mercantile and share supper at the Covington Hotel dining room. Become acquainted with extraordinary people living in a troubled time. Experience their fear, courage, pain, and simple joys.

Discover how it feels when prayer and laughter are the only effective coping mechanisms.

Book Two: The Courtship of
Miss Loretta Larson

A Thirty-Something Woman Discovers True Love

It is 1908. Loretta Larson has enjoyed many blessings in her life. Attractive and accomplished, she has so much money she barely notices her salary she earns from teaching. In her thirties, she is living in the village of Taylorsburg, a south Mississippi railroad town. She suffers in a damaging relationship with a cruel and dishonest banker. Will she ever find the love she longs to know?

An unusual woman for her time, she is an independent, strong-minded person, who has a cloud over her past, a quirky style in the present, and boundless hope for a joyful future.

With compassion for the down and out, she shows little regard for what others think of her. To live her life requires courage and ingenuity. She relies on the Lord to help her through her problems. Sometimes the help comes in unusual ways. For example, her cat Pinkie saves her from disaster.

The story contains fun-filled pranks, the joy of being alive, and outrage over social injustice. Come spend more time with Caroline, Jacob, and Chad from Book One. Return to the

Covington Hotel and MacGregor's Mercantile. Although *The Courtship of Miss Loretta Larson* is the second in the series, the enjoyable reading stands independent of *Secret Promise*.

Celebrate the fun of having the last laugh.

Book Three: The Dream Bucket

A Young Girl Coming of Age, Her Mother Facing Unspeakable Challenges

In 1909 a wife has no right to know specific details about her husband's finances. The man handles the money, but what is a woman to do if she loses him?

Ten-year-old Trudy Cameron, who adores her father William, hears him slap her mother for asking where he keeps his money. Two days later, he dies in a fire that destroys their antebellum mansion. The girl's goal becomes taking care of Zoe, her mother, while Zoe's goal is taking care of Billy, the twelve-year-old son, and Trudy. Destitute, the three family members move into a rat-infested shack leaky as a colander.

Terror fills their lives. Zoe, a mixture of savage strength and feminine weakness, shoots a black bear and faints afterwards. Risking her life, she defends her children with a long-bladed hog-slaughtering knife. When existence becomes as complicated as she can imagine, new problems arise.

Down the road the neighbor Samuel Benton, a widower who was like a brother to William, cares for his six-year-old twins. While Samuel offers Zoe unwelcome help with her problems, he faces hardships that challenge him to maintain the wellbeing of his own family.

The summer of 1909 is a time for learning to cope with grief and to grow in the realization of God's love. After sharing in the lives of Jake and Caroline, come spend some more time at MacGregor's Mercantile and the Covington Hotel. Even though *The Dream Bucket* is third in the series, it is an independent story.

What riches have you overlooked?

The Dream Bucket placed second in the prestigious Texas Christian Writers Conference for book proposal.

www.ingramcontent.com/pod-product-compliance
Lightning Source LLC
Chambersburg PA
CBHW020824260626
47169CB00003B/820